# *Louisette*

Lewis Marshall

# Louisette

A novel by

# LEWIS MARSHALL

Matador
5 Weir Road
Kibworth Beauchamp
Leicester LE8 0LQ UK
Tel: 0116 279 2299
Email: books@troubador.co.uk
Web: www.troubador.co.uk/matador

ISBN 9781848763463

A Cataloguing-in-Publication (CIP) catalogue record for this book
is available from the British Library.

Typeset in 12pt Sabon by Troubador Publishing Ltd, Leicester, UK

**Matador** is an imprint of Troubador Publishing Ltd

Printed in Great Britain by the MPG Books Group, Bodmin and King's Lynn

*For*
*Joe Gordon*

# CHAPTER ONE

Nathaniel Owen, Sailing Master of His Britannic Majesty's brig-sloop *Vixen*, was not comfortable. His tarpaulin coat was leaking, and rivulets of icy water periodically trickled down his neck. His nose and ears were frozen, and his eyes were stinging from continually trying to peer through a mixture of mist, sleet and freezing rain. He was standing harbour watch, and the weather was foul. Two hours previously, *Vixen* had finally picked up her mooring in Plymouth after a battle with the rising easterly wind. The last few miles had been touch and go, with *Vixen* beating into the freezing wind which bore a thin, icy rain and had lashed up short, steep seas from the rising tide as the little fourteen-gun brig had clawed her way towards the harbour. Several times, the Skipper had been on the point of turning to run for Falmouth, but they had finally made it as the tide had slackened. Mr. Kirton, the First Lieutenant, had immediately gone ashore on some errand or other. The harbour watch should have been stood by one of the midshipmen, but the youth was suffering from a filthy cold and the Skipper had taken pity on him, sending him below an hour into his watch. Owen knew perfectly well that Captain Johnston would have been happy to stand the rest of the watch himself, but, like a fool, he had volunteered. He stamped his numb feet and cursed himself. Then he cursed the weather. It was supposed to be spring, not bloody winter. He glanced up at the mainmast, shivered and cursed again as another icy trickle started on its way down his back. Then he thought of the mug of hot grog which would await him at the end of the watch, and of the possibility of a run ashore and a warm tavern in the evening. He brightened somewhat and groped in his pocket for his pipe, turning his back as another sleet-laden squall hissed towards *Vixen*.

He was engaged in filling his pipe when there was a sudden shout from forward. He turned and looked up to see a shape looming out of the rain and sleet. It took him less than a second to recognize her as one of the local traders, a snow-rigged collier about the same size as *Vixen*, and less than another second to realize that she was adrift and out of control. There appeared to be no-one on board, and she was bearing down rapidly on *Vixen*, carried by the wind and the tide which had by now turned. Stuffing his pipe back into his pocket, he shouted, "Fenders! Fenders, there!" and ran to the side. He had barely had time to heave one of the massive rope fenders over the bulwark before there was a cry of alarm and a splintering crash from forward. *Vixen* lurched violently, almost throwing him off his feet, and he grabbed at the rail. He saw that the other vessel had turned slightly and her quarter had struck the brig's larboard bow. Seconds later, the Skipper appeared beside him, a pen clutched in his right hand. By now, three men had appeared on the snow's deck. One of them ran to the wheel, but the other two seemed paralysed by what was going on, in spite of the shouts from *Vixen's* crew. Owen and Johnston could only watch helplessly as the other vessel scraped down the brig's larboard side and disappeared into the murk astern, trailing her mooring-cables and various parts of

*Vixen's* rigging and leaving a sizeable portion of taffrail draped over her cathead.

⚶

Some two hundred miles away, a flurry of blinding, stinging sleet swept over Horsham common, presaging the arrival of yet another heavy snow shower. The majority of the small crowd gathered round the gallows hunched their shoulders and turned their backs to the icy blast. The squall eased in intensity, and several people turned their attention back to the two bodies swinging in the wind. The crowd had turned out in spite of the weather (quite un-seasonal for March, said some, though others recounted their memories of several such in the past), some to assure themselves that these particular rogues who had terrorised the roads around the county were really no more and it would now be safer to travel, others to derive some grim satisfaction from seeing their assailants brought to justice. Some were slightly disappointed. Three highwaymen (or 'Inspectors', as they preferred to call themselves) had been taken and there were only two men on the gallows. Although there seemed to be some doubt about the third, who was little more than a youth, he had been found in their company and the jurors at the Assize had been as swift to condemn him as they had the others, since he must have been an accomplice. He had, unfortunately for the crowd, but fortunately for him, died in the gaol that very day, cheating the hangman by barely one hour before Justice could be done. Justice, however, had been applied to the other two and the crowd had seen it done. The crowd was satisfied. The only slight dampener on the proceedings had been that the hangman, wet through and cold

3

to his very marrow, had been keen to get the execution done with as quickly as possible and had therefore despatched his victims with a drop, breaking their necks rather than letting them strangle to death. Some members of the crowd who wanted to see the 'hangman's dance' felt they had been cheated of a 'proper' job, but in view of the worsening weather perhaps his use of the drop was as much a mercy to the onlookers as to the condemned.

In fact Grundy, the hangman, had not been at all happy about the verdict on the third man. Scarcely more than a youth, he had seemed bewildered by the court proceedings. He had had no-one to defend him in court. The judge, anxious to climb back into his carriage and be away back to London before being benighted in the town, had summarily condemned all three to death and hurried away. When Grundy heard that the youth had died, he had hurried to the gaol to ensure that this was not some ruse to spirit the youth away but, when he arrived, there was the body, stretched out on a filthy straw mattress. He had arranged with the gaoler for the body to be brought out after the execution to be carted off with the others, then left to be about his duties. Grundy was an essentially kind man who did not relish the spectacle of suffering. Having already decided to make it swift for the youth by using the drop, he had thought it best to despatch the other two by the same method, particularly in view of the fact that he himself had lost practically all sensation in his hands, feet and the tips of his nose and ears.

A second icy squall, much heavier than the first, howled across the common. Several members of the crowd broke away and began to move away across the common towards the inn. After a brief pause, a third blast, this time laden with thick, heavy snow, drove the rest of the crowd in the same direction. The body of the third prisoner had already been brought from the gaol and dumped unceremoniously beside the gallows to await the cart that would take it away. Wet snow was now settling thickly on it. The hangman, his assistant, the gaoler and the prisoners' escort of cavalrymen endured for a few minutes more, then followed to the inn as driving snow began to settle thick and fast. They would wait for the storm to pass, then go and cut the hanged bodies down and transport all three to the gibbet at North Heath, where they would hang them in chains as a warning and an example to others. In the meantime, this weather was not such as any Christian soul should be out in. One of the inn's excellent mutton pies and some mulled ale would serve to thaw them out.

The heavy oak door of the Dog and Bacon Inn closed with a thud behind the last of them. The wind slackened for a few seconds, and two ravens settled on the gallows cross-bar. The bodies swung in the wind, snow settling on them.

The wind picked up again and began to blow steadily, driving heavy snow before it. The ravens flapped heavily off the cross-bar and flew off towards the church, there to seek shelter under roof of the lych gate. From an alleyway near the inn came a scuffling noise, followed by a muffled curse as someone slipped on the snow.

"Get on, Charlie, damn yer lights! Hurry!"

Unseen from the inn, two figures, pushing a rickety handcart, appeared out of the alley. Bent double against the wind, they moved quickly across the common to the gallows. "Get on, Charlie, afore they sees us."

One of the two figures, a sharp knife between his teeth, attempted to shin up one of the uprights. He failed, and as he slithered to the ground again he noticed the body of the youth. "'Ere. This 'un'll do!" Between them, the two men seized the body by the arms and feet, the elder of the two remarking, "They ain't tied 'is 'ands. Makes it easier for us, at any rate." Together they unceremoniously dumped the body on to the handcart, then returned to the gallows and cautiously peered towards the inn. At that moment, the snow eased a little, the door of the inn was opened, and a figure walked out. There was a shout, the figure turned on its heel and disappeared back into the inn. "Let's be gone. One will 'ave to do." The two men returned to the handcart and hastened away across the common with it and its macabre cargo, one of the corpse's hands lolling limply out from underneath the piece of old sacking which they had hurriedly thrown over it.

A quarter of an hour later, having circled round the common under cover of the snowstorm, the two men pushed the handcart with its grisly burden through an anonymous, weathered wooden door almost hidden by ivy in a high wall which surrounded the gardens of an affluent house in a quiet area on the edge of town. They trundled the handcart across the stable yard and stopped outside another door, on which one of them rapped a coded knock. After a short delay, the door was cautiously opened a crack and the elder of the two men murmured, "Some trade for the doctor, Jessie." The chain was removed with a rattle and the door was thrown open. The woman's eye settled briefly on the hand lolling from the side of the handcart, but she made no reaction apart from to beckon with a jerk of her head and the two men stepped into the scullery. "Wait here. I'll fetch him."

Doctor Aloysius Russell was a slightly portly man of average height, with a faintly dishevelled appearance, as if age and weather had taken their toll on his clothing as well as his countenance. His face was kindly and somewhat weatherbeaten (a legacy of having spent some years as a physician in His Majesty's Navy). He was wearing grey breeches, silverbuckled shoes, a frock coat of rather old-fashioned cut over a stained waistcoat, a rather grubby medical bob wig and a pair of round pince-nez spectacles, which he had taped with court plaster in a attempt to stop it chafing the bridge of his beaklike nose.

He now regarded his 'Resurrection Men' carefully through the pince-nez, which he then removed and began to polish with a none-too-clean handkerchief fished from his coat pocket.

"A nice fresh one, yer honour, d'rect from the gallows," ventured the elder of the men. The doctor sighed. "Oh, John! You know they are supposed to be left there for an hour, and I did not bid to buy one from the hangman. How come you have it here, and not half an hour after the hanging? You have stolen it, have you not?" The two men looked at their feet and shuffled uncomfortably. "Nobody saw us, sir. The snow's that thick..." The doctor sighed again. "Very well. Now you have brought him it would be a waste not to dissect him. I haven't had a good fresh one for months. We'd better get him into the laboratory."

A few minutes later, the body was laid on its back on a slab in one of the outhouses and John and Charlie had departed with a guinea apiece, promising to return in three days' time to remove what was left after the doctor's attentions and dispose of it quietly somewhere in return for a further ten shillings. Russell gazed sadly after the men as they vanished with their handcart through the same gate by which they had entered. By eight o'clock in the evening they would both be blind drunk in one of the ale-houses and would probably have been robbed of whatever was left of the money. He sighed again, shook his head, removed his coat and donned an old, bloodstained smock, which he had taken from a peg on the wall. He had not been able to be present at the execution, but Grundy, the executioner, had told him that morning that he had decided to use the drop. Russell had not seen the 'drop' used, and had secretly wondered if he could get hold of one of the cadavers so he could dissect it to see how effective was the method. Anxious to make a preliminary examination of the neck before the onset of *rigor mortis*, Russell turned back the piece of sacking which shrouded the body and looked critically at the cadaver's face. It looked serene, as if sleeping. There was none of the usual tumescence; no protrusion of the tongue. In fact, the face did not even have the pallid, parchment appearance of death. It was very pale, but there was still a slight flush to the cheeks. There was a small bruise in the angle of the left jaw and some abrasion of the neck just below and above it, but no actual injuries or marks he could positively associate with the hangman's halter. The injuries could equally well have been caused by a blow. Interesting, he thought, that this method of execution had apparently cut life off so swiftly. He reached out and laid a finger on the body's left cheek. Curiously, given that the cadaver must have been lifeless for an hour now – it still seemed to have some warmth, in spite of the freezing temperature.

He straightened up, rubbing his back, and turned towards the small table on which his instruments were laid out. He would start his investigation by making a careful examination of the mouth, recording the condition of the teeth and tongue. He picked from the table a notepad, an inkwell, a pen and a small mirror. He placed the pad and the inkwell carefully beside the body, laid the pen on the pad and uncorked the inkwell. Then, holding the mirror before the cadaver's face, he turned back to the table for a spatula with which to open the mouth. Having selected a suitable instrument, he turned back to his work – and froze. There was a fine mist on the mirror, which had been clear when he had placed it there a few seconds before. He waited, and a few seconds later, the mist thickened slightly. He put the mirror back on the table, removed his pince-nez and rubbed the lenses again with his wipe, then felt for a pulse in the neck. He could not detect one. He turned back to the table and retrieved the mirror. It was by now quite clear. Again, he held it before the mouth and again, after a few seconds, a faint mist appeared upon it.

Russell turned back once more to the table and picked up a pair of scissors. He unbuttoned the youth's coat and rapidly cut the shirt from the body over the chest area, then placed his ear to the chest. He could not detect a heartbeat, but he could feel a faint warmth on his ear. He stood back and watched. The chest was, almost imperceptibly, rising and falling.

"Jessie!"

The urgent edge in his call brought Russell's housekeeper hastening across the courtyard. "What is it, Sir? What's the matter?"

"Jessie, it would seem that this young man is not quite as dead as he is supposed to be. Pray go you make up a fire in the small guest room. We must get him in the warm as soon as possible." After a quick sideways glance at the body, then at the doctor, Jessie hurried away. Russell turned back to the slab, removed the pen from the inkwell, wiped it, corked the inkwell and placed it back on the table. As he returned the pen to its rack and the pad to the table, he reflected, somewhat ruefully, that he had just laid out two guineas…

Half an hour later, the youth had been laid upon the bed in the guest bedroom and covered with a thick blanket. He was still cold to the touch, but a slight flush of colour had begun to show on his cheeks, his breathing seemed slightly deeper and Russell could detect a weak, thready pulse. He had examined the boy thoroughly, and could find nothing apart from a few bruises, scrapes and a fresh contusion in the area of the left eyebrow, which he presumed to have been caused by a fall or a blow. He had tried to bring the lad round with hartshorn and by blowing pipe smoke into his nostrils, but there had been no reaction. Russell crossed to the fireplace, poked the fire and added some more sea-coal from the scuttle. Then he returned to the bedside, extracted a hunter from the pocket of his waistcoat and took the wrist once more. The pulse was rapid and slightly irregular, but he fancied it was stronger than when he had last taken it twenty minutes ago. He laid a hand on the forehead. It still seemed icy cold. Russell frowned in puzzlement. The lad was evidently comatose, but he showed no signs of having fitted, nor was there any other evidence as to the cause of this condition. He had not suffered any major blow to the head, and while he seemed a trifle malnourished, he was not starving. Deciding that he could usefully do no more for his patient for the moment, Russell pocketed his watch, walked from the room, leaving the door ajar, and headed for his small library. Perhaps one of his books would provide an explanation.

"Doctor, Doctor! He's awake!" Jessie's voice from the doorway brought Russell out of his musings. He immediately rose and followed her to the guest room. The lad still looked very pale, but his eyes were open, revealing themselves to be a startling shade of blue. They followed Russell as he approached the bedside. The mouth opened as if to speak, but the only sound was a hoarse croak.

"Jessie, water, if you please." Russell sat on the chair beside the bed. "Don't try to speak yet, lad. I am a physician. Just nod if you can hear me." The head nodded stiffly, then the youth suddenly raised himself on his elbows and grimaced with pain. "Easy, lad." Russell supported him with an arm round his shoulders and pushed the bolster behind him. He relaxed back on to it and looked around him. Jessie arrived, bearing a tray on which stood a jug and a tumbler. Russell smiled at Jessie, filled the tumbler and proffered it to the youth, who painfully extended a hand and took it. He drank greedily, then coughed. Russell re-filled the tumbler and, when it was empty, placed it on the bedside table. The youth looked wistfully at it and at the jug. "Not too much at once," said Russell. "You obviously have a very great thirst, but too much at once will bloat you and make you ill. You shall have some more in a few minutes." The youth sighed and nodded. "Yes, sir. Thank you, sir."

Russell stared at his patient in astonishment. Although the voice had been somewhat faint and croaky, it sounded well-bred and refined, not at all what he would have expected to hear from the mouth of a common thief and footpad. He removed his pince-nez and fished in his pocket for his handkerchief. He found it, and was bringing it towards his spectacles when it was suddenly whisked from his fingers. "Oh,

Doctor! You can't be using that filthy thing!" He turned in time to see Jessie disappear from the room, her demeanour showing exasperation. He glanced at his patient and pulled a rueful face, receiving a raised eyebrow and a faint smile in return.

Jessie returned a few moments later, bearing a severe expression and a clean wipe which she handed to Russell, who mumbled thanks, took it somewhat sheepishly and, forgetting why he had wanted it in the first place, pushed it into his pocket. Then he turned his attention back to his patient.

"How do you feel?" he asked. The youth frowned slightly and moved his head gingerly from side to side. "I have a terrible headache, Sir, and I feel very weak. I have pain all over. I must have had another episode of my illness."

"What illness?" enquired Russell.

"Well, Sir, I don't rightly know. Nobody seems to know. I cannot say what happens, but I have been told that some part of me seems to go someplace else, and sometimes I go to sleep for days, or I seem to be sleepwalking."

"I see." Russell did not see, but the youth was evidently very unwell and Russell was worried about overtaxing him. "Do you know what day it is?"

"No, Sir." "Well, can you tell me the month and year?" The youth seemed to struggle to recall, then "February, I think, Sir. Yes, February, or – no, I'm not sure, Sir. The year is seventeen ninety-two."

"Very well," replied Russell "and what is your name?"

"Poitiers, Sir, Hugo Poitiers."

"Well, young man, you have had a very lucky escape. You must be tired. I will ask you no further questions for now, but will ask Jessie to bring you a little soup, if you think you could manage it."

"If you please, Sir, but Sir?"

"What is it, young man?"

"Escape, Sir?"

"Yes, do you not remember?"

"Remember what, Sir?"

"Do not try. It is better that you have no recollection. You have been very ill. Try to rest." I will return soon with something to relieve your pain. Ah! Jessie, could you find our patient a drop of broth? Not very much: just a few spoonsful. He is very weak. I think we should treat him as a convalescent who is just beginning to recover from a severe ague, and we should avoid taxing him with too much in his belly or with tiresome questions."

Russell left Jessie to minister to his patient, and retired to his study, where he opened a cabinet and extracted from it a tumbler and a decanter of whisky. He examined the level in the decanter and frowned. He would soon have to obtain some more, but his usual source of supply was fitful. Brandy and rum, licit or smuggled, were readily available, but Russell disliked both. Whisky, Scotch or Irish, he did like, but it was scarcely even heard of in England. Russell had developed his taste for it on visits to Scotland and Ireland in the course of his travels, but obtaining it here in Sussex was difficult, to say the least. He poured himself a moderate measure, added a similar amount of water, and sat down at his desk to ponder. Unless he was a consummate liar, the youth evidently had no knowledge of what had happened to him over the past few days. In fact, Russell realized with a start, he appeared to have no knowledge of the last couple of months, since he had stated that he thought it to be February. What had happened to the youth in the intervening six or so weeks? What was the nature of his 'illness'. His name seemed vaguely familiar, but Russell could not remember why. What were the circumstances that led to his ending up being condemned as a common criminal?. Too many unanswered questions, and he dare not tax his patient yet – the lad was too weak. Russell sighed to himself again, picked up his tobacco pipe, and crossed the yard to retrieve the youth's jacket from his laboratory.

His examination of the jacket puzzled him. It was spattered with mud, but it was of good quality, made of black broadcloth. It had originally carried facings, which had been stripped off. He went through the pockets, but, finding nothing, placed it on the bench and removed his pince-nez, which he then absently proceeded to wipe with the hem of the jacket. He turned back to the side table and uncorked the inkwell, selected a pen, checked it, sighed and picked up a pen-knife. When he had re-cut the nib, he opened his laboratory journal and wrote steadily for a few minutes, wiped the pen on the clean handkerchief which he discovered in his pocket, replaced it in the rack, re-corked the ink bottle, picked up the jacket and walked slowly back to the house. The jacket had provided him with no answers. He looked in on his patient, who was by now sleeping deeply as a result of the laudanum which Russell had administered, and headed for his study, where he wrote up his diary and leafed through some medical books until Jessie summoned him to his supper.

An excellent chop, followed by an apple tart and a glass of good port, restored him sufficiently for him to decide that he would like to know a great deal more about this youth, but without asking him direct questions to which he might not receive satisfactory answers. However, there were others who might know. He walked to the kitchen and told Jessie not to wait up for him. He returned to the hallway, seized a silver-topped cane from the stand by the front door, and headed out into the night. About a half-minute later, he returned through the front door, accompanied by a flurry of snow, to find Jessie holding out a heavy cape. Affecting not to notice the dumb insolence of her raised eyebrow, he donned the proffered garment, fumbled the chain over the hook on the clasp and selected a thoroughly disreputable – looking tricorn hat from a peg. Ignoring Jessie's protests concerning the hat, he crammed it on over his medical bob, pulled the cape closely around him, gave Jessie a lop-sided smile and once more headed into the night. As the door closed behind the Doctor, Jessie gently shook her head, then returned upstairs to look in on the youth, whose presence in the house had evidently slipped the Doctor's memory for the moment. She would not be able to retire to her own room until Russell returned from whatever urgent mission he had embarked upon, and on a night like this, too!

The youth was apparently sleeping peacefully. Jessie returned to the kitchen, poked the fire and set a kettle on the hob. A slightly plump and rosy-cheeked woman of some forty-five years (she was not sure exactly how old she was) she had kept house for the Doctor for almost ten years now. Her husband, a gunner's mate on Russell's ship, had disappeared during a storm in the Bay of Biscay. It was assumed he had been swept overboard by a heavy sea and had drowned. Only a few months later, the Doctor, on his retirement from the Royal Navy at the outbreak of peace in 1783, had set up practice here in Horsham and had offered her the position of housekeeper, which she had gratefully accepted. She was quite used to his eccentricities and absent-mindedness by now. At first, he would periodically disappear for months (once for two whole years) on end at short notice, having taken passage on a merchant ship to some remote place to collect specimens, but he had not ventured far for the last two years, and appeared to be content to stay at home, writing and conducting experiments in his laboratory. She was no longer shocked by his gruesome dissections or his collections of bizarre biological specimens, and quite content in her position. She would have a nice cup of tea and put her feet up for a while.

# CHAPTER TWO

R ussell was soon picking his way between piles of refuse in a back-street in a none-too-salubrious area of the town. He eventually came to a green-painted door, at which he rapped with the head of his cane. After a few moments, the door was thrown open and a small mongrel puppy emerged and began to bark at him. He bent down to pat it, then straightened up as the bulk of its owner loomed into the doorway, lanthorn in hand.

"Ah, Grundy. I am sorry about the lateness of the hour, but I was wondering if I could have a few words with you."

The hangman was as used to Russell's foibles as Jessie was, so he simply grunted and moved back from the door, allowing Russell room to pass inside. He put the lanthorn down on a table, scooped up the puppy, which was dancing around Russell's legs, yapping excitedly, and tickled its ears. "Mary, Doctor's here. Will you take a spot of ale, Doctor?"

"Indeed I will. Most kind of you, Grundy."

Grundy's wife appeared, bearing a jug and earthenware tankards, which she set down on the scrubbed table in the centre of the room. "Give me your cape, Doctor, and sit you down."

"Thank you, Mary. God bless you," said Russell. He relinquished his cape to her and eased himself into the proffered high-backed Windsor chair. Mary took the puppy from her husband and carried it out of the room while Grundy poured mulled ale into the tankards. Mary returned and she and her husband drew up two more chairs. They sat down and looked expectantly at Russell as he took a long pull at his tankard.

"Mary, your mulled ale is excellent. What is your secret?"

"Now, Doctor, I've told you before it's the herbs, but I'm still not telling you exactly how!"

Russell grinned at her. Mary had teased him for years because he was unable to replicate her recipe. He thought he knew what was in it, but there seemed to be some secret ingredient that he could not identify. He would wheedle it out of her somehow, some day.... He took another pull at his tankard, then placed it carefully on the table and looked around him. Apart from being the hangman, Grundy also acted in a semi-official capacity as a thief-taker, law-enforcer and tipstaff, but actually made his living as a slaughterman and butcher. Although he was moderately successful, he still lived in the cottage in which he had been born, and he had no intention of moving. The cottage, built about one hundred years previously for a gamekeeper, had originally been outside the town, but in the intervening fifty or so years since his birth the town had expanded to engulf the estate in whose grounds it had originally stood. The area had once been quite well-to-do, but hard times had overtaken many of the inhabitants, while others had improved their station and moved away, the result being that many of the surrounding properties were now little better than slums. Grundy's neat little cottage stood like a little oasis in the midst of a desert of deprivation and neglect. The woodwork was neatly painted, the roof was in good order, and the wicket-fenced garden full of flowers and vegetables.

Inside, all was neat and tidy, the wood scrubbed and the brass gleaming. Shelves in the parlour where they were sitting contained some exquisite pieces of porcelain, mostly Chinese, and there was a small bookcase containing about three dozen volumes whose subjects varied widely. Grundy was an intelligent man who liked to 'improve my mind', as he put it.

Russell's attention was brought back to the reason for his visit by Mary's gentle voice asking, "Well, Doctor, are you going to tell us why you are out and about on a night such as this?"

"Oh, er, indeed, yes, umm," he mumbled, then "Did you attend the hanging, Grundy?"

Grundy regarded his old acquaintance for a moment, then replied gravely, "Indeed I did. It would have been very strange had I not done so. It must have temporarily escaped your notice that I am the hangman."

"What? Oh, yes, of course you are, my dear fellow. How silly of me! Er..."

"Doctor Russell, do I take it from your demeanour that you are in possession of the body that was stolen from beneath my gallows this afternoon?"

"Er, no. Well, yes, that is to say..." Russell looked at his friend, who was watching him carefully, one eyebrow raised interrogatively. Mary was sitting with the jug poised over his tankard, also regarding him steadily. Grundy picked up his tankard. "Doctor, you are a bad liar. It was obvious to me where the body had gone the moment I saw it was missing, particularly since I later saw your two 'assistants' getting themselves pickled in the ale-house opposite my shop. I put two and two together, and I make four. But you would not normally come to me in such circumstances. What is wrong?"

"Very well, Grundy. I do indeed have the body. The problem is that it is not dead! In matter of fact, it is very much alive, though unwell. It has just taken some broth and is now sleeping."

Grundy slowly put his tankard down on the table. "He was stone dead. I was told he was dead, and I saw him with my own eyes"

"I know," replied Russell, "the drop is an humane method, and I applaud your decision to use it, but it is evidently not as effective as might be hoped." Grundy picked up his tankard, took a long pull at it, and sat peering into it, swirling it gently. Finally he said, "Possibly, but I did not use it in his case." In response to Russell's raised eyebrow he went on, "He died in the gaol about an hour before the execution. I checked the body. It was cold. It was taken from the gaol to the gallows to be taken away with the others, but it mysteriously disappeared, I presume under cover of the snowstorm." He slumped on his chair, looked into the fire for a few moments, then straightened up and banged his tankard down on the table. "Good. I was troubled about having to hang that one. It would seem that Higher Authority was also troubled about it."

He lifted the jug. After a moment Mary took it from him and disappeared into the kitchen. Russell said quietly, "I am concerned that your erstwhile victim, who must now be regarded as my patient, should not be taken up again. I find myself unwilling to believe that he could be a common criminal. He seems too well-bred, and his apparel is, or was, of good quality. He is also apparently unaware of the circumstances which brought him to the gallows. In fact, he seems to have no memory of anything for several weeks. I have yet to question him more closely. He is not at all well."

"Well, Doctor," said Grundy, "I do not think taking him up again would be a problem. Even if he *were* taken up, I do not believe that it is possible to condemn a man twice. As you say, he is now your patient. How much has he cost you so far?"

"Two guineas, dammit!" said Russell, then grinned ruefully at Grundy, "and I cannot now, in all conscience, dissect him. I conjecture that he might object!" Grundy laughed, then stood up and poked the fire. At that point Mary returned with the re-filled jug. Grundy added some more logs to the grate and sat down again. "You say you were unhappy about hanging him," said Russell, "will you tell me why?"

"You have already discovered the reason. He just didn't seem to know what was going on and, yes, come to think of it, you are right about his clothing. He seemed to be in a trance. I was at the trial, and he seemed almost asleep through all of it, such as it was. He didn't get a fair hearing. Well, he didn't get a hearing at all. No-one even seemed sure of his name, which was given as 'Peters', and he seemed unable to speak, so he did not confirm it. The court seemed to regard his silence as proof of his guilt, and he had no counsel. It was all quite irregular. I was not happy at all, but I just had to do my duty. I am grateful that the Almighty saw fit to relieve me of it."

"Hmm," murmured Russell, "that is most odd. He told me his name is Poitiers. Hugo Poitiers."

"Sounds French to me."

"It does indeed, but he speaks very good English, with not a trace of an accent. I wonder who he *really* is. No doubt all will be revealed, in time. I am loath to overtax him at present: he is not at all well."

"You say he seems well-bred," ventured Grundy, "so why not enquire of Sir Horace? He may have heard of the family."

Russell slapped the table with the flat of his hand. "Of course! Thank you, my friend. I shall call upon him at once!"

"I would suggest that tomorrow would be a better idea. I doubt he would welcome a visit at this hour, even from a friend. Besides, I also doubt you would get there by walking, and you are unlikely to find anyone willing to lend you a horse on a night like this. How is your old nag, by the way? Still wheezing and blowing?"

"She is much improved, I thank you. I may even give her a gentle run when the weather improves. However, I feel that you were right when you said a few months ago that she is now past any hard work. I shall have to find myself a younger and fitter mount. The expense of it all..." Russell's voice tailed off and he stared gloomily into the fire. Grundy grinned and winked at Mary. The Doctor's parsimony was well known, to the point of being a joke. He had been an excellent and skilled naval physician, and, having been present at several successful actions, had made a small fortune in prize money. Now, his practice in the town was also successful. He must be one of the richest men in the area, but he resented parting with as much as a farthing. He could afford a whole stable full of fine horses, probably a coach-and-six as well, but his stable contained just the one broken-down old mare who was not much use for anything any more – except eating, Grundy reflected. She should have gone to the knacker a couple of years ago, but Russell seemed strangely reluctant to part with her. So she remained in her quarters, eating herself silly, and the Doctor, for all his parsimony, didn't seem to notice what she must have been costing him. Grundy grinned to himself.

After a few moments, Russell sighed and stood up. "You are right," he said, "it is late. I shall call upon Sir Horace tomorrow. Now I must thank you for your advice – and for the excellent ale." He smiled at Mary, who inclined her head graciously to him and fetched his cape.

⁂

Sir Horace Markham, Baronet, Justice of the Peace and a shrewd operator in government circles, sat at the large mahogany desk in his library, poring over a series of documents which he extracted from official-looking buff-coloured files tied with yellow tape. The contents of the files were known only to a small handful of people in government, Horse Guards and the Admiralty. They contained a great deal of sensitive information concerning various matters and individuals, all of which related to security. The next day, Sir Horace would post to London. On arrival in the Whitehall area, he would pay off the chaise and walk several streets away before entering an unremarkable building through a plain door in a back alley. There he would preside over a small meeting which would collate the information gathered over the past week by various people working, unofficially for the most part, on behalf of the His Majesty's Government, and decide upon plans of action. The department of which Sir Horace was the head did not officially exist. Neither did its agents. If any of these spies were caught or compromised, the government would deny all knowledge of their existence. Tomorrow's meeting should be very interesting. The news from France was the cause of a great deal of concern. The situation could de-stabilize the whole of Europe, if not the world. The threat to England's peace and security was very real, and it was necessary to try to formulate some plans to safeguard the country should the political turmoil across the channel show signs of spreading nearer home.

There was a knock at the door. Sir Horace carefully closed the folder which was open in front of him, placed it on top of the others, picked them all up and put them into a drawer of the desk. This he closed and locked before calling "Enter."

The door opened to reveal Taylor, Markham's butler, who announced "I am sorry to disturb you, Sir, but Doctor Russell is here and would like a word with you."

Markham glanced at a bracket-clock on the mantelpiece. "It seems an appropriate time for some refreshment, and I have all but finished anyway. Show him in, and see if you can find us some coffee, if you please."

"Certainly, Sir." The door closed, and Markham stood by his desk, listening to the tapping of Taylor's shoes receding down the marble floor of the corridor. Then he moved to a window which looked out over the grounds of the park. A warm breeze from the south-west had sprung up overnight. Yesterday's snow had all melted, leaving just a few rapidly-shrinking patches beneath the hedges, and the estate was now basking in warm spring sunshine. Two gardeners were working in one of the borders, surrounded by the nodding heads of daffodils. The window was wide open, and Markham could hear loud birdsong and, in the distance, childish laughter mixed with the barking of dogs as his children (evidently released from the watchful eye of their tutor after their morning lessons) and household pets played by the lake. It would soon be time to send his son to finish his schooling. Markham had been at Winchester, and he had Gerald's name down for the same establishment. The son should follow in the footsteps of the father. Markham nodded to himself. Life was good. It had better damn' well stay that way. If the mess the bloody Frogs were making should arrive here there would be chaos, and no knowing what might happen.

His musings were interrupted by Taylor's announcement: "Doctor Russell, Sir." He turned and, as the butler ushered the Doctor into the room, strode across the fine Turkish carpet to shake his hand. "It is good to see you, old friend. It has been quite a while, eh?" "Several months, I believe," replied Russell, easing himself into the proffered chair. Markham sat on another opposite Russell and regarded his friend benignly. They had been at Winchester together, and were a similar age, but Russell looked, thought Markham, older than his forty-eight years. He seemed to have put on a bit of weight in the past few months, and his slightly dishevelled appearance gave him the air of a down-at-heel country parson. At Winchester, Russell had been a bookworm, happy only when reading or soaking up knowledge, for which he seemed to have an immense capacity. He had shown little or no interest in physical or sporting activities, and had spent his first two terms at the mercy of the many bullies who proliferated at the school. He had finally been rescued from the situation by Markham, who, sickened by the sight of one of the ringleaders attacking Russell for the third time in a day, had given the thug a severe thrashing, breaking his nose in the process. Thereafter, Russell had been left strictly alone and their friendship had developed to their mutual benefit. Markham had, up to then, struggled academically, and he soon grew to admire the mind trapped within Russell's then rather puny and short-sighted body. Russell had proved to be an able teacher who delighted in sharing his new-found knowledge with his new–found friend, and Markham's academic progress had advanced by leaps and bounds, to the astonishment of the academic staff.

After leaving Winchester, Markham to take up a commission in the Army, purchased for him by his father, and Russell to read Natural Philosophy at Oxford, they had kept in touch. Markham had initially been surprised when Russell had written to tell him that he had accepted a post as a naval physician, but soon realized that Russell would be able to use his spare time in the further pursuit of his interest in all things scientific, and at the Navy's expense. Their paths had crossed on a number of occasions, invariably connected with intelligence. Russell possessed an almost photographic memory and was an excellent observer. Some of his observations and sketches, made during his voyages, had proved very useful, if not invaluable, to some of Markham's more clandestine operations. Russell was no stranger to the little committee-room in the nondescript building in Whitehall, but Markham did wonder if his friend realized the significance of the meetings in that room. Now Markham was in charge of his non-existent department and Russell was a physician in a small country town. They lived some six miles apart, Markham with his beautiful and elegant wife, his son and two pretty little daughters and a full household, Russell alone in a house much too large for him, with only a housekeeper for company and a groom-*cum*-gardener who turned up on the few occasions when he was sober enough to be useful until Russell paid him, at which point he would go to the nearest pot-room, get blind drunk and vanish again.

Markham dragged himself from his reminiscences and realized that Russell was gazing at a painting on the wall. It depicted the grounds of the park, with the house in the distance and Markham's late father, the fourth baronet, standing rather inconsequentially to one side of the middle distance. It was not a well – executed painting. The figure was nowhere near any of the golden means, and unbalanced the picture. Russell found himself idly wondering if it was supposed to be a picture of the Park or of Markham's father – perhaps the two should have been the subjects of two separate paintings, but had been unsuccessfully combined in order to save money. Russell smiled to himself and then caught Markham's eye. Markham was regarding him with mock severity, as if daring him to comment. At the same time, Markham was making a mental note to have the painting moved to a less conspicuous place. It seemed good to him, but there had been several adverse comments concerning the painting of late and he had to admit he knew nothing of art. The Doctor's expression was enough to convince him.

Instead of the expected criticism, Russell enquired, "When was that painted?"

"Oh, er, about forty years ago. I just remember it being done. The grounds had just been laid out. I was a small boy at the time. My father grumbled about the amount of time he had to pose for the artist. He did not much like having to stand still."

"Quite so. Most tiresome." Russell avoided Markham's eye and continued, "The park has grown up well since. It is a pity that your father cannot see it."

"It is still not fully mature. With luck, I might just live to see it as he intended it to be. He had a vision of the future for this place. It is to be hoped that the atmosphere across the Channel is not contagious, or there may be no-one around to appreciate his efforts."

"I think you are being excessively pessimistic, but your

remark brings me conveniently to the reason for my visit, since it may concern the French. Have you heard of the name 'Poitiers'?"

"In what connexion?"

"I have in my care a young man who is suffering from loss of memory. He is also quite gravely ill and has, I fear, been the victim of some injustice. He has given his name as Hugo Poitiers."

He was interrupted by Taylor's arrival with a silver tray on which stood an elegant silver coffee pot, cups, saucers, cream and sugar. Both men were silent as Taylor set the tray down and poured two cups. As the door closed behind him and his footsteps receded once more down the corridor, Markham leaned forward and pushed the sugar-bowl towards his friend. Then he picked up his own cup and said quietly, "I know of one Henri, the Comte de Poitiers. He is known to me personally, (though I do not know him well), and also to the committee. He is married to an Englishwoman. They moved to England, to Kent, I believe, a year or two ago. He is a staunch supporter of the French Monarchy and has been, er, helpful, in the past. About six weeks ago, he returned to France to sort out some affairs. He should have returned within a few days, but he did not. We had no word of him, and the committee's enquiries at the time came to nothing. He just disappeared, and I fear for his safety, particularly in view of the political climate in France, which has deteriorated noticeably in the past few weeks. 'Aristos' are in considerable danger, as you are doubtless aware. I did, however, receive intelligence from one of my colleagues a few days ago. It would appear that his whereabouts may have been identified. More than that it did not say. Anyway, that aside, he has a son by the name of Hugo.

I have never met the boy, though he must be about twenty years old by now. To the best of my knowledge, he is a midshipman in the French navy, and doing rather well. His father spoke proudly of him the last time we met."

"Which was when?" asked Russell.

"Just before he left for France. I recall he mentioned that Hugo's ship was on a diplomatic mission somewhere off West Africa, and that it was confidently expected that Hugo would be made *Lieutenant* on his return to France. It seems most unlikely that your patient is that young man. What on earth would he be doing here?"

Russell stood up and walked over to the fireplace. "You have just mentioned that the political situation in France is not healthy for 'Aristos'. I wonder what his reception would be now? Also, his father has disappeared. It is possible that Hugo came to England to be with his mother."

Markham picked up the coffee pot and shook it. Finding it empty, he replaced it on the salver and said, "Give the bell a tug, Aloysius. The coffee seems to be at full ebb." Russell pulled gently at the tasselled silk bell-cord by the mantelpiece and turned to face his friend, who continued, "The Comtesse is also missing in France. When Henri failed to return, she went to look for him."

"Oh, indeed? Then it does seem unlikely. Maybe my patient is not the same young man, but the name is unusual and I have a strange feeling about this. Are there any brothers or sisters?"

"There is an older sister. She is married to a successful businessman, a minor aristocrat. He owns sugar plantations in the West Indies – Saint-Domingue, I believe."

"And they live there?"

"Yes, though I believe that Charlotte is not at all happy, and wants to return to France. However, in the light of recent events, I think that would be unwise, particularly for her husband."

"They have been there long?"

"Several years, I believe."

"Then it is surprising that they have so far escaped the Yellow Jack."

Taylor appeared, bearing another pot of coffee. Russell waited while he replaced the empty pot with the fresh one, then went on to describe, in some detail, the events of the previous day.

When Russell finished, Markham was silent for several seconds. Then he said, "It all sounds most irregular, and very odd indeed – it almost suggests that someone was trying to dispose of the young man. We need to establish the identity of your patient. I suggest that, when he is well enough, you permit me to ask him a few questions – that is, if you are unable to discover anything yourself. If he *is* the Comte's son, he may be in possession of useful information, and we may be able to help him find his parents." Russell nodded in agreement. Markham poured more coffee and said, "I do not think we can proceed any further until we know for sure. Now, tell me what you have been doing since I last saw you, but, before you do," he glanced at the clock, "I trust you will dine with us?" He saw Russell glance at the clock, too, and went on, "I insist on dining at one: two at the latest. I cannot abide this modern fashion for dining late. It does not suit my constitution. It wants only an hour to dinner. We can take a turn round the garden, and you can tell me what you think of my new shrubbery."

Before Russell could reply, there was a sudden commotion outside the door, which burst open to reveal Markham's two small daughters. Both were plastered in mud. Around them bounded two small terriers, equally plastered in mud and yapping excitedly. Behind them came Markham's son, sopping wet to his waist, covered in green slime, and bearing a bundle wrapped in his coat. The bundle wriggled feebly and made occasional hissing sounds. "What on earth...?" began Markham. He was interrupted by the two little girls, "Oh, Papa, Papa, we were by the lake and there was this poor duck - one of your new ones, Papa, and it is all tied up and it was drowning and Gerald went in and pulled it out and we all got wet and..." The girls' voices trailed into silence as Markham held up his hands. "One at a time, please, my dears! First of all, you must greet Doctor Russell properly. Then Gerald will tell us what you have found."

Order restored, Russell listened to Gerald's rather breathless description of events, then took the bundle from him, laid it on the table by the window and unwrapped it to reveal a bedraggled Aylesbury duck snared in fishing-line. The line trailed from the bird's beak and around its legs and one wing, effectively pinioning it. Markham took one look at it and exclaimed, "Damn' poachers! They are always after my fish!" Russell looked sternly at him over his spectacles and fished a lancet from his pocket. Deftly he cut away the fishing-line and gently extracted the hook, which had caught in the bird's beak. Then he set the bird down on the table, where it shuffled its ruffled feathers and began to preen.

"Well done, Doctor. Thank you. I do not like to see any creature suffer unnecessarily," said Markham. Then, "Children, my thanks to you as well, but you had better go and get yourselves cleaned up before your Mama sees you in that state. Gerald, please take the dogs to the yard and put them under the pump – yourself, too! Annie and Lizzie…"

"What in heaven's name is going on? Children, how have you got into that state of filth? Horace, have you completely taken leave of your senses? And what is *that creature* doing in here, on the table, too? Oh, it's you, Doctor. I might have known! You sow chaos wherever you go!"

"My dear, it is somewhat unfair to blame the Doctor, or indeed the children. Between them they have rescued 'that creature' from drowning."

Caroline Markham looked coolly at her husband for several seconds, then turned her gaze on Russell, who gave her a weak and sickly smile. She pursed her lips, gave a sniff that said more than a thousand words, glared at Gerald, who had scooped up the terriers and was standing by the door with one under each arm, shooed the girls out of the room and swept out. Markham grinned at Russell, dismissed his son with a wink and a jerk of his head, marched to the table, picked up the duck and dropped it out of the window. After a few seconds it came into view, apparently none the worse for its ordeal, waddling across the terrace in the general direction of the lake. Markham watched it for a few moments, then strode to a cupboard, from which he extracted a decanter and two glasses. "A drop of Madeira, Aloysius?" In response to Russell's nod, he poured two generous measures. "I think discretion might well prove to be the better part of valour just now. Let us take our drinks to the shrubbery. Fortunately, I had the foresight to have a seat installed there. It affords a delightful prospect!"

# CHAPTER THREE

"Doctor, will you please to tell me again about your patient. It all sounds very mysterious." Caroline Markham, the events of two hours ago forgotten, waved away the decanter which Taylor was hovering near her glass. "We will take coffee in the drawing-room, Taylor, and some *petits-fours*, if there are any." She looked expectantly at Russell, who related his tale for the third time. When he had finished, Markham shook his head in puzzlement and rose from the table. "Extraordinary. It becomes more mysterious at each telling. Shall we…?" He moved to the door and held it open for his wife and Russell. All three filed into the drawing-room. Russell settled into an armchair and a maid appeared with a tray.

Taking up his cup, Markham said, "I am going to London tomorrow. There will not be time to question this young man beforehand, even assuming he is well enough, which I doubt from what you have told me, Aloysius. I shall, however, make some discreet enquiries. Someone may be able to shed some light. I shall be back on Saturday morning, early. How are you fixed for transport?"

"My old mare is, I fear, no longer fit for work. I walked here, "replied Russell.

Markham set his cup down, rose and tugged at the bell-pull. "Take a mount from the stables. I still have that nice steady grey mare that you borrowed to follow the hunt two years ago. She doesn't get much work, and some exercise will do her good. Bring her back on Saturday, if you have anything to tell me. If not, send me word and bring her back when you do have something for me." There was a discreet knock at the door and Taylor entered. "Do you require more coffee, Aloysius? No? Very well, then. Taylor, please go and tell Nicholls to saddle Bluebell for the Doctor. Tell him to find a *comfortable* saddle."

Just over an hour later, the grey mare clattered to a halt in Russell's own yard. He dismounted and looked around. Clapp, sober for once, appeared from the direction of the kitchen garden. Without a word, he took the reins and led the mare towards the stables. Russell entered by the servants' entrance. There was no sign of Jessie, so he walked up the passage into the hall. He was hanging up his cape when he heard laughter from upstairs.

The door to the sick-room was ajar. Russell could hear Jessie's voice, scolding gently. He pushed on the door. It swung open to reveal his patient sitting on the edge of the bed, his feet on the floor, with Jessie fussing around him. Both looked up as he strode in. "Oh, Doctor, thank goodness you're back!" exclaimed Jessie, "Your patient has taken it into his mind that he is well enough to get out of bed. He must have come down with a terrible crash – I heard it from the parlour."

Russell switched his gaze to the youth, who said simply, "I wanted to look out of the window, but my legs turned to jelly." Russell regarded him for a moment. "Never mind. I perceive a considerable improvement. A few hours ago, you could not have even made the attempt. You did not hurt yourself?"

"I only bumped my elbow on the floor, Sir."

"Good, no lasting damage, then. Now back into bed with you. Tomorrow, we will see if you are well enough to get up for a short while. You have been very unwell, and you must not over-tax yourself too soon. In the meantime, if you are bored, perhaps you would apply yourself to answering a few questions for me?"

"Why, of course, Sir."

"Very well. Could you tell me again what your name is? I am afraid my memory is somewhat defective."

"Hugo Poitiers, Sir."

"Poitiers? Not Peters?."

The youth looked at him with faint surprise. "No, Sir, not Peters, but my father was proposing to change the name to Peters. He said we are English now, so the family name should be English. He decided he would do it at midsummer. It is supposed to be a secret. Did I blurt it out, Sir?"

"You did not, but somebody knew. Why is it supposed to be a secret?"

"There are people who, well…. My father is the Comte de Poitiers, Sir, and I serve in the French Navy."

I understand. I know of him, and of what is going on in France. How is he?"

"I – I don't know, Sir. I have not seen him for some time. My parents live here. Father went to France to meet me when my ship returned. He had received word that I was ill, and wanted to send me to a specialist in London. He met me when my ship docked, and took me to see a specialist in Paris, who agreed that I should see the man in London. I stayed in Paris with my father for a week or two, then he took me to Calais and saw me aboard a boat coming to England. He told me he had sent word to my mother that I was safe. Then he was going to go to see some of his staff at the one of his estates, give them instructions on what to do in the event of, er, unrest and so on, then catch a boat to England himself. I was to wait for him in Dover so we could both travel together to London, and then to the new house. I don't even know exactly where our new home is. I have never been there."

"So you arrived in this country, evidently. What then?"

"My father did not arrive. I waited several more days, but there was no sign of him. I asked among the fishermen if there had been any report of a vessel lost or sunk, but they said there was none."

"What did you do then?"

"I could feel another attack of my illness coming on. I had money and I knew the address of our new home, so I decided to hire a chaise to take me there. Mother and I could decide what to do."

"And then?"

The chaise was attacked. I remember being dragged out. I was beaten. I must have lost consciousness. I can remember nothing more until I woke up here."

Russell dragged his pince-nez off his nose and polished them with the corner of the counterpane. He replaced them and asked gently, "How long have you had this illness? Many years?"

"Oh, no, Sir. It began on my last voyage to Africa. I was in a fever for several weeks. I think the ship's surgeon despaired of me, but I recovered. Then it struck me down again when I was on leave, and again during the most recent voyage, but I recovered from that, too, or I thought I had."

"You speak good English. I can detect no trace of an accent."

"My father speaks English. My mother *is* English. I also speak Italian, and some Spanish and Russian." He shifted uncomfortably and grimaced.

"Indeed? Well, you are getting tired. You must rest and try to gain strength. It will be some time before you are strong enough to travel." Russell peered at the water-jug on the bedside table. "I will ask Jessie to bring you some more water. You must have a raging thirst. When you need it, the usual receptacle is in the cupboard to your left. How are you feeling now?"

"I still have a bad headache, Sir."

"I shall prepare you some Willow-bark. Jessie will bring it to you soon."

❧

Two days later, Bluebell, trotting easily, bore Russell back up the long gravelled driveway to the Park. It was another fine spring day, with some promise of real warmth in the sun. Russell, jogging gently in the saddle, felt pleased with himself. His patient had made excellent progress. He had wobbled unsteadily around his room the previous day, and today Russell had left him sitting in a comfortable chair on the terrace of his garden, wrapped in a blanket and reading one of Russell's medical books, with Jessie fussing round him from time to time.

Bluebell, scenting her own stable, slowed to a walk, snorted and turned into the yard. A groom appeared as if from nowhere. "Good morning, Doctor. Sir Horace arrived about an hour ago. He told me to look out for you."

"Most kind. Thank you." Russell dismounted, gave the mare an affectionate pat on the neck and headed for the house.

He was half-way across the courtyard when Markham's booming voice called from an upstairs window, "Ha! Aloysius! There you are. I hope you have some news for me. I have some for you. I will be down in a few minutes." Russell doffed his hat in the general direction of the window and headed for an open door, where he was met by none other than Caroline. "Good morning, Doctor." Russell swept his hat off again and made a leg. Caroline bobbed in reply, then took him by the arm and ushered him to the morning-room.

"Where is the worthy Taylor?" enquired Russell, settling on to a chair near to the French windows, which were open.

"I have sent him to Horsham to buy china. The maids are so clumsy that there is scarcely a teacup left in the house. He took the dog-cart and one of the grooms with him. I don't suppose they will return for several hours. I think there may be other attractions in Horsham. You did not meet them on the road?"

"I did not, but I did not come directly by the main road. I made several detours, and looked in on two patients on my way. How are the children?"

"Cleaner than when you last saw them. How is your patient?"

"Improving rapidly, but I will tell all when Horace arrives – ah, here he is. Good morning, Horace."

"Good morning, Aloysius. I trust you have returned my property intact? She is not missing a leg, or anything? You have a great propensity for dissecting things on a whim."

"Horace, don't tease Aloysius so. It is not fair, and unbecoming!"

"My dear, you clearly do not remember the occasion that Aloysius dissected one of my fowling-pieces to discover how the mechanism worked. I recall that he was unable to put it together again. It cost me four guineas to have it put to rights at Gamble's." Markham winked at Russell.

"Oh fie, Horace! That is even less fair and less becoming! You know perfectly well that Aloysius only dismantled your piece at your behest, because you had somehow managed to break it! For shame! Ignore him, Aloysius. It must be the town air. It has addled his wits more than usual." Caroline marched to the bell-pull and gave it an irritated tug, while Markham chuckled to himself and Russell shook his head in mock sadness.

"Horace, do please try to behave yourself. It is bad enough having to deal with the children, without mischief from you as well, and with a guest present. You are impossible, sometimes." Caroline gave up her pretence of outrage and, grinning, cuffed her husband round the ear, eliciting a yelp and a gust of laughter. "You must think us mad, Aloysius."

"I have encountered more hopeless cases," said Russell gravely, "but I cannot remember where. Certainly not in the Bedlam Hospital!"

"I thank you for that professional endorsement of our sanity," said Markham, giving Russell a mock bow. "Would you care for a glass of Sillery? We could take it in the garden: it is warm enough."

A maid arrived and was despatched to fetch the wine. Caroline led the way out on to the lawn, where a table and some rather flimsy-looking cane chairs had been set out. Russell lowered himself gingerly on to one of them and looked expectantly at Markham, who began immediately, "Well, I have managed to discover a few things, but not as much as I hoped. Has your patient been able to throw any light on the situation?"

"He has. He is making a rapid recovery. It would appear that he is who he says he is, and his father is definitely the gentleman of your acquaintance. The lad says that he suffers from some condition. He was on his way to the family's new home in Kent, but became ill and was waylaid. He is aware that his father has vanished, but knows nothing of his mother's disappearance. I thought it best not to break that to him until I had at least consulted you."

"Very good. I had also managed to ascertain that he is indeed Hugo Poitiers, and my sources tell me that the driver of the chaise in which he was travelling reported that they were attacked only a few miles from the house in Kent. There were two assailants, he claims. He says they first threatened him, then told him that he would come to no harm if he co-operated with them – they only wanted 'Mr Peters'. The one who spoke to him had a foreign accent. The other one dragged the young man out of the chaise and beat him senseless. They then bundled him on to a cart, stole the chaise's horses and fled, heading west."

"Where exactly is the house?" enquired Russell.

"Near Tenterden. My source also reports that the two highwaymen hanged at Horsham could not have been the two men who stopped the chaise."

"How so?"

"Because at the time, they were attempting to rob the mail coach at Dorking. Their attempt was foiled, but they escaped, nonetheless. Besides, neither had a foreign accent."

"Where were they finally taken up?"

"In the woods by Henfield Common. They had a hideout there, but they had become careless. They were blind drunk and asleep. Earlier, someone tipped off the guards at Horsham barracks, mentioning the name 'Peters'. A search party was sent out and the smoke from their fire was spotted. Young Hugo was with them. He was insensible."

"How, and by whom, were the guards tipped off?"

"Apparently, a lone man on horseback just rode up to the gates of the camp and handed over a note, then rode away before anyone had time to read it."

Russell swirled the wine in his glass and held it up to the light. "Henfield? It is many miles from Tenterden to Henfield."

"Quite so."

"Did the two rogues claim that Hugo was with them?"

"No, but they would not have had much chance. All three were held separately, and the two villains did not recover from their stupor until the next day. They would not have seen him again until they were all three brought to the dock together to be sentenced. Neither would have had any reason to know that Hugo was supposed to have had anything to do with them, or, if they did, they chose to keep silent."

"It is a pity that no-one asked them. Still, it is too late now."

Caroline Markham placed her glass carefully on the table. "It does not make sense to me," she said. "If someone wanted Hugo dead, why not just murder him there and then? Why take him all that way?"

"Perhaps his abductors knew of the highwaymen and hoped they would murder him for them," replied her husband. "Or maybe they had some 'arrangement'. Do you know if he had any money or valuables on him, Aloysius?"

"He did, but how much I did not enquire. He must have had sufficient to pay for the chaise."

"Apparently, he had none when he was taken up, so someone must have robbed him," said Markham.

"Unless, of course, they were only interested in him and not in his money, in which case it would still be in the chaise," countered Russell.

Caroline stood up. "Well, my dears, it would seem that you need to have a few more words with the coachman. There may have been more than enough to compensate him for the loss of his horses. I will leave you two now. I must see cook about the arrangements for next Sunday."

When she had moved out of earshot, Markham said, "The horses were recovered not far away. Whoever took them did so only to prevent pursuit." He picked up the decanter. "This is excellent Sillery. May I press you to a drop more?"

"If you please, dear fellow. It is getting rather warm." Russell removed his wig, revealing a sizeable bald patch in the midst of his greying hair. It looked very like a monk's tonsure, thought Markham. Russell stuffed the wig into a pocket and said, "There is something much more to this than meets the eye. It is all most puzzling."

"It is downright fishy, if you ask me," replied Markham. "I am beginning to suspect underhand dealings. The family is French and aristocratic. I detect a faint whiff of revolutionary methods in this, though to what purpose I have no idea. I have encountered a similar *modus operandi* before."

"What? Surely they are not carrying out their revolutionary business here in England?"

"They most certainly are, and have been for some years. Their revolutionary fervour is not limited to their own aristocracy. It is their wish that it should be world-wide. *Liberté, Egalité, Fraternité* for all, damn' them. If they are up to something, I'm damned if I can see what it could be. As Caroline said, it makes no sense."

"Then perhaps we should make further enquiries. I will start by asking the lad a few more questions."

"Please do, and as soon as he is well enough I should like to meet him, if possible."

"Give him a few days more, then by all means."

"Good; we are decided, then. You had better keep Bluebell for a while longer. I am sure you will need little persuasion to dine again. Let us go inside. You can inspect my new rifle. I acquired it in London. It is quite the thing for game – amazing range, and accurate, too."

❧

Late in the afternoon, Bluebell plodded once more into Russell's yard. There was no sign of Clapp, so Russell ministered to Bluebell himself. That done, and the mare settled into her stall, he went in by the back door. Jessie, her arms covered in flour up to her elbows, was busy at the kitchen table. "Ah, Doctor, sit you down. I am just about to make a pot of tea." Russell sat and watched her bustle over to the fire. "What are you baking?"

"Scones, and tarts, and a game pie for your supper. Hugo can have some, too, if you agree he is well enough. He got rather tired, and I packed him off back to bed. I gave him one of your old nightshirts." Russell glanced up at the drying-rack over the fire. On it, washed but not yet repaired, was the youth's shirt, together with his breeches and hose. His shoes, stuffed with hay, stood on the hearth. "Where is his coat?" asked Russell suddenly.

"I've seen no coat, Doctor. Perhaps it is still in your laboratory?"

"Ah – oh, no, it is not. I left it in the library. I will fetch it later for you, though I feel it is much the worse for wear."

"Let me have it and I'll see what can be done. It can't be much worse than some of yours." She placed a mug of tea on the table beside Russell. "And where is your wig? You were wearing it when you went out. I suppose you have left it at the Park."

"My wi-? oh, here it is!" Russell produced it from his pocket. Jessie took it from him and shook it. "Oh, Doctor, just look at it! It is all crumpled! It will have to be washed and straightened. I'll take it to Preece's presently. You will have to use your spare."

Russell sighed resignedly and sipped his tea. Jessie was still fussing over his bob, so he decided to change the subject. "Where is Clapp?" Jessie, by way of reply, simply looked at him and shrugged her shoulders. She disliked Clapp for his drunkenness and for the way he leered at her. Russell said suddenly, "I need a reliable groom. Could you make any recommendations?"

"So you'll be keeping Bluebell, then?"

"It would seem so. I have a feeling in my bones that Sir Horace is trying to inveigle me into buying her." Jessie hid a smile. She was well known below stairs at the Park, and it was common knowledge that that was precisely what Sir Horace had been trying to do for nearly two years. There were even bets among the household as to whether he would succeed in getting the Doctor to part with money, and, if so, how much. Indeed, a penny sweepstake had been organized, with valuations of Bluebell from ten guineas (too little) to one hundred guineas (far too much). Jessie, as an 'impartial' observer, held the book.

"You'll be needing a gardener too, Sir."

"Oh, yes, I suppose I will. That is two recommendations, then, Jessie."

Jessie sat down and picked up her tea. "Well, Sir, as to the groom, there's Mrs. Carter's nephew. He is looking for a position. His father is in service at a big house in Devon, near Tiverton. The lad was an apprentice groom, and good, too, but the owner has died and they no longer need all the staff. He's staying with his aunt at the moment. As to the gardener, there's no need to look further than old Philpott who was at the Park. He's retired, but wants to 'keep his hand in', as he puts it. He says he'll seize up if he doesn't."

"Oh, yes, Philpott. Splendid." Russell drained his mug. "How old is the lad?"

"About eighteen, Sir. His name is George Trecott."

"Good. That's settled, then. He can start as soon as he likes."

"But, aren't you going to interview him, Doctor?"

"Jessie, I may own this household, but you run it. You may pass the word round the ale-houses that Clapp need not bother to re-appear here. Should he do so, send him to me." Russell stood up and strode to the door. "I shall be in the library." He turned and grinned at the astonished Jessie.

As the door closed behind him, Jessie put her mug slowly down on the table. "Well, bless me!" She rose and topped up the teapot, poured herself a celebratory second mug, sat down and put her feet up on the chair just vacated by Russell. "Well, bless me," she murmured again.

※

Ten minutes later, Russell, the youth's coat draped over his arm, peered around the door of the sick-room. Hugo was sitting up in bed, one of Russell's books open before him.

Russell coughed and entered the room. "I have come to check on my patient." he said, "What are you reading?" Hugo smiled at him. "It is about 'Diseases of the Tropics'."

"Ah, yes, quite so. I have brought your coat. It is still a trifle damp, I fear, but I will hang it before the fire and it will soon dry."

"I beg pardon, Sir, but ..." Russell turned and saw the look of incomprehension on Hugo's face. "That is not my coat, Sir."

"Not yours? It is the one you were wearing when you were," Russell just checked himself in time, "found."

"It is certainly not mine, Sir. Mine is brown."

Russell gazed at the coat for a few seconds. "Well, none of mine will fit you," he patted his belly. "And I have noticed that the pocket is torn. Jessie is attending to your other garments, so I will give her this as well. You can wear it until you can obtain another. Do you have any money?"

"I had a hundred guineas, Sir, but I am sure whoever robbed the chaise has them now."

"Mmm, yes, of course. Well, I will pass this to Jessie. There is game pie for supper. If you feel well enough, you are welcome to join me."

"Why, thank you, Sir."

"Very well, young man. I look forward to our first social meeting. Do not set too much store by what you read in that book, or you will discover that you have every disease described in it, with the possible exception of Yellow Jack, which, I can assure you, you do not have!" Russell winked at his patient and walked from the room without waiting for a reply.

# CHAPTER FOUR

Citizen (for so he liked to call himself) Pierre Chabot paused for a moment from shovelling chicken into his mouth, sighed and transferred his gaze out of the dirty window which overlooked a small square by the harbour. Rain pattered against the glass and ran in grimy rivulets down the panes. Chabot disliked seaports, and he disliked Dieppe more than most. His family was from Aveyron in the south. He found the north too cold and windy – and it was always raining. Had he realized, when planning this operation, that he would have to spend days in this grey, windswept, sodden, tedious place, he would have altered his plans accordingly, though he did have to admit that it was, quite fortuitously, an excellent choice. There was a brisk trade in contraband in both directions between France and her old enemy across *La Manche*, and the activities of the fishing vessels went un-remarked, whether they were actually carrying fish or more irregular cargoes, and they and their counterparts across the channel provided a means by which he could have agents smuggled to and from England. The 'fares' were not cheap, but there was a good deal of risk involved, mainly on the other side, where Revenue Cutters and the Royal Navy could make life very difficult for the operators, so he felt they were justified. However, he disliked the strange smells, the noise and the bustle and felt vulnerable amongst all the comings and goings, particularly here since he felt too uncomfortably close to England for his liking. Well, it would do no good to complain: he had his work to do. As a good Jacobin, his duty to the Revolutionary Cause must necessarily involve some personal sacrifice. In fact, he reflected, there was really no need for him to be here at all. Lessard, his deputy, a man seasoned in espionage under the Bourbon regime and who had now joined the revolutionaries, was running the operation. Chabot could have stayed in Paris, where he would have been more comfortable, but he felt he should take some sort of active part in the operation, at the same time getting away from the political atmosphere in the capital, which he had been finding rather cloying and frustrating of late. Having arrived, he found that for several days there was nothing for him to do except to watch the daily life of the harbour, much of which centred around the activities of the fishermen, and which resulted in a permanent aroma of fish. Still, he had finally managed to make arrangements for the aristo and his lackey, who had been arrested about a month ago while trying to board a packet for England, to be taken to Paris. Tomorrow, he would travel with the prisoners, who were now confined to an upstairs room in the inn, and their escort. He took another mouthful and glanced down at his plate. In fact, not only did everything smell of fish; it seemed to taste of it as well.

As if to reinforce his distaste, two men, evidently fishermen, entered, looked around the room, chose a table a few feet from Chabot's and sat down. After a minute or two, one of them stood and walked to the counter. After flirting briefly with the innkeeper's daughter, he returned to the table with two mugs and a flagon of cider. He and his companion then started a muttered conversation which seemed, from the few words that Chabot could hear, to concern the state of a fishing-boat, and some scandal concerning a local prostitute. Chabot strained his ears to hear more, but the conversation was lost in the general low hubbub of other customers and he gave up. A heightened aroma of fish drifted across from the other table.

Chabot sighed again, pushed his plate aside, belched and reached for his glass. The wine was more reminiscent of vinegar than of Bordeaux, and his nose wrinkled as it hovered over the glass. He sighed once more. It was the best the house could offer, or so he had been told. He regretted not having brought some of his own supplies with him – he had managed to acquire some quite passable vintages in the course of his rapid rise to his present office. Well, if there was no decent wine in this hovel, he would have to drink something stronger instead. He glanced to his left and caught the eye of the inn's proprietor. The man affected to ignore him for a few seconds, then sauntered across to the table at which Chabot had eaten alone. Chabot gestured at the still half-full jug. "Citizen, this wine is disgusting. Take it away, and bring me some brandy. Not that revolting local stuff which you make from apples, but proper Cognac, or Armagnac. I should also like some cheese, and some bread that is not three days old, and coffee, if at all possible."

Dufay, the innkeeper, grunted and took the carafe from the table without a word. He disliked being addressed as 'Citizen'. He was '*Monsieur Dufay*'. He bit his tongue. He knew exactly where he could sell the remainder of the contents of the carafe, at an apparently knock-down price. As for the brandy, this ex-peasant couldn't tell the difference between a good Cognac and polishing-alcohol. He had some stuff that had been concocted in Spain. Though extremely fiery, even when considerably watered down, it tasted vaguely like brandy. This idiot had already drunk two carafes of the rot-gut which he passed off as wine, so the fool should not be any the wiser, though Dufay had to admit there was little enough alcohol in the wine he had served his unwelcome guest, since it consisted of the results of a very swift and perfunctory fermentation of the dry remains of grapes left over from a first pressing, bulked up with water and weak vinegar and adulterated with cochineal and sugar of lead, amongst other things. As for the coffee, some of the brew he made from roasted and ground-up acorns would probably pass this palate. He grinned to himself. It was good to hit back, in never mind how small a way, at the puffed-up, self-important, ignorant fools who had effectively ruined his business by frightening away, exiling or even murdering many of his best customers. These 'Republicans' had succeeded in confining the King to his palace at the Tuileries last year, and were now stirring up trouble everywhere. They seemed to think themselves beyond the law, and this particular one seemed to expect to be treated with some sort of deference. At least his previous clientele had been appreciative of his hospitality and generous in the matter of gratuities, but this one seemed to expect everything for nothing. The cretin could damn' well wait at least twenty minutes for his coffee and brandy. That would be sufficient time to gather a few tail-ends of bread and cheese left by other diners and trim any tooth-marks from them, arrange them neatly on a nice plate and place over them a silver cover, to be removed with a flourish on its arrival at the table...

"And butter, Citizen!" Chabot's voice followed him

through the door. Dufay shrugged his shoulders and continued toward the kitchen.

Chabot hunched his own shoulders and frowned at the table. He knew there were shortages, but he was sure that Dufay was swindling him. Chabot suspected him of being a Royalist sympathiser. One day, he would have him arrested, but to do that now would be effectively cutting off his nose to spite his face since it would be difficult, if not impossible, to find other accommodation in this god-forsaken hole, and he would probably need to return in the near future. Besides, there were more pressing matters at the moment. He would deal with this cheating bastard at leisure. He sighed and drummed his fingers on the table, then took from his pocket a small leather toilet-case. Opening it, he extracted an ivory tooth-pick and was carefully searching a cavity in a molar when a shadow loomed over him. Alarmed, he looked up at the man, who was already easing himself into the empty chair at the other side of the table, then relaxed as he recognised the craggy features of his deputy, Henri Lessard.

"Oh, Lessard, it is you. You gave me a shock. I wish you wouldn't creep up on me like that!"

"You are much too jumpy. You should have stayed in Paris."

"Not with the Legislative Assembly in its present frame of mind. At the moment it is all talk and no action. I cannot imagine what they are waiting for. They are still discussing the Austrian threat. Let the Austrians threaten all they like. They can do nothing, and it is none of their business. Meanwhile, the Bourbons are sitting in the Tuileries making fools of us. We should dispose of them and declare the Republic. The revolution will soon spread to Austria, and then there will be no problem with threats."

By way of reply, Lessard reached into his coat pocket and produced a copy of *Le Moniteur*. He held it out to Chabot and said simply, "You are out of touch. The Assembly declared war on Austria four days ago." Chabot took the paper and turned it to the fading light from the window.

Dufay appeared with a covered plate, a bottle and a glass, which he deposited on the table. He glanced at Lessard, gave him a brief nod, walked over to the counter and fetched a second glass. Chabot laid the paper on the table and glowered at the plate.

"You are right. I should have stayed in Paris."

Lessard removed the cover from the plate to reveal two chunks of bread and two pieces of cheese at which Chabot peered closely. At least he could not see any signs that rats had been at them, so that was an improvement on yesterday. Lessard seized one of the hunks of bread and tore off a piece with his teeth, while Chabot waved Dufay away and slopped brandy into the two glasses. Lessard swallowed his mouthful, made an appreciative noise and said casually, "The operation was completed. Now all we have to do is wait."

Chabot looked at him. "Completed? There were no difficulties?"

"I gather not. The agents returned about an hour ago aboard a lugger. They were picked up at a place called Brighthelmstone yesterday. They report that they lay in wait near the house in Kent and ambushed young Poitier's chaise. They drugged him, though one of them remarked that he didn't seem to know his arse from his elbow anyway. Perhaps he had been taking something stronger than snuff! They had found out where the nearest active highwaymen were, though it was much further away than we had expected and it took them two days to get there – the next county, apparently. Anyway, they asked questions and pretty soon found their hide-out. The rest of it went exactly as planned. They sent Marcel to tip off the nearest authorities, then left the drugged brandy where the highwaymen would be sure to find it and kept watch. After one of the villains took it, they waited a couple of hours, drugged the boy again, put the coat on him, left him at the edge of the camp and lit a fire, putting plenty of green stuff on it. Then they hid and watched again. It wasn't long before the smoke from the fire was spotted. They waited until the three were dragged off, then made their way to the coast. I have sent them to Paris. They did well. Marcel has remained in England, at a place called Horsham. There is a garrison there. He might be able to get some useful information. This brandy is disgusting!" He pulled a wry face.

"They did do well." Chabot sat back in his chair and allowed himself a small satisfied smile. "Very well. Now, as you say, all we have to do is wait. When the English find that document all hell will break loose. Just imagine! The boy will protest that he knows nothing about it, but who will believe him? The revelation that a French aristo is involved in a plot to murder King George will cause more than a stir. By the way, our prisoners are comfortable, I trust?"

"Yes, we have put them in the small room over the kitchen." He gestured upwards.

"They are secure?"

"There is no lock on the door, but do not worry. They cannot get down the stairs without being seen, and Jacques is watching the stable yard. There is no exit for them. The aristo seems agitated, and he does not look well"

"You searched them?"

"They were unarmed. They have a valise. It contains mainly clothes. The aristo has a pocket-book, some keys and a purse. I have let him keep them, for the moment."

"Well, he is not so important to us now – more of an insurance than anything. The odious Markham will deny everything, but the document implicates him, too. I wish I could be present when he dances on the gallows."

"They shoot aristos in England: they don't hang them." said Lessard quietly.

"Ah, well, no matter. He will be just as dead." Chabot smiled grimly.

Lessard regarded his superior steadily for a some moments. The man was really not suited to this sort of business at all. Apart from being too nervous, he had apparently developed a deep personal hatred for Sir Horace Markham. It was perhaps not surprising, since it was Markham who was responsible for foiling his attempt to have William Pitt, the British Prime Minister, assassinated last year. The operation, planned by Chabot, had been a miserable failure which had degenerated almost into farce. Pitt's life had never been even remotely in danger, and Lessard had ended up losing two good men, killed in a fight with British Revenue men and the local militia, miles from where they should have been and having been taken for smugglers. Chabot's failure irked him, but in the shady world in which Lessard had operated for many years there was no room for personal vendettas. However, Chabot was a prominent member of the committee in Paris which now directed these operations, though how he managed to achieve that position Lessard was not sure. He just wished the wretched man would stay in Paris and let professionals such as himself get things done.

"It may be a little longer than we anticipated before we hear anything." He said finally. "The place where they found the highwaymen is further from London than is the house in Kent, and we do not know if the communications are as good. They probably aren't, and we have no agent in the area. My men said it was rather remote."

"Then we must exercise patience. Do we have any agents in Kent?"

"Fournier is watching Dover, Millard is at Chatham, gathering information about the dockyard. We have two men in Sussex as well, but they are in the east of the county. As far as I know, we have no-one else between there and Portsmouth, except, of course, for your man Marcel now, but it will be some time before he will be able to glean anything useful. Of course, another department may have people in place, but…"

Chabot drained his glass. "You are right. This brandy is foul. Where is the coffee? And the dolt didn't bring the butter I asked for. How long do you think it will be before your two arrive in Paris?"

Lessard considered for a moment. "It is difficult to say, with the state of the roads. Two days, probably." He stood up and walked to the counter. "*Monsieur* Dufay, I think you have forgotten the coffee, and are you quite sure there is no decent brandy?" He placed some coins on the counter.

Dufay looked down at the coins and a smile spread slowly over his face. "I will look again, *M'sieur*. Do you require more bread and cheese?"

"If you please, and I would like a bowl of your excellent onion soup, if you have any."

"Certainly, *M'sieur*. I will bring it in a few minutes."

"Thank you." Lessard turned and made his way back to

the table. Dufay swept the coins into his pocket and headed for the kitchen.

※

At about ten o'clock, Chabot rose from the table, yawned and said to Lessard, "It has been a long day. I think I will retire. I would like to get back to Paris early tomorrow. Good night, citizen."

"Good night," replied Lessard. Chabot disappeared up the stairs. Lessard finished his brandy, stood up and went to the door to the yard, which he opened. "Jacques? All is well?"

On hearing the affirmative grunt, he closed the door, turned, nodded to the two fishermen and walked out of the inn, pulling his cape around him. He would spend the night at the brothel – much better company than that at the inn.

A few minutes later, the two fishermen rose from their table, bade the innkeeper's daughter goodnight and left. The girl crossed to clear the table. The flagon of cider had hardly been touched. Perhaps it had not been to their liking. She shrugged and picked it up. She could sell it again…

※

About an hour later, Chabot was awakened from his slumber. What it was that woke him he was not sure. He lay and listened for a minute or so, then rolled over and prepared to go to sleep again. As he did so, he caught a whiff of smoke. The damned chimney again, he thought, then realized that the smoke was coming through his window, which he had left slightly open by mistake. He was just considering whether to get up and close it when he heard the sounds of a sudden commotion from outside. He rolled out of bed and went to the window. He could see nothing, but he could hear shouts and running footsteps. A few seconds later, boots thundered up the stairs and someone was hammering on his door. Whoever it was yelled "Fire, fire!" and the boots thundered away again without waiting for a reply and before he could reach the door. He threw on his clothes and hurried from the room. There was chaos. People were running everywhere, bumping into each other in the darkness. There was no sign of Jacques. Chabot found his way downstairs and out of the building, where the rain and mist were lit by the glare of flames coming from the rear of the building. The stables! Damn! His horse was in there! He hurried in the direction of the gates to the stable-yard.

As he vanished into the mist and smoke, two figures detached themselves from the darkness and loped, stooping, to the window by the table at which Chabot and Lessard had been sitting. They wrenched it open and slipped through it into the building.

꿏

Hugo Poitiers sat back in his chair and watched as Russell helped himself to more cheese. It was a long time since he had eaten so well. The game pie had been delicious, the bread fresh and the wine of good quality, but he had, on Russell's advice, eaten only enough to satisfy his immediate hunger and taken just one glass of wine. Russell himself, in spite of his slightly portly frame, had eaten only a modest amount. Hugo studied the room. Though the house was old and the windows rather small, it was light and airy. The furniture was mostly of oak, and dark with age. Hanging on the walls and displayed in cabinets were mementoes of the Doctor's travels – curious small sculptures, weapons (Hugo recognized an assegai and a scimitar), paintings and tapestries. Pride of place on a side-table was given to a large and finely-made model of a seventy-four gun ship, accurately rigged and correct to the last detail. Their conversation over the meal had centred largely around these items and their shared maritime backgrounds. It was evident to Hugo that Russell was much-travelled. He himself had visited Africa and the West Indies, but Russell had been to India and Indonesia: places to which he longed to travel. The pictures which Russell painted, both verbally and the ones on the walls, made him even more determined to see these strange lands for himself. For Russell's part, he found the youth to be in possession of both intelligence and an enquiring mind. He asked intelligent questions and appeared surprisingly mature for his years. During the course of the meal, Russell had warmed to him: he should like to know more about this young man who seemed strangely at ease. He pushed his plate away and fumbled in his pocket for his pince-nez, jammed them on to his nose and peered over them at Hugo. "Well, young man, I suggest we take some coffee in my library." He rose from the table and led the way to the door.

A few minutes later, Hugo was gazing into a cabinet of curios when Russell said, "I should like to take you to meet a friend of mine tomorrow, if you feel well enough. He may be able to throw some light on your father's whereabouts."

Hugo dragged his eyes from the cabinet and replied, "If you please, Sir. I should be most grateful for any help."

"Very well, then. Oh - I have forgotten to give your coat to

Jessie. You will need it tomorrow. I will fetch it now. Do make yourself at home, and I shall be pleased to answer any questions you may have concerning my collections, if they interest you."

Russell strode from the room, went to the sick-room and took the coat from the hook where he had left it. It was still a little damp. A few moments later, the coat draped over his arm, he walked into the kitchen where Jessie was tidying up. "Jessie, I forgot to bring you this. I hope you can do something with it by tomorrow." Jessie gave him a stern glance and took the coat from his arm. She shook it out and held it up. "It doesn't look too bad to me, Sir. The pocket is nearly off and it is still damp, but the mud will brush off." She opened the coat and examined the lining, then paused, a frown on her face. "Look at this, Sir." Russell peered at the patch of material which Jessie had turned toward him. "It has been repaired, I see." "Yes, Sir, but not well, and why is it such a big patch? You may get tears in the lining, but that is a very strange repair."

Russell reached out and took the coat from her. He examined the patch more closely. It was very roughly sewn on. He poked it with a finger. It seemed much firmer than the surrounding material and made a slight crackling sound. He poked it again, with the same result, then looked up at Jessie's puzzled frown. He fished in his pocket and produced his penknife, cut through the stitches and peeled the patch away to reveal a thin packet, wrapped in oiled silk. Without a word, he handed the coat to Jessie, laid the packet on the table and opened it. It contained two sheets of paper, twice folded. Russell unfolded them and began to read. Jessie, still holding the coat, remained stock still. When Russell had finished, he folded the papers again and returned them to the packet, resettled his pince-nez and said quietly, "Most interesting. I am sure Horace will agree with me. Is the coat repairable, Jessie?" "Yes, Sir. It wasn't damaged." She held the patch away to reveal the intact lining. "Please to keep the patch safely when you have finished removing it" said Russell, " I must have a word with our young friend." With that he was gone. Jessie sighed, hung the coat on the back of a chair and moved it closer to the fire.

"You are quite sure that you have never seen the coat before?" asked Russell. He was standing with his back to the fireplace, the packet hidden in his pocket. "Absolutely certain, Sir." Russell regarded Hugo for a moment. The youth had a perfectly open expression on his face and was looking steadily at him. Russell could see no reason to suspect him of lying. "May I ask why, Sir?"

Russell considered for a moment longer, then made up his mind. He produced the packet from his pocket. "You may. I have just found this in the lining. It is written in French, and my knowledge of that language is not good, though I think I have the gist of what is in this document. Perhaps you would be kind enough to assist me with some of its finer points. Read it for yourself first." He opened the packet, extracted the papers and placed them on the desk.

Hugo leaned over the desk, smoothed the papers down and began reading. After a few moments, Russell heard him gasp. He flashed a glance at Russell, who merely inclined his head gravely and motioned him to continue. Having finished, he read through again, more carefully, then straightened up.

He looked pale and very worried. "Sir, this, this document…"
"Purports to implicate both you and your father in a plot to murder King George," said Russell quietly.

"Yes, Sir, it does." Then, "You said your knowledge of French was not good, Sir."

Russell smiled grimly at him. "I lied. I just wanted to see your reaction. You have passed the test. Now we must decide on a course of action." He picked the papers up from the desk, re-folded them and put them back in the packet, which he placed in a drawer of the desk. "Let us have some more coffee, and I think perhaps a little of something stronger might be an aid to the grey matter. Brandy or Whisky?"

# CHAPTER FIVE

Horace Markham rested his elbows on his desk, clasped his hands together and studied the young man standing before him. As Russell had intimated, he found Hugo Poitiers open and honest. He could detect no sign of shiftiness or unease – nothing to suggest that his story was anything but the truth. He glanced over to where Russell was standing before the fireplace, then looked back at Hugo, to find the bright blue eyes still fixed steadily on him. Markham straightened up, removed his elbows from the desk, shifted back on his chair and placed his hands, palms down, flat on the document which lay in front of him. "Well, young man, I believe you. Now we must decide what to do. The situation regarding your father is grave, and that your mother is also missing makes it more so. In addition, it is obvious that agents of the revolutionary movement in your country are not content with confining their fomentation of rebellion and anarchy to their own borders, but are hell – bent on spreading it as far and wide as possible. We know of some of their activities in Europe, but hitherto there has been only one bungled attempt at interference on these shores, or, rather, only one of which I have knowledge. This document," he picked it up and waved it, then replaced it on the desk at looked down at it, "is of singular interest. It is most fortunate for you that things did not go quite as its perpetrators intended, or you would by now be facing some very difficult questions indeed. It is also your good fortune that you chanced to have fallen into our hands. Had you not, you might well by now be dead."

He glanced up at Hugo again. The youth was looking very pale and rather shocked. Hardly surprising, thought Markham, in view of the fact that in the past ten minutes I have informed him that not only had an attempt been made to have him executed as a common criminal, and that at the probable instigation of some of his own countrymen, but also that his mother, whom he believed to be safe in Kent, had disappeared. He has taken it well: he could be useful to us.

After a moment he asked, "Have you heard of a man called Pierre Chabot?"

"I have not, Sir, but I have heard the name Chabot – François Chabot. I believe he is a member of the Legislative Assembly, and a Jacobin."

"Yes, we know of him. Pierre is a cousin. We believe him to be connected with certain departments of the Assembly which are concerned with spreading the revolution, and who are not too fussy about the methods they employ. This," he indicated the document, "smacks of some of those methods. I suspect Chabot's hand in it somewhere, since we have learned that he was responsible for the previous bungled attempt. I am informed that he was most displeased at our foiling of his little scheme and that he is the sort of man who bears a grudge. I am also informed that he knows something of me: hence this attempt to implicate me in this sordid little affair." Markham smiled. It occurred to Hugo that there was something distinctly sinister about the smile. He decided that he would not wish to get on the wrong side of Sir Horace Markham, despite all his apparent amiability. The smile, thought Hugo, did not bode well for Citizen Pierre Chabot.

He looked up and caught Markham's eye. As if reading his thoughts, Markham winked at him and said, "I believe some of your compatriots regard us in these islands as '*La perfide Albion.*' Well, as a result of this, I intend that Citizen Chabot should discover what the true meaning of perfidy is. He will find that we are capable of far worse than his," he flicked at the document with the back of his hand, "risibly pitiful little attempt at it."

Again the smile. There was something vulpine about it. Hugo swallowed. No, it was possibly more reptilian than vulpine. He swallowed again. Markham suddenly threw his head back and laughed. "Aloysius, I think I have frightened your patient enough for one day. You are standing near to the bell. It is time for some refreshment." He stood up, picked up the two sheets of paper, folded them, returned them to the packet, opened a drawer of the desk, dropped the packet into it, closed the drawer and locked it. He walked round the desk, clapped Hugo on the shoulder, and turned to Taylor, who had made an almost silent appearance. "Ah, Taylor, we will take some wine – on the terrace, if you please. Come, gentlemen."

A few minutes later, feeling dazed and without really knowing how he came to be there, Hugo found himself seated at a small table outside the French windows of the morning-room, with Russell facing him and Markham on his left. Taylor poured three glasses of claret, placed the decanter on the table and retired through the French windows. He looked up to find Russell looking gravely at him, and Markham watching Russell. "How are you feeling, young man?" asked Russell.

"I am well, Sir." He replied.

"Your appearance implies something less than that, which is not surprising given the undoubtedly unwelcome revelations of the last hour or so." Russell turned to Markham. "I think it might be prudent for me to get my patient home as soon as possible. He is still far from well, and I should like him to have a few days to recover from the shock which you have visited upon him. Perhaps we should meet again in a few days' time?"

"By all means, dear fellow. Young man, the doctor is perfectly correct. I am sorry to have had to be the bearer of bad tidings. I have sent instructions for the curricle to be readied for your journey. If you feel you can help us, I am sure that both His Majesty's Government and I will be very grateful." He picked up his glass and examined the light through its contents. "When you are quite well, I should like you to meet some friends of mine. Oh, and I was forgetting, I have something for you. Taylor! Taylor! Dammit! He cannot hear me, and we have not brought out a bell. Taylor!"

"Sir?" Taylor had approached from the entrance to the stable yard, where he had been relaying Markham's instructions concerning the curricle.

"What? Oh, there you are. What the devil were you doing in the stables – oh, yes, I remember. Well, stop creeping about like a curate in a whorehouse and fetch me the package which you will find on my desk, if you please." Taylor, grinning, disappeared through the French windows. Markham glared after his retreating form and announced, "I sometimes wonder who is the head of this household. Whatever I propose is, more oft than not, vetoed by my wife; my children run rings around me and that man is insufferable."

"How so, Sir?" ventured Hugo.

"Because he is nearly always right, damn' him, and he seems to know what I want before I know it myself. He also somehow contrives to nag me, and it is all too obvious should he disapprove of something, yet he never says a word."

"I believe those to be indicators of a good servant, Horace," interjected Russell. "He has been with you for many years. Your father engaged him, did he not? He chose well. You do need someone to rein in your wilder schemes, and I think your good lady has given up on that front. It is just as well that Taylor has known you since you were quite young. He must have the measure of you by now. You should be grateful. Without him, I fear your household would collapse into anarchy."

"I know, I know…" Markham's voice trailed off into silence. He picked up the decanter and removed the stopper. "But even so…" He poured more wine and said suddenly, "He never seems to age. Now I come to think of it, he cannot have been very much older than I was when my father took him on as a footman. It was only a few years after that Mudge died and suddenly Taylor was everywhere. That was while I was in the army. I recall coming home on leave and that was it. He has remained in his position ever since, though by God I should have removed him from it many times over for his insolence!"

Russell, grinning, took his lancet from his pocket. "Now, Horace, you are becoming over-animated. If you do not calm yourself you will do yourself a mischief, and I shall have to bleed you."

"Oh, ah, yes, um. Have some more wine, Aloysius." Markham grimaced at the lancet which Russell was waving under his nose. "And put that infernal instrument away, there's a good fellow." Russell put the lancet away and turned to Hugo. "You see, he is not as fierce as he makes himself out to be. More like a lamb, really. He should know better: the consequences of blaspheming Taylor are likely to be dire."

Markham opened his mouth to reply, but caught sight of Taylor approaching from the house, thought better of it and snapped it shut again. "The package, Sir." Markham gave him an almost sickly grin. "And the curricle is ready, gentlemen," this with a slight bow to Russell and Hugo.

Russell inclined his head slightly. "Thank you, Taylor. You are a very good fellow."

"Yes, thank you, Taylor," said Markham to the man's already retreating back. He placed the package on the table and untied the string. He unfolded the hessian wrapping to reveal a small wooden box, which he pushed towards Hugo. "Yours, I believe."

"It is, Sir. How did you find it?"

"Some of my men paid your coachman a visit. He suddenly remembered that your box was left in his chaise when you were abducted from it. He had apparently removed it for 'safekeeping'." Again Hugo noticed the sinister smile. "I am afraid the lock is broken, but as you have undoubtedly been so careless as to lose the key, that is probably an advantage. You had better make sure it is all there."

Hugo opened the box, poked about in it for a few moments and said simply, "It is all there, Sir. I thank you."

"Good." Markham nodded in satisfaction. "My men are very good, you know. Very, very good."

"I trust they left the coachman in good health," said Russell quietly, with a sideways glance at Markham.

"Oh, yes, indeed. He was not damaged at all, well, hardly

at all. Just a little frightened, perhaps. Now let us adjourn to the yard. Mustn't keep your carriage waiting, you know."

⚜

Russell hitched up his coat-tails, turned his backside to the fire and watched Hugo as he peered into one of the collection cabinets in the library. Hugo had been very quiet over supper. He was evidently pre-occupied by the events and news of the day, but Russell did not want to intrude too much on his thoughts. Hugo suddenly straightened up, turned to Russell and said, "Sir, what do you think I should do? My life is all turned about. I am supposed to be taking my lieutenant's exams, but I have realized that the Legislative Assembly has effectively expelled me from the navy. I am cast up on the beach."

"They have not only expelled you from the navy, but also from your country. You cannot go back: they are likely to murder you." replied Russell. "Perhaps you now have to decide where your loyalty lies. It must be very difficult for you, and nigh impossible for me to offer any constructive comments."

"And my parents are both missing, unless this, this Chabot has already had them murdered." Hugo began to pace up and down. "My father feared this some years ago. That is why he decided to move to England. The rest of us thought he was mad, and the unrest would soon be forgotten, but he was right. I have heard that mobs are rioting in the streets, and anyone with a title or land is in danger of being attacked, even killed."

"A good many have fled the country," said Russell. "Your father had considerable foresight, as many of the refuges escape with just their lives and the clothes on their backs. Your father has property, and he was able to get his wealth out of France because he acted early."

"But that is no use to him if he is dead. He should not have gone to France again. Surely there must have been someone who could have done his business for him."

"You forget that your own health was part of the reason for his visit."

"Oh, yes, Sir, of course. I am sorry."

"Do not be. It is not your fault."

Hugo sat down on a chair by the fire and looked at Russell. Then he said, "I have lost my career, I have lost my country, and I have lost my parents." After a long pause, during which Hugo stared into the flames, Russell said, "At least you will inherit."

"That is not important, Sir, not to me. I have little interest in money or property." There was another long pause, then Hugo said, "I like Sir Horace. Do you really think he can help?"

"I do," replied Russell. "If he says he can help, that means that he can. He is a man of his word. I am pleased you like him. I think he likes you. Many people find him intimidating."

"But he is not. I saw his reaction to your threat to bleed him."

"Indeed. Like all of us, he has his weaknesses. One of those is the sight of blood, particularly his own. Strange that his profession should involve the shedding of so much of it! At least when I draw blood, it is with kindly intent."

"What is his profession, exactly, Sir?"

Russell considered for a moment. "Well, let us say that he is a sort of counterpart of Monsieur Chabot, but much better at it. I would loosely describe his profession as 'intelligence'."

"Well, Sir, if you agree, I should like to see him again, and to meet these friends of his. I would like to do whatever I can to help England, since she offered my family a refuge, and if Sir Horace can help me find out what has happened to my parents, I would be greatly indebted."

Russell let his coat-tails drop, drew his pipe from his pocket and said, "Very well, young man. We shall pay him another visit very soon. He has been called to London on urgent business and will be away for a few days, but we can spend those usefully. I suggest we start tomorrow by visiting my tailor." He grinned as Hugo looked down at his patched breeches.

❧

As dusk closed in on the little village of Saint-Pierre, about ten miles from Dieppe, a farm cart, drawn by a tired donkey, drew up in the yard of a modest farmhouse. The driver descended and walked to the rear of the cart. He prodded with his whip at the heap of hay on the cart and announced, "We have arrived." The hay stirred and two figures crawled stiffly off the cart. The carter reached under the hay and pulled out a canvas valise, which he deposited on the ground beside the men, who were trying to massage some life back into their limbs and brush the hay off their clothes.

The carter waited patiently and watched as the taller of the two fumbled in his pockets, eventually finding his purse, from which he took some coins. He counted some out, spread them on the palm of his hand, looked critically at them and counted out some more. Then he proffered them to the carter, who took and pocketed them with a nod and a grunt of thanks. The other man picked up the valise and both turned to walk towards the house. The carter watched them for a few seconds. The tall one, his aquiline features silhouetted against the fading light, was evidently an 'aristo', the other possibly a servant. What the two were doing and why they had asked to be conveyed in secret were no longer the carter's business and he had been paid handsomely. He mounted the cart and clicked his tongue at the donkey.

Henri, Comte de Poitiers, stood at the door of the house for a moment, listening to the clop of the donkey's hooves and the creaking of the cart fading into the distance. Then he sighed and nodded at his companion, who knocked on the door. After a few seconds, it opened a crack.

"*Qui va là?*" demanded a gruff voice.

"*Chasseur.*"

There was a moment's pause, then, "*Mot de passe?*"

"*Oriflamme.*"

"*C'est bien.*" The door closed again, there was a rattle as a chain was removed, the door opened wide and a man, short and rather fat, with a ruddy complexion, beckoned them inside.

"You were not followed?"

"I think not," said Poitiers, "we were well hidden."

"Good. The carter is reliable. He is unimaginative, and very stupid if he needs to be. I was expecting you. I had word two days ago. You have made good time." He shook his head sadly, "These are dangerous times. The English Gentleman came. He told me his men helped you to escape."

Poitiers nodded. They had been 'arrested' by militia and held at a run-down boarding-house in Dieppe until two days ago, when they had been handed over to a small group of men who were apparently from Paris, and whose leader had introduced himself as 'Citizen Chabot'. They had been taken to an inn set at the side of a square. Unbeknown to them, the 'English Gentleman's' men had witnessed the 'arrest', had followed the militia and their prisoners to the boarding house, and had kept watch on the place and all its comings and goings until the prisoners were moved to the inn. They had followed them there, watched again, and at about midnight they had set fire to the inn's stables. In the ensuing confusion they had hustled Poitiers and his servant out of the inn, pushed them on to a cart and given them the password before melting into the shadows. The cart had taken them out of town and they had been passed from one safe-house to another, travelling mostly under cover of darkness for the first part of the journey. Like thieves in the night, thought Poitiers. "He is here?" he asked.

"No, he has gone back to England. He told me to tell you that arrangements are being made to collect you, but it may take some while, as there are now possible extra difficulties. You may not have heard – the Assembly has declared war on Austria. You will be safe enough here, and word will come when it is time to move."

"Austria? That is madness. When did this happen?"

"I do not know exactly when. It was a few days ago. The English Gentleman told me. He had to hurry home to consult with his superiors, otherwise he would have been here to meet you. He told me the situation is very grave, law and order have broken down in many places and there are murderous mobs in many of the towns. Thank God it has not spread this far."

"I fear it will, my friend, I fear it will. What is the English Gentleman's name?"

"I do not know, and I do not wish to know. The less I know the better. I do not even know your name. I know you only as 'Chasseur'. That is sufficient. Your companion I shall call Jean. I am known as 'Rameau'. Welcome to my home. He extended a hand. Poitiers and Gaston shook it each in turn, then 'Rameau' picked up the valise and said, "I will show you to your rooms. You must be tired."

"Rameau?" said Poitiers, "Twig? A strange alias…"

The other turned at the foot of the stairs. "Yes, 'Twig'. The English Gentleman gave me the name." He patted his belly. "I think it is the English sense of humour, no?"

In Dieppe, Chabot and Lessard picked over the burned-out remains of the stable. A groom had managed to rescue the horses, but Chabot's had suffered from inhaling smoke and was still not fit enough to make the journey to Paris. The inn's chaise had been destroyed in the fire, so it was evident that Chabot was likely to be stranded in the port for several more days. It had not been until the next morning that the disappearance of the aristo and his man had been noticed. Lessard, returning to the inn in the morning, had immediately gone to check on the prisoners, to find the room empty. It was only then noticed that Jacques, too, had vanished. His body was discovered soon after in the alleyway behind the stables. His neck was broken. An examination of the building had revealed that the window in the dining-room was open, but it was assumed that someone had chosen that way to escape from the fire, which had not, in the end, spread to the inn itself. Lessard was suspicious. Jacques' body had been found some distance from the inn. His neck was broken, but Lessard could not see how a fall could have accounted for that, unless he had somehow climbed on to a roof. Yes, perhaps that was it. He must have found himself trapped in the hayloft and climbed on to a neighbouring roof to escape the flames, then lost his footing. Lessard stirred a fused and blackened mass, which had once been some harness, with his boot, then straightened up and said, "We are wasting our time. We shall find nothing here."

"You think the fire was deliberately started?" asked Chabot.

"I do – to create a diversion to allow Poitiers to escape."

"The English?"

"I doubt it. You worry too much about the English. It is more likely royalist sympathisers. There are plenty around here, and no doubt Poitiers has friends."

"He is probably still in Dieppe," said Chabot. "The roads are watched. Organise a thorough search of the town."

"As you wish." Lessard turned away. The roads were indeed watched, but in the confusion caused by the fire, it was likely that not much attention would have been paid to a couple of men leaving the town. The watchers would probably have rushed to help with putting out the blaze. Poitiers could be many miles away by now. He was small fry. He would eventually be caught. Meanwhile, Lessard had other matters to deal with, not the least of which was getting his superior out from under his feet and on his way to Paris. That would leave him time and space to deal with the pimp who controlled the women at the brothel, and whom he feared might possibly attempt to denounce him. Good Jacobins were not supposed to make use of prostitutes, but Lessard had his own ways of dealing with blackmailers, and, besides, he was no Jacobin. His loyalty was only to the highest bidder. He had served the King well in the past, and had had no compunction about transferring his loyalty when it became apparent to him that the King would not be his paymaster for much longer. He did not trust the Assembly, but, at least for the moment, it paid him well. In the future, well…

Chabot sighed and turned away. He felt trapped in this dismal hole of a town, with its dreadful smell of fish.

# CHAPTER SIX

The morning of Saturday, the 28th of April, 1792 was bright and clear. There had been rain overnight, but this had cleared in the early hours, leaving everything looking washed and fresh. The air was warm, the sky was a vivid blue, and fluffy cumulus clouds moved sedately from west to east.

Halfway along the gravelled drive to the Park, a lone horseman reined in his chestnut hunter and cocked his head to listen. After a few moments, the cuckoo called again. The horseman smiled. Spring at last! The English Gentleman thought this the finest time of year, and was always glad if he could be in England during April and May. The sight and sound were particularly welcome after his rough passage across the channel two days ago, he thought. He was not a good sailor, and was violently seasick in anything other than a flat calm. The cuckoo called again, this time from nearby, and he swivelled his head in time to see the bird fly into a spinney off to his left. He sat for several more seconds, then clicked his tongue at the chestnut, who moved off at his usual easy walk. A few minutes later, The English Gentleman dismounted in the stable yard, unhitched his saddlebag, waved away the footman who had come running and nodded to the groom, who led the chestnut away.

Hugo was standing together with Russell in Markham's library, a little apart from two men whom Markham had introduced as Major Fletcher and Sergeant-Major Lloyd. As they waited while Taylor served drinks, Hugo studied them. Neither was in uniform, and neither had a particularly military appearance. Fletcher, in particular, had more of the appearance of a society fop than an army officer, reminding Hugo of some of the dandified, perfumed higher ranks of the French Army. Lloyd, on the other hand, seemed to have an air about him that suggested he would be very much at home as a librarian, but this impression was marred by the presence of a livid scar which ran from his left ear almost to his chin. The two men obviously knew each other well, and there was a good deal of good-natured bickering between them. They also teased Markham gently, to Russell's evident amusement. He chuckled at one of Fletcher's jibes and turned to Hugo. "I think you will like Fletcher. He is actually Lord Augustus Fletcher, but, being his father's third son, he does not stand to inherit unless something calamitous befalls his two older brothers. He was something of a rogue in his youth, but he eventually joined the Army, where it was discovered that he has a talent for clandestine activities. He doesn't use his title, except if he is in the sort of company which absolutely requires it. He is very well connected, and plays the dandy a little 'to relieve the monotony of London society', as he puts it." Hugo glanced at Fletcher's face, which appeared good-natured, if slightly aquiline. He was not wearing a wig, and his fair hair was pulled back and tied in a queue at the nape of his neck, in the naval fashion. He caught Hugo's gaze, smiled and crossed the room, hand outstretched. "Don't listen to whatever scurrilous details Russell is telling you about me. They are probably true, for the most part." Hugo shook the proffered hand and replied, "Indeed, my Lord?"

"Ah! I thought as much. You have been taking my name in vain, as I suspected, Russell. Take no notice of him, young man. Augustus is the name – 'Taffy' to my less kind friends, for some strange reason which I have lost in the mists of time. I prefer 'Fletch', which is what my men call me." He gave Russell a wolfish grin and wandered back to join Lloyd, who was peering at something out of the window. Russell smiled at Hugo and said, "He has not really forgotten the reason for his sobriquet. Apparently, when he was young, he disliked being called 'Gus', which is the common contraction. Some learned wag at his school suggested that the first person to dislike the name Augustus was the first person to be so called – the Emperor Octavian, so he began to call him 'Tavvy', short for Octavian. It soon became corrupted to 'Taffy'."

Taylor finished serving the drinks and retired from the room. After a few minutes of small talk, the door opened again and Taylor announced, "Gentlemen, Sir Charles Goodrich." Everyone rose to their feet and Markham hurried over to the new arrival, his hand outstretched. "Welcome, Jack. I trust you had a good journey?"

"Abominable, thank you, Horace. Quite the worst storm in the channel I have ever experienced, but you knew that, of course, damn' you!" Goodrich punched Markham gently on the shoulder and seized the glass of wine which Taylor proffered. "How is your good lady?"

"She is very well, I thank you, Jack. I have no doubt she will appear when we have finished our business. Before we begin, I should like to introduce you to this young man. His name is Hugo Poitiers." Goodrich's eyebrows shot upwards. "Poitiers! Indeed! How d'ye do, young man." Hugo found his hand taken in a vice-like grip and shaken firmly. "Then I have news for all of you. I think it best that we start now, and I shall make my report immediately." He opened a leather document case and extracted several sheets of paper, a copy of *Le Moniteur* and another journal, which he passed to Russell. "There you are, Doctor, as promised." Russell thanked him.

Markham ushered them all to a large table at one end of the room and waved vaguely at the chairs surrounding it. "Please be seated, gentlemen. Let us not stand upon any sort of ceremony."

When the scraping of chair-legs had subsided, Goodrich looked straight at Hugo and said, "Well, Mister Poitiers, I take it that you are the son of Henri, Comte de Poitiers, who is missing in France?" In response to Hugo's nod, he continued, "Then it is my pleasure to inform you and the members of the department who are present that he is no longer missing, although he is still in France, and extracting him may be difficult. I can assure you all that he was alive and well two days ago. He is now in one of our safe houses. I had word of his arrival there from the keeper of the house just before I sailed."

"What had happened to him, Sir? Where had he been?" blurted Hugo before he could stop himself. Goodrich gave him a smile and continued. "It seems that he and his man Gaston were seized by revolutionaries as they tried to board a channel packet at Dieppe. I am afraid the department's enquiries as to his whereabouts arrived too late, otherwise our usual other arrangements would have been made. It was, I believe, only a matter of minutes too late." He glanced at Markham, who merely nodded. "They were held at a boarding-house for some while, then handed over to some people from Paris, who took them to an inn. The man who was apparently in charge is, I believe, known to you, Horace. His name is Chabot."

"Ah, I suspected as much," said Markham quietly. Glancing at him, Hugo noticed again the sinister smile creeping across his features. "Pray continue, Sir Charles," he added formally.

"It would seem that Chabot was careless. He and a man called Lessard, who appears to be his deputy, put up at the inn, or at least Chabot did. They had a couple of thugs with them to act as guards, but they all seemed rather complacent. My men were able to extract Poitiers and his man without too much difficulty."

"Your men?" interjected Markham. "I was not aware you had men in place."

"Not exactly 'in place', as you put it. They were the men whom I had alerted to receive him had your message arrived in time, so they were in the area. As a matter of fact, they were able to observe Poitiers' detention, and they had no difficulty in following him. They kept watch the whole time, and when he was moved, they followed again. They are, ahem, fishermen, though I suspect they do more fishing for bottles than for whiting. They are originally from Guernsey, and speak fluent French. They are quite well known, and their presence in several of the channel ports goes un-remarked. They come and go without interference from the French authorities. It is necessary only to arrange for certain individuals to receive - how shall I put it? - certain 'sweeteners' from time to time."

"I have heard of Lessard," said Markham. "He used to work for the King. Has he become a revolutionary?"

"It would seem so, but I have it on fairly good authority that he is prepared to prostitute his skills and services in the field of intelligence to the highest bidder. He may be useful to us, even unwittingly."

"Please, Sir," Hugo interrupted the silence which followed, during which Markham's sinister smile broadened and the others nodded, "How did your men get my father away?"

Goodrich turned his steady gaze on Hugo. "Well, Chabot and Lessard had a habit of eating together in the inn's parlour. Unusual – the French tend to take meals in their rooms. My men simply occupied a nearby table and listened to their conversation. When Lessard left – my men knew he stayed at a local brothel, yes, Horace, that could be useful to us," he added, noticing Markham's raised eyebrow, "and Chabot went to bed, they waited a while, then set fire to the inn stables."

"What about the guards?" enquired Fletcher.

"One of them attempted to interfere, but he unaccountably slipped and broke his neck, poor fellow. My men took advantage of the ensuing confusion to release the prisoners. They smuggled them out of Dieppe on a cart, since their vessel had sailed some time before. A stay of more than a few hours would have attracted attention – they were, after all, supposed to be fishing, and the other vessels sailed as usual with the tide. We know the harbour is watched. The only thing I do not really understand is why Chabot should be so interested in Poitiers. It is not," inclining his head toward Hugo, "as if the family is of especial importance or a particular threat to the revolution."

"I think we have the answer to that," said Markham, pushing a document across the table towards him. "Young Poitiers here found himself caught up in something rather unsavoury. This document was planted in his clothing, evidently with the intention that it be discovered." He went on briefly to describe the circumstances leading to Hugo's presence.

"I see." Goodrich nodded and picked up the document, which Hugo recognized as the one which had been sewn into the lining of the coat, glanced briefly at it, exclaimed, "Aha!" and read it through. Then he nodded, replaced it on the table and said simply, "Yes, that does indeed make everything much more easy to understand. As a matter of fact, my men in Dieppe overheard Chabot and Lessard discussing this very document. They could not hear every word of the conversation, but what they did hear they reported to me. I was going to suggest that we organize a search for it, and for young Hugo here. That is now unnecessary, it would seem." He looked at Hugo. "Your presence among us has saved a great deal of work, young man." After a few moments' silence, he turned to Markham. "Was it not Chabot who was responsible for that business last year."

"The same," replied Markham.

"Bastard."

"A dangerous bastard. He needs to be stopped. Fortunately, he does not appear competent."

"Perhaps not, but Lessard does."

"Hmm. What other news?"

"Nothing much, except that a week, no - eight days ago now, France declared war on Austria."

"What? Are they mad?" exclaimed Markham.

In the ensuing hubbub, Hugo looked across at Russell, who raised his eyes slowly from the journal which Goodrich had given him, and which he had been reading rather than pay any particular attention to the proceedings going on around him. Their eyes met. Russell gave him a brief nod and laid the journal on the table. Hugo dragged his attention back to the conversation.

"What will Mr. Pitt do?" Russell enquired of Markham.

"I cannot say. I would imagine that the government would wish to avoid war, but I cannot see this country standing by if the French are attempting to spread their revolution over Europe. We must necessarily become embroiled."

Goodrich nodded vigorously in agreement. "It means that we must take advantage of the present state of peace to complete our business on the Poitiers affair, and neutralize Chabot and Lessard before we find ourselves at war. A state of war would only make our task more difficult. So, gentlemen, I propose that we see if we can agree on a course of action."

&

Half an hour later, the chairs were being pushed back from the table. Markham stood up and stretched himself. He glanced at Russell, who was still reading one of the pamphlets. "Well, Aloysius, have you discovered anything which might be of interest before we break up?"

"I am not sure if it is of particular interest to us, but the French have apparently adopted a new means of execution."

"Oh, how so? They usually behead people."

"Quite so. It is just that they have developed a machine which they claim does the job more accurately and efficiently than an axeman. This reports that Antoine Louis, the secretary of the *Académie Chirurgicale*, as saying that he believes it to be more humane because of its accuracy and swiftness. There is an engraving of it here."

The others crowded round to peer at the sheet, which had been hastily printed. Markham, after studying the engraving for a moment, said, "That is nothing new. It is a Scottish Maiden."

"What, pray, is a Scottish Maiden?" asked Fletcher.

"Much the same as this," said Russell, gesturing at the page. "It was used as a method of execution in Scotland until about an hundred years ago. The only difference I can see is that whereas the Scottish Maiden used a straight blade, this one is angled."

"Why 'maiden', Sir?", enquired Hugo.

"Ah, it resembles a particular type of frame which is used for drying clothes. We know it as a 'horse' in this part of the country, but it is called a 'maiden' elsewhere." He read on for a few more lines. This paper refers to the device as a 'Louisette' – oh, I see, after M. Louis. The machine has been tested, and it is planned to execute a highwayman, one Nicolas Pelletier, with it tomorrow." He looked to the top of the page for the date. "This is dated the twenty-fourth, so… I wonder how it went." He took off his spectacles and groped for his handkerchief. "You would." muttered Markham. "Not well for Pelletier, I'll be bound. Come, Hugo, let us leave the doctor to his ghoulish musings, and join the others for refreshments."

❧

Hugo stood gazing out of the big windows of the morning room, only half paying attention to the conversation around him. He felt rather hot, and hoped it was not the onset of another attack. He was suddenly conscious of Fletcher standing next to him. "Well, Poitiers, do you like our plan?" Hugo nodded. "Yes, but it seems dangerous. I am concerned for my father and…" his voice trailed off and he looked at Fletcher.

"And? Out with it. If any of us has any reservations, now is the time to voice them."

"Well, Sir, I am wondering why Sir Charles could not have brought my father with him."

Fletcher regarded him almost pityingly, then suddenly smiled. "Of course, you are not used to our ways. A very reasonable question. Sir Charles is well known to the French authorities, such as they are, but they assume him to be running a smuggling operation, which is very lucrative, not least to those officials in charge. They are well paid to fail to observe his comings and goings. However, he is always alone. Suspicions would be aroused were he to suddenly have companions. It is our intention that our Jack should continue to come and go as he pleases, so we could not have jeopardized his access to France by doing something unusual. As far as we know, he is unknown to Chabot. I think we should all prefer it should Chabot remain in ignorance, do you not agree?"

"Of course, Sir. I understand now. Why do you call him 'Jack'?"

"One of Markham's little jokes, I am afraid. Sir Charles is a very poor sailor – always sick, so Markham had to call him 'Jack'. It is what people call all sailors in this country."

"He does not object?"

"Heavens, no. It would take a great deal more than that to offend him, or, for that matter, any one of us here. I am afraid that you will have to get used to our sense of humour, which you may find rather strange. By the way, you will find that our little group does not stand on ceremony. We are distinctly informal, amongst ourselves. You will find this even when you meet the more junior members of my little outfit. Although I am nominally in charge, Lloyd is my Sergeant-Major, and we are technically soldiers and therefore subject to military rules, you will see little evidence of it. Markham refers to us as his 'Irregulars'. That is an apt title, in more ways than one. Our methods can be – how shall I put it? – unorthodox."

"What are your other men like?"

"Rogues, for the most part. The majority of them should have been hanged years ago. They are a collection of ruffians. There are two murderers, two thieves, a cut-purse, a house-breaker, two poachers, an exciseman who proved to be more on the side of the smugglers than of the Revenue and an ex Royal Navy Commander who was dishonourably discharged for fiddling his ship's accounts. There are several others whose backgrounds are a little less unwholesome – frauds, smugglers and so on. On the whole, I think you would have to go a very long way to find a more disreputable bunch of villains, but their skills are very useful indeed. You should fit in very well. I am sure you will be most welcome." Fletcher glanced at the expression on Hugo's face and suddenly roared with laughter, slapped him on the back and said, "There you are! Your second lesson in English humour. They are not as bad as I have made them out to be, but you shall meet them ere long and be able to judge for yourself."

Hugo smiled weakly and looked up to find Lloyd had joined them. He was grinning, and the scar gave his grin an almost unpleasant quality. He seized Hugo's hand and shook it firmly. "Take no notice of this primped-up fool. He has been too long away from the salons of London. Our men are good fellows – reliable. I prefer to forget their backgrounds."

"As I prefer to forget yours," rejoined Fletcher.

"And I yours." Markham's voice boomed suddenly from behind Fletcher, who turned and gave him a lop-sided smile.

"Where are your fellows at present?" Markham asked him.

"At Aldershot, for the most part. The 'naval' fellows are at Rye."

"Doing what, exactly?"

"Assisting the excisemen. We must continue to foster good relations."

"Quite so. Our operations would be nigh impossible without their co-operation. When do you think we can make a start?"

Fletcher considered for a moment. "It will be several days yet. We must all get to Pevensey, and it will take some time for the Navy to provide us with a suitable vessel as an escort. Jack tells me he has someone in mind, but he believes the gentleman and his vessel are in Plymouth. Even assuming that the wind favours him, It will be at least a week or ten days before we are ready… Hugo, are you quite well?" He caught Hugo's elbow, took the glass from his hand and steered him to a chair. "Russell! I think your patient is ailing."

Russell detached himself from the group around Goodrich and strode over to Hugo. The young man was deathly pale. Russell laid a hand on his forehead. It felt hot and clammy, and Hugo had begun to shiver. A few moments later, his eyes rolled upwards beneath the lids and he slid from the chair, falling in a heap to the floor.

❦

Half an hour later, the door to Markham's library opened and Russell entered the room. Markham looked up from his desk and Goodrich and Fletcher left the window, through which they had been admiring the park. Goodrich took several paces toward the doctor and asked, "How is the patient?"

"Not well," replied Russell. "It is a recurrence of the condition from which he has been suffering for some time. I have bled him and administered Jesuit's Bark and Laudanum. He seems more comfortable, though he is still not with us."

"Can you cure him?" asked Markham.

"I do not know. I have not encountered the symptoms before, and I find them puzzling. His condition appears to be a form of catalepsy, or a severe and sudden ague; of that I am certain. I have treated many cases of the ague. It is the sudden loss of faculties and the high fever in this case which worry me. The onset of the attack was extremely rapid, and the debility is total. In the cases I have encountered, the ague is more gentle."

After a few moments, Fletcher said suddenly, "Did you not tell me he had been in Africa?"

"Why, yes," replied Russell.

"What part?"

"The Slave Coast, he said."

"You have never visited that part yourself?"

"Sadly, no. Have you?"

"Not the Slave Coast as such, but I was in Sierra Leone. There was a disease which we called 'Sleepy Sickness'. What young Hugo has sounds very like."

"I have read of it," said Russell, "but I do not think Hugo has it. I have not encountered it, but I will consult a colleague in London who has knowledge of it. However, that information is very relevant. That knowledge may prove useful. Thank you, Fletcher. For the moment, I shall treat his condition as a severe ague. The treatment I have administered so far appears to be moderately effective, but there may be something better and more specific."

"I take it he cannot be moved?" said Markham, and, without waiting for a reply, he added, "He must stay here until he is well enough. You stay too, Aloysius. Send home for whatever you need, unless, of course, you have other patients?"

"I do, I am afraid. One is quite gravely ill. I was planning to visit on my way home."

"Then why not do so? You can gather what you need and return later."

"I will do that. Russell shot a glance at the clock. "I had best leave now."

As the door closed behind Russell, Markham turned to Goodrich. "Will you be staying, Jack?"

"No, Horace, I thank you. I must away to London. The sooner I pull strings at the Admiralty, the sooner I will be able to arrange for the escort for our men." He, too, glanced at the clock. "If I set off soon, I will be there before dark."

"Of course," replied Markham, getting up from his desk and crossing to the bell. "I will write a note for you while your horse is readying." He took his keys from his pocket and unlocked the desk drawer in which he kept his secret files. "I wonder if I might impose on you to deliver some papers to the usual place for me?"

"You may indeed, Horace."

"You will be going the Admiralty. Shall you be passing Horse Guards?"

"I shall be doing more than passing. I need to see someone."

"Ah, excellent. Well, I have a letter for the Chief of Staff. I was going to send it by courier tomorrow… Ah! Taylor.

Please to pass the word to have Sir Charles's horse readied for him."

Taylor had entered the room carrying a tray on which stood a jug and two tumblers. He acknowledged his new instructions with an inclination of his head, placed the tray on a side-table and withdrew, closing the door quietly behind him. Markham pushed his chair back from the desk, stood up and walked over to the side-table. "What have we here?" The jug had been covered with a circular lace cloth, to the circumference of which were attached coloured glass beads to hold it in place on the jug. Markham whipped the cover off and peered into the jug. "Ah! Iced lemonade! Splendid! Would you care for a glass, Jack?"

"If you please, Horace. You still have ice?"

"Of course – Oh, I didn't tell you. As you observed last year, the new ice-house was incorrectly constructed and badly sited, which was the reason we always ran out of ice by Easter. Well, last summer, I had the old ice-house excavated and repaired, and it appears to be working properly. There is still a large quantity of ice in it. It is so much better than the one my father had built."

"I fear your father was the victim of sharp practice in the matter of that ice-house. The builder told him the old ice-house was beyond repair," said Goodrich.

"Yes, and, what is more, he then proceeded to take two years to construct a new one a quarter the size, and charged my father a small fortune for it. It was simply not large enough to work, never mind its siting. Nor was it deep enough underground. My father was extremely displeased."

"Could he not have pursued the builder through the courts?"

"He could have done, but he was already a sick man. He just did not bother in the end. Anyway, the builder went bankrupt within months of completing the job, so there would have been little point in pursuing him. As it was, it would seem that the builder was also a sick man. He died about eighteen months later, a few months before my father."

"Had your father won the case, he could have had the builder imprisoned."

"Jack, what would casting the fellow into a debtor's prison profited my father, save for revenge, and he not a vengeful man? It would not have made the ice-house satisfactory, or recovered even a penny in damages. Besides, as I said, he was a sick man. The action would probably have hastened his death. It just meant that we had to spend all summer, every summer for ten years, begging or buying ice." Markham grinned ruefully, ladled ice out of the jug into his glass, clinked it against Goodrich's, and took a deep pull of lemonade. "Excellent!"

"It is very good," replied Goodrich. There followed a short silence, which was broken by the clinking of ice as Markham re-filled the glasses. Then Goodrich said, "What do you make of young Poitiers?"

"I like him. He seems honest and open. He has 'the makings', as they say. Russell likes him, and Russell is a quite shrewd judge of character. How did you find him?"

"I concur with your opinion of him. I have never met his father, but the lad seems to take after what I have heard of him. He was quite dashing in his youth, I am told. He served with credit as a cavalry officer before retiring to marry Hugo's mother, settle down and make wine. I suspect that Hugo also takes after his mother. I knew her, before she married the

Count. I was only a lad at the time, but I was captivated by her. She was a rare beauty, and also very dashing, particularly for a woman. I remember one day when she turned out with the hunt. She was mounted on a magnificent dapple-grey, but no long skirts and side-saddle for Margaret Howard, as she was then! She wore breeches and rode astride. The Master was a retired Colonel of the Militia. He was absolutely outraged – nearly choked on his stirrup-cup when she appeared - but he dared not say anything to her." Goodrich laughed at the memory. "Her father was also a cavalry officer, and the Master was a tenant of his."

"I see," said Markham, grinning at the idea. "It would hardly have been politic for the Master to have complained."

"Quite so. Not that Margaret's father would have done anything. He was not that sort of man. I fancy he would have told the Master to address his remarks to Margaret, who would have given him very short shrift. I suspect he was actually terrified of her, for all his pomposity and bluster. Still, it was most amusing to hear the Master snorting and spluttering and muttering 'Scandalous!' and 'Don't know what the world is coming to' for days afterwards." Goodrich took a pull at his lemonade and went on, "I recall that she had every young blade for miles around falling at her feet and practically eating out of her hand, but she showed no inclination to marry any of them. I believe some of them even quarrelled over her, and at least one duel was fought. The result was declared a bloodless draw by the seconds."

"How so?"

"They were only lads, not much older than me. They chose pistols at twenty paces. Their seconds, also lads, but much wiser, ensured there was only sufficient powder in those pistols to propel the balls a few feet from the muzzles. Honour was, apparently, satisfied."

Markham chuckled. "I suppose the dashing French Count found the dashing Englishwoman quite enchanting, then."

"Or just *formidable*," replied Goodrich. "Either way, they seem to have produced a fine son and heir. I wonder what the daughter is like."

"No doubt out of the same mould. Yes, Taylor, what is it?"

"Sir Charles's horse is readied, Sir."

"Thank you, Taylor." Goodrich drained his glass, picked up his portfolio from the desk, received the two packets from Markham, shook hands with him, and allowed Taylor to escort him towards the door.

# CHAPTER SEVEN

Simon Curzon Johnston sat at a scrubbed table near the fireplace in the side parlour of a small inn in Plymouth. On the table in front of him stood a bottle of cheap wine, a pewter goblet and a board on which sat a hunk of bread. He had cleared his plate. The food at the inn was good, but not what one would call plentiful. He had just eaten a mutton chop. It had been excellent, but he could not afford two. He was in funds at the moment, but that situation would change at the end of the week. For the present, he was Master and Commander of the *Vixen*, and until three days ago he had expected to continue in the post. In the incident with the collier *Vixen's* bowsprit had been sprung and the larboard cathead badly damaged. The following day, Johnston had visited the Port Admiral to arrange for repairs to be made to the brig, but the Port Admiral had informed him that he had no real need of a vessel the size of *Vixen*, and in view of the damage she had sustained to her bows he was giving orders for her to be paid off and laid up. Her crew would be scattered and her officers put ashore to kick their heels on half pay. Johnston would cease to be Master and Commander and would revert to being a Lieutenant. He sighed and poured himself more wine. The Port Admiral's orders had been like a slap in the face. *Vixen's* little company had become very adept at apprehending smugglers and had learned to operate in close co-operation with the Revenue cutters. They were all seasoned seamen, they knew their little ship well and could use her armament, just fourteen little six-pounders, - not much more than pop-guns, to great effect. In spite of the peace and the mass laying-up and even sale of the Navy's ships, Johnston and his little crew had always found steady employment – until now. He sighed again. Fate could be cruel. He should by all rights be approaching being made post by now, not cast back on the beach to join all the other half-pay Lieutenants pestering the Admiralty for an appointment, any appointment. In fact, had the country still been at war, he would have almost automatically have been made post several years ago. He was now approaching thirty years of age, and the prospect of having no employment in his chosen profession was not an attractive one. He could always go home and throw himself into the affairs of the estate which he would one day inherit, but not yet. Please, dear God, not yet… Meanwhile, his little *Vixen* would be unrigged, her masts taken out, her pop-guns taken ashore, and she would be towed away to be stored with all the other laid-up vessels in a creek up the river. He had made the sad announcement to the ship's company immediately on his return from the Port Admiral's office, and had been met with a stunned silence. He had immediately gone ashore again to make some arrangements with the dockyard. On his return, he found that the crew had put *Vixen* into mourning – yards a-cockbill, black ribbons tied to the rigging. He had been angry at the time, but he had said nothing, just gone below to his tiny cabin. When he went on deck about half an hour later, she had been back to normal again. No-one had said a word, but he knew what they were all thinking. *Be damned to you, Port Admiral!*

He often stayed at the inn, which was plain and unpretentious, not much frequented by either officers or other ranks, and quiet. He liked peace and quiet, and Morris, the innkeeper, respected his need for them. Besides, Morris was good in the matter of extending credit. He knew that a Lieutenant's pay was not riches, but he also knew that Johnston would always settle his account. He could obtain funds from his father, but Johnston preferred to pay his own way and wanted to experience the same ups and downs as anyone not in the same position of privilege as himself. Besides, he was not on very good terms with his father at present, they having disagreed last month about his younger brother, who had started a promising career in the Army, but had been invalided out after only a few months and was now back at home. His father now wanted him to take the cloth, but, as Simon had pointed out, he would need some years of studying before taking orders. He had also pointed out that he thought it would be rather a waste of Matthew's talents, and, besides, he did not think it right for his father to make decisions of that sort without even bothering to find out Matthew's wishes on the matter. His father had stormed out of the room and Simon had not seen him again before he had to leave for Plymouth the next day. It would take a week or two more, but the old man would 'simmer down' and he would be very welcome on his next visit, but he knew it would take some time. He also knew that, by the time he next visited, his father would have sought Matthew's views on the matter, and he would himself be involved in a family decision. In the meantime, his mother would soothe his father's ruffled feathers.. Simon knew that she agreed with him, not with his father. She had said so at breakfast on the morning before he left. His father had not been present. His mother had said, "He is suffering with his gout again. Simon, dear, why do you have to provoke him when he is like this?" She had given him a severe look, the smiled and said, "Actually, I rather fancy he is sulking. He knows you are right. I shall wait a day or two, perhaps until Doctor Green has bled him. Bleeding always seems to put him in a better frame of mind, and he does suffer, poor lamb. Then I shall gently broach the subject." Johnston sighed again and reached for his goblet.

His musings were interrupted by the appearance of Morris. "Was the chop to your liking, Sir?"

"It was excellent, thank you, Morris. What is for pudding?"

"A boiled baby, Sir, but it wants a few minutes more yet. You were early today."

"I know." Johnston stared gloomily at his empty plate. "I am afraid I am bad company at the moment, Morris."

"Not to fret too much, Sir. Something will work out. At least *Vixen* is not to be sold out of the service or scrapped."

"No, I suppose that is some small consolation." Johnston gave Morris a weak smile, then sat back on his chair. Morris scooped up the plate and left the room. Johnson picked up his spoon and fiddled with it. He was concerned for his crew. They had all been together for four years now. Breaking the crew up seemed to him an act of almost criminal folly. He put the spoon back down on the table and brushed some crumbs from the lapel of his coat, glancing up as the window darkened. He peered out and watched as a cart stopped to allow a chaise to pass, then moved on. A lone horseman passed the window and turned into the inn yard. Johnston picked up the spoon again and was listening to the jingling of the chaise's harness fading in the distance when Morris reappeared, carrying a plate which he placed on the table. "There you are, Sir. Another chop, on the house. The pudding will be ready when you have finished it."

"Why, thank, you Morris. That is most kind in you."

"We must keep you young gentlemen well fed, Sir, or you'll not be any use to us next time we need you."

Morris bustled out of the room and Johnson set about the chop. He had just finished pulling the last shreds of meat from the bone with his teeth when he became aware of a disturbance in the main parlour. Cocking his head and straining to hear, he caught Morris's voice saying, "In there, Sir." A moment later, the door opened and a young and travel-stained Lieutenant walked in. "Mr. Johnston?"

"I am he," replied Johnston. Then his eye fell on the package which the Lieutenant was carrying. It looked like orders. He stiffened. Already? No, there must be some mistake.

"Special from Admiralty, Sir, and this is from the Port Admiral. I had to call at the office on my way."

"Thank you." Johnston took the envelopes and examined the seals. He wiped his knife on his napkin and slid it under the seal of the envelope from London, pulled out the sheet of paper and read it. He shook his head in disbelief and put the paper down on the table. Then he picked it up and read it again, after which a broad smile spread across his face. He beamed at the young Lieutenant, who ventured, "Good news, Sir?"

"Aye, indeed, very good news. You'll join me for a glass?"

"Thank you, Sir, I will."

Johnston waved him towards a chair. "Forgive me a moment. I had better read the other one." He opened it, extracted two pieces of paper, read through the contents, then announced, "There you are, Port Admiral. Put that in your pipe and smoke it!" He grinned mischievously at his young companion and called out, "Morris!"

Morris poked his head round the door. "Sir?"

"This young gentleman is joining me. May we have some claret, if you please, and is my coxswain still here?"

"He is, Sir, in the back bar."

"Then my compliments to him and would he please to remove his attentions from whatever unfortunate doxy is enduring them and present himself in here at the double."

Morris vanished. Johnson pushed his chair back from the table, slapped his hand on the papers and laughed aloud. In response to the messenger's quizzical look, he said, "Forgive me. This time last week, I had a ship. Two days ago, I had no ship. Now I have one again." Morris appeared, bearing a decanter and two glasses. After a few seconds, there was a tap at the door and Hicks, Johnston's coxswain, appeared, wiping his mouth on the back of his hand.

"Ah, Hicks, there you are. I have some good news for you." Johnston seized the glass of claret which Morris had just poured and thrust it at Hicks, who regarded it suspiciously. "Get that down you, then double to the brig and tell them to avast de-commissioning. Then take this to the dockyard." He pushed one of the papers across the table. "It is a chit for urgent repairs to *Vixen*. It would seem that something has given the Port Admiral cause to change his mind. Then go and find the First Lieutenant and ask him to repair on board again. I will return aboard when I have finished here."

Hicks gaped at him for a moment, then took the glass, knocked it off at one go, placed it on the table, picked up the chit, grinned broadly at Johnston, said "Aye, *aye*, Sir!", nodded at Morris, who was standing open-mouthed by the fireplace, and practically ran out of the room.

"I told you, Sir, I told you! I'll fetch the pudding." Morris dusted his hands together and strode out. Johnston regarded his companion for a moment. "Is there any other news from London?"

"Well, Sir, it seems the French have declared war on Austria."

Johnston whistled quietly. "Oh, have they, now?"

"Surely that does not affect us, Sir?"

"Not directly, perhaps, and not in the immediate future, but I would regard it as significant, and I would regard it also as having some bearing on your being sent all the way from London with this." He prodded at his orders. "Something is stirring. May be good for all of us, eh?"

"If you say so, Sir. I am afraid I am just a messenger." The young Lieutenant picked up his glass. "To your new orders, Sir."

"Thank you. Please to inform the Admiralty that I shall endeavour to carry them out to the best of my abilities. Ah! Morris, that looks and smells delicious. I am sure this poor starving officer would like a portion!"

In response to the vigorous nodding and grinning, Morris headed for the door. "I'll fetch another plate, Sir."

⁂

Nathaniel Owen sat wearily down on a heap of cordage, rubbed his back and pulled his tobacco-pipe from his pocket. It had been a long morning, during which he had supervised the unreeving of a quantity of running rigging and the hoisting on to the dockside of the larboard six-pounders. He felt depressed. He disliked de-commissioning a ship. The process took the life out of her. It also felt, this time, as if it was taking some of the life out of him, too. At the age of fifty-one years, or thereabouts, he did not fancy his chances of another appointment. Still, he had accumulated a tidy little sum in prize money and could afford to retire and set up a little business on shore. Just what, he was not sure. Many retired seamen bought inns, but the idea did not appeal to Owen. Maybe if he had a word with the Captain – he might have some suggestion to make. After all, he was well-connected. He sat up straight and watched as some hands prepared to shift one of the starboard guns ready for hoisting ashore. The Gunner was fussing about. There was no need for Owen to interfere.

A sudden shout from the dockside made him turn his head. It was Hicks, out of breath, waving his arms about and looking agitated. What the devil was he doing here? He was supposed to be keeping an eye on the Skipper. Owen stood up as Hicks practically catapulted himself aboard, shouting "'Vast, 'vast, there!" Owen strode a few paces across the deck towards him. "Steady, man! What's up?" Breathlessly, Hicks blurted out his news, men appearing as if from nowhere to hear him. When he had finished, Owen became aware of the sound of wild cheering. He let it continue for a few moments, then jumped up on to the capstan-head and raised his hands for silence.

"Well, lads, that is good news, but I dunno what you're a-cheering about. Get set to and sway those guns back on board, then the topmen can set about setting the running rigging up again!" He gave the assembled company a toothless grin and jumped down from his perch to a chorus of groans and a call of "Miserable old sod!" He chuckled to himself and pushed his pipe back into his pocket. The day suddenly seemed brighter. The hands would now have to spend hours re-doing everything they had already spent hours undoing, but they would do it cheerfully. He turned to the still puffing Hicks. "Where is the Skipper?"

"Still eatin' his dinner. He sent me to find the First, but he's not in his lodgings. I dunno where he could be."

"Try the whorehouse," replied Owen.

"I heard that! Take that man's name!" came a growl from the quayside. Owen turned to see the Lieutenant Kirton's lean figure striding down the gangplank. "You impudent old bugger!" He paused and looked around him. "What the hell is going on? Why has the work stopped?"

Hicks related his news again and, to his surprise, the First Lieutenant slapped him on the back. Then Kirton turned and shouted, "Right, lads. Get this lot shipshape again and we'll get her warped round to the dock." He swung round and glared at the grinning Owen. "I would remind you that not all of us indulge in the same pastimes as you, Master!" Then he strode off towards the forecastle. Owen pulled a face at Hicks. Kirton was, like Johnson, of aristocratic origins, a fine seaman, and good-natured. Owen teased both of them from time to time. They both took it in good part, and the *Vixen* was a happy ship. The Skipper did not believe in flogging except as a last resort. The usual punishments were extra duties, fines and – pumping ship. At least once a week, weather and duties permitting, Johnston would have the sweetening-cocks opened to flood the bilges to the depth of several inches. After allowing the water to slosh around for a few minutes, the pumps would be manned and it would all be pumped out again. It kept the bilges fresh and was an ideal punishment which achieved something useful. An extra hour at the pumps was the Captain's standard sentence for most minor misdemeanours, two hours for offences which, aboard many other ships, would have attracted a dozen strokes at the grating. Owen rubbed his back again and turned to a group of men who were standing by the tackle hanging from the mainyard. "Let's be getting 'em back on board, then."

❦

An hour later, Johnston found himself sitting on an uncomfortable chair in the Dockyard Master's office, regretting the boiled baby which seemed to be sitting very heavily on his stomach. He regarded the Master with increasing irritation. The Master knew Johnston and liked him, only partly because he was good at oiling the unofficial wheels of the Master's domain.

"Well, now, Sir, I might be able to fit *Vixen* in next week, but I've got Captain Small's bomb ketch to finish, and…"

"Have you read the order?" Johnston interrupted him. "I think you will find that it states 'with all despatch'."

The Master peered at Johnston over a pair of small spectacles. "Well, Sir, I suppose something could be arranged…"

"Oh, dammit!" Johnson fished in his pocket, produced five guineas and slapped them down on the desk. A slow smile spread over the Master's face. He removed the spectacles and said. "If you would care to have her warped round now Sir, I'll see what we can do."

Johnston rose to his feet, placed his hands palms down on the desk, leaned over it towards the Master and said quietly. "I should report you for malpractice, but I am too busy. Another five if you can finish by Monday evening. I want to catch the early tide on Tuesday – and my men will remain aboard while you are working. They will work all weekend, and I expect yours to do the same"

The Master opened his mouth to protest that his men would not be happy about having to work on a Sunday, but caught the expression on Johnston's face and changed his mind.

"Very good, Sir." He picked up the five guineas.

Johnston walked the short distance back to the brig and went aboard. He immediately went straight aft to the tiny cabin, threw his hat on to the cross-bench which ran beneath the stern windows and sat down. After a few moments there was a tap at the door and Kirton walked in. He took one look at Johnston and raised his eyebrows.

"Do not dare to say a word," snarled Johnston. "Ten guineas! That's practically all I had left of my pay. The shark ought to be court-martialled."

"Sounds cheap to me. Perhaps he was impressed by the urgency, or maybe it was your personality."

"Bah! The man is a crook!"

"They all are. Count yourself lucky to have got off so lightly. You have evidently over-eaten again. Shall I send for the surgeon?"

"No," snapped Johnston. "The man is a butcher!"

"What was it this time?"

"Boiled baby," mumbled Johnston. "It really was very good."

"That may be so," rejoined Kirton, "But I am reliably

informed by the 'butcher' that it is the matter of balancing quality against quantity which appears to be beyond your comprehension."

Several heavy thuds sounded from on deck, followed by shouts. The hull rocked slightly. Kirton glanced towards the cabin door, moved to a locker, opened it and extracted a decanter of brandy and two glasses. He placed the glasses on the table and sloshed brandy into them, plonked the stopper back into the decanter and handed a glass to Johnston, who seized it, grunted thanks, and downed it. He gasped and held out the glass. Kirton re-filled it and Johnston this time took a sip, then placed the glass on the table, sat back, unbuttoned his coat, belched, loosened his belt and sprawled on the bench. "That's better. Thank you, Rupert."

Kirton seized hold of a chair and attempted to move it. Discovering that it was still held down by a lashing from a ringbolt on the underside of its seat to a ringbolt on the cabin sole, he rotated it instead and sat down. The two men sipped their brandy and discussed the sudden upturn in their fortunes, until they were interrupted by another heavy thud from the deck. The hull rocked slightly again.

"That's the last of the guns aboard," said Kirton. "Did the rogue at the Dockyard give us a time?"

"As soon as we like."

"Ah – oh, that soon?"

"Yes, that soon. So, if you are ready, Mr. Kirton, let us commence."

Kirton picked up his hat. "Aye, aye, Sir." He paused in the doorway. "Ten guineas? That was very cheap."

"Actually, I have only paid him five. I promised him the rest if he completes by Monday evening."

Kirton shook his head. "And *you* call *him* a rogue…" He closed the door. From the little quarterdeck he could hear Johnston chuckling quietly. He nodded. The Skipper was happy again. They had their ship back. All was well with the world. He straightened his shoulders. "Mister Owen! Where is the bosun?"

Some two hundred and fifty miles away, the ring of steel on steel sounded faintly through the open window of Markham's library. Goodrich and Russell stood at the window, watching as Hugo and Fletcher circled each other warily on the lawn outside. Suddenly, Hugo darted forward. Fletcher tried to parry his blade, but found himself off-balance and stepped backwards, raising his arm in the process. There was a flash of steel and a ringing sound, and Fletcher found himself staring at his weapon, which was now lying on the lawn some eight feet away from him. He spread his arms wide and grinned ruefully at his youthful opponent, then bowed to him. "Yours, Sir. I yield the contest." Hugo returned the bow, then picked up Fletcher's sword and handed it to him. Fletcher produced a large silk handkerchief and mopped his brow. "I used to fancy myself as a swordsman, but you run rings round me."

"You lack practice, and you do not use your feet sufficiently," replied Hugo. "My fencing – master taught me that in order to fence, one should first learn to dance. A thrust will always beat a hack, but you must be properly balanced to achieve it. If you are off-balance, your instinctive reaction is to step away and start to wave your arms about to regain your equilibrium. Once you do that, all is lost. Your guard is down, and I have you."

Fletcher pulled the cork button from the end of his sword. "You make it sound simple, but it is very difficult to put into practice. How are you feeling? I trust that has not tired you too much. The Doctor," he nodded towards the window "says you must not over-exert yourself."

Hugo smiled and picked up his jacket. "Perhaps I am a little tired. He waved his blade in the direction of the window. We had better go inside."

As the two walked out of sight, Goodrich turned to Russell and said, "That young man is an excellent swordsman. I am pleased to see how quickly he has recovered from that last episode."

"Aye," replied Russell, "I am still not sure of the diagnosis, but I seem to have hit on the right treatment. I think the swift administration of Jesuit's Bark was the key. It brought the fever down quickly. I fear he will never be entirely free of the attacks, but they may become less frequent and less severe as time goes by, and as long as he can take the Bark as early as possible, he should do well."

"Will he be fit to take part in our little adventure?"

"I see no reason why not. I would have recommended a sea voyage to build up his constitution again, and they are likely to spend some while at sea, I should think."

"Good. I shall break the news to him in a minute. We should be setting off for Pevensey early next week. I am just waiting for word that the vessel I have requested is on her way. When that has been confirmed, we can make the rest of our preparations."

# CHAPTER EIGHT

Hugo Poitiers glanced nervously from left to right. He had been walking for about a quarter of a mile through the wood, trying to make as little noise as possible, but twigs snapped under his feet and he could hear his own breathing, loud in the still air. He was uncertain as to his exact whereabouts in relation to the woodman's hut for which he was supposed to be heading, and he was beginning to think he had lost his bearings. He had a roughly-drawn map which he had made when they had arrived here two days ago. He decided to consult it. He fished it out of his pocket, unfolded it, and looked around him. Deciding that he was indeed lost, he moved a few yards into a small clearing, where he spotted a fallen tree. Had he seen that before? Unable to decide, he stood beside it and looked back in the direction from which he had come. He could see nothing which he could recognize, so he turned and sat down on the trunk of the fallen tree. He studied his sketch-map again and was trying to smooth out the creases when he heard a sharp metallic click, apparently just inches from his left ear. He turned his head slowly and found himself looking into the muzzle of a pistol which seemed to be growing out of a bush a few feet away from him. With a sinking feeling, he realized that the bush had not been there when he had arrived in the clearing. It had somehow simply appeared in the minute or two during which he had been engrossed in his map.

"Gotcha!" said the bush conversationally.

Hugo sighed and slumped his shoulders. The bush suddenly lowered the pistol and transformed itself into a small wiry man with features reminiscent of a weasel. He was wearing a jacket made of loose-woven material to which he had attached sprays of leaves. From a few feet away he looked just like – well, a bush.

"You'm goin' to 'ave to do better than that, young Sir. I been trackin' yer for a furlong or more. Yer makes more noise than a 'erd o' cattle, an' yer doesn't keep a lookout, Sir. I can't think 'as 'ow yer didn't spot me a-creepin' up."

The bush sat down on the log beside Hugo and produced a water flask. "You'm lost too, ain't yer?"

"I'm afraid so, Hankins. It is all very confusing for a poor sailor like me. I cannot seem to get my bearings in this damn' wood. It all looks the same from every angle."

"I told 'ee afore, Sir. The moss grows thicker on the north side o' the trees. 'Tis easy!"

"Oh, yes, of course. So I am here and…" Hugo gestured vaguely at his sketch-map.

"The 'ut is over yonder. You was goin' the wrong way again. Yer passed Fensom about forty yards back. 'E was standin' up straight, an' you still didn't see 'im. I don't think you'd 'ave seed 'im if 'e'd been a-wavin a flag an' hollerin'."

"Oh, dear, I'm not very good at this sort of thing at all. Shall we try it again?"

Hankins relented somewhat. "Nah, Sir. It'll be getting dark soon, an' I've 'ad enough for one day, so I'm sure yer 'ave too. I been doin' this all me life. You'm been tryin' it for two days. Yer'll get the knack in the end. It takes time. Put me on a ship an' I wouldn't 'ave a clue. 'Orses for courses, I says." He rose from the log, tucked the pistol into his belt, put two fingers in his mouth and let out an ear-splitting whistle, so loud it made Hugo wince. Several other figures, previously unnoticed by Hugo, rose from their hiding-places and the whole band started towards the house, Hugo trailing somewhat disconsolately a few yards behind.

An hour later, the group was assembled in the snug of the Barley Mow Inn. Tankards of ale sat on the scrubbed tables and tobacco-smoke drifted across the room, mingling with a smell of something good from the kitchen. Sergeant-Major Lloyd took a long pull at his tankard and said, "Well, Corporal Hankins, how is our new recruit shaping up?"

Hugo cringed, not wanting to hear what Hankins would say about his abysmal performance.

"Well, Sarge, 'e'm not too good at the woodcraft, but it's early days, an' I reckon 'e'll do. I wouldn't want ter tangle with 'im if he 'ad a sword in 'is 'and, that's for sure."

There was a ripple of chuckles around the table. Earlier in the day, Hankins had challenged Hugo at swords. The result had been much the same as Fletcher's experience, the defeat even more rapid, and Hankins' surprise all the greater.

"Well, I wouldn't worry too much about creeping around in a wood. I don't think Mr. Fletcher has much of that sort of thing in mind. He thinks Mr. Poitiers will be rather more useful attached to our 'more nautical operation', as he put it."

The conversation was brought to an end by the arrival of the landlord's wife with a large pot of stew, followed by her daughter with a basket of bread, and the landlord himself with another jug of ale. Hugo helped himself, then sat down to eat and observe his companions. They were much as Fletcher had described them. Apart from Hankins and Fensom, both of whom had been poachers, there was Gibbs, a one-time costermonger who had supplemented his income with the proceeds of house-breaking, Holden the ex-pickpocket, who looked like a little cherub, and Walters, tall, lean and gaunt. He was the fallen exciseman. Across the room sat Good, who was anything but, having allegedly murdered his wife. Hugo was not so sure about him. The case had not been proven and no body had ever been found. The man himself was quiet, and seemed to be of a gentle disposition. However, he had finally been sentenced to transportation for stealing a watch, but had somehow escaped. He was deep in conspiratorial conversation with the most villainous-looking member of the group, A Neapolitan (or so he claimed) by the name of Costa. Costa was short and wiry, with typically swarthy features, missing most of his right ear and with a livid scar above his left eye, which he sometimes covered with a patch. He was, Hugo had been told, adept at silent killing, which he generally achieved either by the use of a thick needle about nine inches in length or by garrotting his victim with a thin cord. Either way, he could achieve his object in complete silence. On a high-backed settle by the inglenook sat Williams and Murrell, the only two members of the group who were not ex-criminals. They were the group's technical experts. Williams, the group's armourer, was a lugubrious-looking individual with a roman nose. He had been apprenticed to a blacksmith in his youth, and had spent a while as a locksmith, but had become bored with the trade and had joined the army, where his skills as an armourer soon became apparent. Murrell was the oldest member of the group, probably about thirty-five years of age. He was a Royal Engineer Sergeant. As far as Hugo could make out, he was an expert on demolishing things using charges of gunpowder.

Fletcher had 'poached' both of them from their units. The two were now comparing notes on something, Murrell waving his arms about to emphasize a point he was making, Williams, his arms folded in front of him, nodding slowly in reply. Hugo had been particularly impressed by the intelligence of all the men. Fletcher had informed him that they were all picked, not just for their extraordinary skills, but because they possessed quick wits, knew how to use them, and could act independently, without orders, if necessary. "Not, of course," he had said with a wry smile, "that that means they do not need handling with a fairly tight rein. Some of them can be rather irritating and irresponsible at times. They are somewhat given to childish pranks, particularly if they are not kept busy. I sometimes think I command a bunch of schoolboys, rather than grown men, but they are very good at what they do. They seem to regard me as some sort of father-figure, which is disconcerting as several of them are older than I." He had pulled a wry face at Hugo's suggestion that perhaps 'schoolmaster' might be more accurate than 'father'.

Hugo finished his bowl of stew and regarded them all again. They were dressed in a motley assortment of parts of military uniforms, none of them matching, and they carried an equally motley collection of weapons. Hugo glanced at the stack of arms which had been propped up against the wall by the door. There were two standard-pattern muskets and two much shorter-barrelled Jäger rifles, favoured by Hankins and Fensom, lethally accurate at long range. There was a naval cutlass, two swords which had started life as cavalry sabres, and even a modified bayonet. The smaller weapons were mostly pistols and various wicked-looking knives. All the equipment was in excellent and clean condition, and all of the men invested considerable time and effort in keeping it thus.

Hugo's thoughts were interrupted as the door opened to reveal Fletcher and Goodrich, who strode straight over to Lloyd. The men did no more than glance at him and continued eating or talking. Fletcher closed the door behind him, placed a curious-looking weapon with the stack of others, looked around until he spotted Hugo in the corner, nodded at him and walked over to the stew-pot. He seized a bowl and ladled some stew into it, picked up a hunk of bread and sat down opposite Hugo. His dandyish clothes were gone. He was wearing trousers and an officer's coat which had once been red, but which was now a sort of dun colour.

"How are you finding our lads?"

"They are very patient. They are trying their best to teach me, but I fear I am a poor pupil."

Fletcher gave a short laugh and spooned stew into his mouth. "This is very good. I get tired of fancy food in London. It is good to have some honest stew for a change." He tore off a piece of bread. "Bread's fresh, too." He noticed Hugo looking at his coat and glanced down at it.

"I thought the English Army all wore red coats," said Hugo. I have seen your marines. They wear red. Why red, and why are none of your men wearing it?"

"Ah, well, I will endeavour to explain. Some many years ago, it was found that if you have a large number of men, it is very difficult to count them if they are wearing red. For some reason, the eye becomes confused. So field army uniform is generally red. You hope that, since it is normally inevitable that you are visible to the enemy, he will be confused." Fletcher paused to spoon more stew into his mouth. "One man wearing red, however, is very conspicuous. We do not want to be seen, so we try to wear apparel that blends in with the surroundings. Makes us very difficult to spot, let alone count. It was a lesson we learned from the rebels in the American colonies. They are masters at concealment, and we suffered greatly at their hands."

"Of course," said Hugo. "That should have occurred to me this afternoon. I was trying to find the hut in the wood. I failed dismally, I fear. I was taken by surprise three times, and I never saw anyone."

"Precisely, because they did not want you to see them. They are very good at it, particularly Hankins and Fensom. Many is the time I have seen one of them creep up on someone and…" He left it there. Hugo, after his experiences that afternoon, could imagine only too vividly what the 'and' implied.

A few moments later they were joined by Goodrich, who plonked himself down on the bench next to Fletcher, leaned across the table and said to Hugo, "We shall set off for Pevensey tomorrow. I have heard the vessel is on her way. I shall be accompanying you, but I shall be making my own way to France, from Rye. We may meet in France, but if not, then I shall see you again in Horsham. Apart from getting your father out, these men," he gestured at the assembled company, "are going to be looking for Lessard, and possibly Chabot, if he has not returned to Paris. We understand that Lessard, at least, is hunting for your father. Henri Lessard, as you know from our meeting at the Park, possesses a great deal of information which would be useful to us. His capture would be a useful one, I think. Now tell me, who knew of your journey to England?"

Hugo thought for a few moments, then said, "Apart from my parents, no-one."

"Hmm, in that case, how did Chabot's men know you were going to Tenterden?"

"Oh, I – I cannot imagine."

"I can. Presumably, your arrival at the house was expected. The staff would have been aware of your impending arrival."

"Oh, yes, of course, I wrote to let them know I was on my way." replied Hugo.

"Do you know who the staff are?"

"Yes, there is a butler. He is English. I do not know his name. My father engaged him soon after they moved to the house. Then there is the cook. She is English, too, and there were two other men, a butler's assistant and a footman. Father brought them from France. I think my mother engaged a couple of maids as well, but I am not sure."

"Never mind. The maids are not of our concern. I have been to the house and interviewed the butler. He was very annoyed. Vallon, his French assistant, disappeared last week. He is trying to train the footman to take his place, but says the man is stupid, and he cannot understand English properly."

"Disappeared?"

"Yes, vanished without a trace, but not without taking his own few possessions, and some of your father's more portable ones, with him."

Fletcher wiped his bowl with the last of his bread. He paused with it poised half-way to his mouth. "So it would seem there is a snake in Poitiers' grass."

"It would indeed," replied Goodrich.

"Have you any idea of his whereabouts now?" Fletcher popped the bread into his mouth.

"None at all. It is a week since he decamped, so the trail is probably cold. We must be watchful. He could still be here, or he may have escaped to France. Hugo, would you please to describe him for us."

Half an hour later, Hugo found himself, in the company of Goodrich and Fletcher, walking slowly back from the inn towards the Park. The others had settled down to playing dominoes and drinking at the inn, where they would billet for the night. The evening was mild and still, and all three walked in silence for a while. As they turned into the long drive to the house, Goodrich stopped as a cuckoo called. "You two go on ahead," he said, "I will catch up with you."

After about fifty yards, Hugo glanced back. Goodrich was leaning on a fence-post, peering through a small telescope. Fletcher also glanced back. "Our Jack is something of an ornithologist. Birds fascinate him. He is always charging off to look at some strange warbler or duck or whatever." He grinned at Hugo at the two walked on. After a minute or so, Hugo said, "Will you tell me what your gun is? The one you brought to the inn. It looked, well, strange."

In reply, Fletcher looked around and, spotting the stump of a tree, walked over to it and sat down. He detached the canvas roll which Hugo had noticed strapped to his pack and from it produced a gun barrel about two feet in length. "Oh," said Hugo, "You have it with you. I thought you must have left it with the others."

"I never leave this anywhere," replied Fletcher. "As you see, it comes to pieces." He handed it to Hugo, who studied it with interest. The barrel was normal enough, but the lock arrangement looked very strange indeed. Out of the left hand side of the rear of the barrel there protruded a metal bolt about an inch square. It stuck out about two inches from the side of the barrel. On the right hand side there was what looked like a second barrel, but it was shorter than the other. Hugo turned the thing round and saw that this second 'barrel' had no muzzle. It appeared to be solid. He then examined the hammer. It looked normal enough, but he frowned at the absence of a flint. There was also no pan. At the rear of the barrel there was a threaded tube with some sort of pin at its centre. He looked at Fletcher and shook his head. Fletcher grinned at him and produced the stock from his pack. It was a curious shape, completely conical. Hugo peered at the narrow end. It was also threaded, and there was something which corresponded with the pin on the barrel. Then Fletcher produced a second stock from his pack, and a third. Still grinning at the gaping Hugo, Fletcher held out his hand, took the barrel from his young companion and screwed one of the stocks on to it. Then his unscrewed the cap from the end of the shorter of the two barrels and dropped a handful of balls down it. He replaced the cap, tilted the muzzle of the weapon upwards, pushed the bolt in and released it. Then he pulled back the hammer and handed the weapon to Hugo. "Have a pot at that tree." He waved at an oak about fifty yards away.

"But it is scarcely within range," ventured Hugo, taking the gun from him. Fletcher shook his head, "Go on," he said. Hugo levelled the weapon. It felt rather strange. He squinted down the barrel and pulled the trigger.

There was a sharp metallic 'Snap'. Hugo, braced for the recoil, staggered in surprise at the lack of it. There had been a little kick, but nothing like what he was expecting. He was so surprised that he failed to observe the result of his effort. "Good shot," said Fletcher. "Now, tilt the barrel up, push and release the cross-bolt and cock the hammer. There, now you are ready for a second shot." This time, Hugo observed a splinter fly off the tree. "And again," said Fletcher.

After the third shot, Hugo stared at the weapon in astonishment. "There is no smoke!" he announced suddenly. Fletcher took the gun from him. "No, because there is no fire. This weapon works on air."

"Air?"

"Aye, air. The stock contains air which is compressed to a high pressure. When you pull the trigger, a charge of this air is released and blows the ball out of the barrel at high speed. The barrel is rifled. The tube holds about twenty balls. It is possible to shoot them all off in about a minute. The range is at least twice that of a musket. Another advantage is that there is no flash and, as you observed, no smoke. When the pressure in the stock drops too low to be effective, you just put on a freshly-charged one, and off you go again."

Hugo shook his head. "How is the air put into the stock?"

"By means of a pump." Fletcher grinned wryly. "That can be hard work. It takes many strokes – some say two thousand – to charge an empty stock. I usually re-charge mine after only about thirty rounds. It takes many fewer strokes, and is easier. The Austrian army has a regiment equipped with these weapons. They actually recharge the stocks by means of a steam pump mounted on a wagon."

"The Austrian army? I have never seen anything like it before. It is amazing."

"It is the invention of an Austrian gunsmith named Girandoni. A very clever man. The Austrian army's weapons are the same size as a normal musket. I managed to get hold of several of them while I was in Austria. I have had the barrel of this one shortened to make it easier to carry and to conceal if needs be. It does not seem to have affected its efficiency, so I have had several more shortened, and most of my men will be equipped with them for our trip. There is also a pistol version. I have several of those, too, but, being smaller, the reservoir cannot hold as much air and they are not as powerful."

"Has it a special name?" asked Hugo

"Not really. It is generally called an air gun, though I suppose 'air rifle' would be more accurate. The Austrians call it a '*Windbüchse*', or 'wind-rifle'."

"I have never seen anything like it before. I wonder it is not more widely known," said Hugo.

Fletcher detached the stock and put it away. "Well, it is something of a secret. The Austrians would prefer it if their enemies knew nothing of it, particularly the French, at the moment, I should think."

"So how come you have several?"

"Sir Horace and Sir Charles both feel that our irregular little group is an ideal way to try out new inventions which may prove to be useful in battle. Sir Horace heard rumours of these weapons a year or two ago. I was sent to Austria to discover if there was any truth in them." He unloaded the remaining balls from the tube magazine and put them in a pouch, then went on, "On behalf of His Majesty's Government, I was able to beg a number of guns for evaluation."

"Have you reached any conclusions?" asked Hugo.

"Yes, I think so. The piece is very useful under certain conditions. It is quieter in use than a musket, and has a very rapid rate of fire. However, there are some disadvantages. The mechanism is rather delicate, so much so that it is not as 'soldier-proof' as a musket, and it requires careful maintenance. So far, only about a third of my men are proficient in its use, and it has taken me many months to train them. It took the Austrians about a month to train me. The Austrian regiment which is armed with these has to give its men special training. Also, the power drops off quite quickly, and there are practical difficulties in maintaining a supply of charged stocks and in re-charging them once their efficacy is reduced. It is a very useful weapon to a group like us, but I fear it would not be practical in general use. It is also expensive to make, and that must be a major consideration to the government."

They both turned as the sound of footsteps heralded the approach of Goodrich. He looked at Hugo. "So, Fletcher has been demonstrating his piece of wind artillery. Are you impressed?"

"Indeed, Sir Charles," replied Hugo.

"Hmm, well. My opinion is that it would be better were it to work on hot air, so we could have the stocks re-charged in Parliament at no extra expense." He glanced up as the cuckoo called again, turned and grinned at the others. "Time to get back to the house. Ale is all very well, but I think it is now time for a raid on Horace's cellar. That hock which he gave us yesterday was excellent. I think we should endeavour to persuade him to part with some more of it."

⚶

Henri Lessard sat at a table outside an inn overlooking a square near the harbour in Dieppe. On the table stood a bottle of wine and two glasses. Open in front of him was a slim file which he had extracted from a leather portfolio. He had weighted the pages down with a coffee-cup. He picked up the wine bottle and poured two glasses, one of which he handed to his companion. Both men sipped their wine and watched as workmen struggled to erect a wooden frame on the far side of the square.

"So that is a Louisette," said Vallon. "I had heard of it."

"It is," replied Lessard. "It has been officially adopted as the means of execution."

"Why are they putting one here?"

"It is to be a sign of the Revolution, a reminder that the old regime is finished, and a warning to any who oppose the cause."

"Is there any opposition?"

"Oh, yes, very much. A lot of aristos are staying, not running away like yours. You did well. I am sure the Committee will reward you suitably." Lessard studied the other's dishevelled and bloodstained appearance in silence for a moment. "But I gather from the state of your clothes that you must have had some difficulty."

"Yes, a little. I met Gerard as arranged and we went to a beach near Rye. The boat was waiting for us, but as we approached the beach we were attacked."

"Who attacked you?"

"I do not know. It was dark. There were three of them. Gerard killed one. The others escaped."

Lessard grunted. If Gerard had done the killing, then how come Vallon's clothes were bloodstained? Vallon looked shifty, and Lessard had known him long enough to mistrust him. Lessard surmised that he was either lying or, yes - that seemed more likely - he had paused to rob the victim before escaping. He did not like Vallon, but he felt that he might be useful. He studied him through narrowed eyes as he turned to watch the men working on the *Louisette*. The sunlight caught more stains on Vallon's coat. They were faint, but Lessard had seen too many attempts to scrub off blood before. He frowned at Vallon's back. There was altogether too much blood. He said, "Are you quite sure you had no other trouble – before you met Gerard?"

Vallon swung round. "No, none at all."

"Good," replied Lessard, "Because, in my line of work, *unnecessary* trouble can lead to unfortunate complications and endanger my men." He looked hard at Vallon, who shrugged and picked up his glass.

❦

The next day dawned grey over Sussex. The countryside lay under a uniform pall of cloud, which discharged a fine drizzle over the little party mounting up in the stable yard of the Park. It was the sort of rain which soaked everything without really trying, thought Hugo as he carefully mounted and arranged his oiled riding-cape. It would be a fairly unpleasant journey. Still, he felt that with Goodrich and Fletcher he was in good company, and at least he had a horse. The rest of the 'Irregulars' would be on foot. They would have set off at the crack of dawn, several of them no doubt nursing headaches after their evening at the Inn. The mounted party expected to catch up with them some miles down the road. He looked round as Markham appeared, carrying two bottles and followed by Taylor, who bore a tray on which stood four goblets of brandy.

"Doctor Russell has ordered that I am to provide warming

sustenance for your journey," announced Markham. "I have therefore provided this fortifying stirrup-cup." He stepped forward and thrust the two bottles into Goodrich's saddle-bag. "And there is some more for later."

"Why, I thank you, Horace. You are not such a bad fellow after all," exclaimed Goodrich, taking a goblet from Taylor. Markham lifted the last goblet from the tray and raised it. "To success, and a good outcome to the operation."

# CHAPTER NINE

Hugo was saddle-sore and weary. He had not ridden a horse for some time, and was not used to it and out of practice. The group had covered over twenty miles since setting out from Horsham, the horsemen catching up with the foot-party around mid-day, when they had stopped at an inn. Now, according to Goodrich, they were within a mile or two of the inn where they would spend the night, but something was amiss ahead, and they had come to a halt. The turnpike was in poor condition, and for the last few miles it had become increasingly busy, with a good deal of traffic in both directions, much of it consisting of heavy wagons. Those travelling eastwards, in the same direction as the group, all seemed to be carrying heavy loads of dressed stone blocks, whereas those travelling in the opposite direction had loads that were closely sheeted with canvas tarpaulins.

Fletcher's men had sat down on the verge and were talking amongst themselves. Goodrich had dismounted and walked on ahead to discover the cause of the hold-up, which seemed to be around a corner some hundred yards or so ahead. Already, there was a long queue of the heavy stone-carts and several smaller vehicles, and Hugo could hear shouts coming from around the bend. After another minute or so, Fletcher slid from his saddle and led his mount to the side of the road, where he hitched it to a fence. Hugo followed his example and the two of them joined Fletcher's men on the verge, where Hankins had already contrived to light a fire. Hugo sat down on the bank and studied his surroundings. For some time, they had been travelling through countryside which was thickly-forested. The forest would, from time-to-time, give way to areas of farmland and occasional villages, and also to gentle hills, the tops of which were bare of trees and covered with heathy vegetation. They were on one of those hills now. Hugo looked along the road at the forest ahead. Here and there, he could see columns of smoke rising above the trees, but what was making that smoke he could not determine. He could see no villages or even isolated farms. He shifted his attention to the heathy clearing. It was now early evening. The weather, so un-promising when they had set out, was now fine and warm and the heather was heavy with the sound of bees. Hugo watched idly as a white butterfly with orange tips to its wings flitted along the opposite hedgerow, periodically pausing at a patch of flowers. Curious, he thought, that it was only alighting on the little lavender-pink flowers which he remembered his mother had taught him were called 'cuckoo flower', because they blossomed at the time when the cuckoo arrived. The butterfly ignored the other flowers. Hugo wondered why. He made a mental note to ask Doctor Russell when they next met.

His musings were interrupted by Hankins' announcement of, "Brew up, lads." He watched as each man contributed a small handful of tea-leaves from his individual stash and the tea was made. He smiled to himself. Tea was evidently the English army's secret weapon. Wherever the party had stopped on their journey, a 'brew' was made. He was not very keen on it himself, but on this occasion he was thirsty and gratefully accepted the offer of a mug. As he sat sipping the slightly bitter liquid, he had to acknowledge that it did seem strangely refreshing, though he did not find it very palatable. Well, if he was to become English, he thought, he had better try to acquire a taste for it.

He had just drained his mug when Goodrich re-appeared, looking grave. He declined the offer of a mug of tea and said, "There has been a bad accident ahead, and the road is blocked. Help is required, so let us go and do what we can. We had best go on foot." He glanced back the way they had come. Two more stone-carts had arrived in the short time they had been there, and another was visible in the distance. He went on, "Had it been earlier in the day, I would have suggested a detour, but it is too late. Leave your kit here, lads. Good – you stay and guard it. Let us be going."

Round the corner, only just out of sight of where they had stopped, the road ran into a dip. The approach from the west was quite steep, and the road was still wet and slippery from the morning's rain. One of the stone carts had got out of control on the downslope and had collided with one of the other heavy wagons coming in the other direction. The stone cart had lost a wheel and overturned, spilling its load of dressed blocks over the road and blocking it, while the other wagon had slewed round into the shallow ditch at the roadside. One of the two men in charge of the stone cart had fallen down in his efforts to stop the runaway, and a wheel had run over his foot. He was lying in the road, moaning with pain, while his mate tried to comfort him. The men of the other wagon had succeeded in releasing the heavy horses from their traces, had calmed them and moved them away from the wreckage. Other people were simply standing around, apparently with no idea of what to do. Fletcher took one look at the situation and began snapping out orders.

Within half an hour, the remains of the stone wagon had been dragged out of the way and left in a nearby gateway and the stone blocks had been piled neatly at the side of the road. The other wagon, which proved to be carrying a load consisting of a single eighteen-pounder gun barrel, had been extricated from the ditch and a stretcher had been made up from broken timbers from the stone cart. The injured man had been gently placed on the stretcher and given a tot of Markham's brandy, and the gun-wagon's heavy horses once more hitched to its drawbar. Hugo found himself walking back up the road next to one of the carters, who was leading the right-hand horse. As the animals plodded slowly up the hill, Hugo commented to him that the road seemed very busy.

"It is, Sir," the man replied, "And it ain't helped by all these here." He gestured at the stone-carts. This time of year, we moves the guns. We could do without all these stone-wagons clutterin' the road up. There's dozens of 'em, and they mean delays and accidents. That was the third one this week, that I know of."

"Where are they going?" asked Hugo.

"Big house a few miles back. The old General who owned it died a couple of years back. The new owner is building some sort of tower. Something to do with a battle, or something. I don't know for sure."

"You 'move the guns' this time of year. Where are you moving them from, and to?"

The carter looked askance at Hugo for a moment, then said, "Why bless you, Sir, you'm not from these parts, are you? They make 'em here during the winter, an' we takes 'em to

Woolwich in the summer. Sometimes they go by sea, but if the weather ain't right, we takes 'em by road."

They had by now reached the point at which the group had left their kit. Hugo bade farewell to the carter, unhitched his horse and mounted. The traffic was now moving again and they soon arrived back at the scene of the accident. There was no sign of the stretcher. Hankins and Fensom had already picked it up and headed on down the road with it.

An hour later, Hugo found himself sitting at a table in a comfortable parlour at a coaching inn in a small village. He was tired, but, from what he could gather, they were over half-way to Pevensey. Tomorrow, they would turn south-east. Goodrich had said they should have an easier journey from here on. Hugo hoped so. He ached everywhere, and his hands were sore from heaving the stone blocks around. He rubbed his back and yawned as Goodrich entered the room. He grinned at Hugo and sat down. "There will be food presently. I am famished."

"How is the carter?" enquired Hugo.

"Fortunately, there is a Doctor in the village. He has examined the carter. His foot is badly bruised, but there is no lasting damage. He was lucky. I suspect that, had we not had all that rain, the road would have been much harder and he would have been much more badly hurt. He won't walk for a few days, but it will take at least that long to set his wagon to rights."

"All those stone-carts," said Hugo. "The gun-carter said something about someone building a tower for some sort of battle, and making guns here. I could not really understand him."

"Well," said Goodrich, "Guns are indeed made here – all over this area, in fact. There are deposits of the necessary iron ore, forests to provide the charcoal for smelting it, and rivers which provide power for waterwheels which run the machines which bore the barrels. Charcoal is made in the woods all around here. It probably explains the name of this place. 'Blackboys' is probably a corruption of the French for Black Wood, though some do say it is more to do with the colour of the charcoal-burners themselves. It is quite an industry, all the way from here into Kent."

"Oh, I see," said Hugo, "But the carter said they move the guns in the summer, and take them to Woolwich. Why summer, and why Woolwich?"

"The roads are better in summer," replied Goodrich, "And there is less water available to power the machines, so the guns are made during the winter. They are taken to the Royal Arsenal at Woolwich. There they are tested, or 'proofed' by being fired several times with double the intended charge of powder. It is quite a dangerous business. If a gun has an invisible flaw, it can explode."

"Oh," said Hugo. "I had wondered about testing guns. I saw one explode once. It killed two of its crew, and injured several others."

"Was that in battle?" asked Goodrich.

"No, it was just practice. We were shooting at a raft of old casks. The barrel had split for the whole of its length. I remember the gunner saying something about its age."

"Yes, it does not do to try to use a gun that is too old. The metal becomes porous – 'honeycomb', it's called – and loses its strength. Does the French Navy have a great many old guns?"

"I dare say it does. The ones on that ship were all of a similar age, or even older. What about the stone carts? The carter mentioned a battle."

Goodrich shifted himself on his chair and leaned an elbow on the table. "Not a battle, exactly. The stone is being taken to a house a mile or two further on. It used to be called Bayley Park, and it was owned by General George Eliott. He was the man who commanded the British forces at Gibraltar during the besiegement by France and Spain. That must have been ten years ago."

"Oh, yes, I have heard of it. It was a long siege, but Gibraltar was not taken."

"Quite so. Well, Eliott returned to England, was made a Knight of the Bath and created a peer, becoming Baron Heathfield. He died in '90. The new owner of the house is a Mr. Francis Newbery, the son of the publisher John Newbery. Have you heard of him?" Hugo shook his head in reply. "He published a great many books, some of them for children. Have you heard of 'The History of Little Goody Two-Shoes?'"

"Oh, yes. I read it as a child."

"And a very good moral tale it is. Well, that was one of Newbery's publications. His son has re-named the house 'Heathfield Park' in memory of Sir George Eliott, and the stone is for the construction of a tower which he has ordered to be built as a memorial to the siege of Gibraltar. The building has only just commenced, but he showed me the plans last year. It will be very grand. We shall pass the house tomorrow."

❦

Simon Johnston winced and cursed himself for a fool, a weak, soft-hearted fool. He was regretting his decision of some days ago, which, he reflected, he must have made in a moment of delirium or alcoholic poisoning. That decision had been to invite Rupert Kirton to practise with his new fiddle in the Captain's cabin. Kirton had long expressed a wish to take up a musical instrument, and Johnston had encouraged him, saying, "By all means, dear fellow. Just as long as you don't take up the bloody German Flute, you shall practise in my cabin." The day before *Vixen* had sailed from Plymouth, Kirton had disappeared for some time again. Some members of the crew had made insinuating remarks and speculations about Kirton's recent disappearances, but it became clear on his return that he had been spending his time, not in a brothel, as most had surmised, but either in a music-shop or taking violin lessons. When he eventually returned from his last foray, he was bearing a violin-case containing an instrument which must have cost him a great deal of money. Johnston was not a very musical man, and could not himself play an instrument, but even he could appreciate the quality of the object which Kirton had purchased. Relieved that it was not, indeed, a German Flute, he had foolishly repeated his offer. How he regretted that now, he reflected as he tried to screw the two balls of cotton-wool further into his ears. He should have made Kirton practise in the ship's gig, towing astern on a very long painter. To make matters worse, Owen could play quite well, and Wilson, a foretopman, was an excellent fiddler who frequently played for the hands. Both of them had been giving Kirton lessons. Johnston grudgingly admitted that Kirton seemed to be learning quickly, so his half-hour of practice was becoming less hideous as the days passed. On the second day, Owen, grinning at his Captain's discomfort, had assured him that Kirton was a good pupil and it would not take long for him to reach a good standard. Johnston sighed, removed the cotton-wool from his ears and picked up his pen in time to hear Kirton play a complex scale, ending in a trill. Johnston suddenly smiled benignly. That was beginning to sound like the real thing, he thought. Perhaps they would even be able to have a ship's orchestra…

"Rupert, that sounded sublime. Play it again."

The second time, the trill ended in a screech, a twang and a muttered curse as *Vixen* gave a skittish lurch. Johnston laid down his pen and turned round on his chair to see Kirton gazing ruefully at a broken string. He looked up from the instrument, shook his bow at the deckhead and cried, "You bitch! You spoiled it for me!" Then he laughed, "*Vixen* is costing me a fortune in cat-gut."

"At least it is beginning to sound less as if the gut were still attached to the cat. That really did sound rather good," replied Johnston. Kirton began to unwind the broken string from its peg, "Thank you, Simon. I am afraid the last few days have been a sad bore to you."

"Oh, not at all," said Johnston, airily. He opened the little drinks locker and extracted two glasses and the brandy-decanter. "I must admit that, as we left Plymouth, it did occur to me to sail straight to the Eddystone Rock and maroon you on it, but I then thought that might be construed as cruelty – to the seagulls, that is." He slopped brandy into the glasses. Kirton carefully wiped his instrument with a cloth and put it away in its case. Johnston handed him a glass. "Owen says you are a good pupil."

"It is kind in him to say so. I must say he is a good teacher." Both men looked up as spray suddenly pattered against the stern lights and *Vixen* gave another lurch. "Wind's picking up," said Johnston, "We should be able to make up a little of the lost time." *Vixen* had set off from Plymouth in a fair westerly breeze, and he had allowed two days for the voyage. However, just west of the Isle of Wight, an ominous splintering sound from her larboard fore-chains had resulted in her putting into Portsmouth, where the damage which had been overlooked at Plymouth was repaired. As a result, she was now a day behind schedule.

"You have not yet told me exactly where we are going, what we are going to do when we get there, or who we are supposed to be meeting," said Kirton. "Are you able to do so, or are our orders secret?"

Johnston looked at the brandy in his glass for a moment, the replied, "Oh, it should be safe to tell you now, and the crew can be told, as well. I had to keep our orders secret while we were in Plymouth, and afterwards in case we had to put into Portsmouth for any reason. You know how dockyards have ears. However, we have now left Portsmouth, so it is safe to tell everyone. We are going to meet a group of Sir Horace Markham's men. He calls them his 'Irregulars'. We are to escort them to France, assist their operation in whatever way we can, and bring them home again three days later."

"Sir Horace Markham? I do not believe I have heard of him."

"Do you remember Doctor Russell?"

"Oh, indeed yes. The mad Doctor who quarrelled with the Physician of the Fleet."

"The very same. Well, Markham is a friend of Russell's. I have met him on a few occasions. I know his second-in-command very well. Sir Charles Goodrich is a friend. It was Charles who requested *Vixen* for this mission."

"What are the 'Irregulars' supposed to be doing in France?

I would not have thought it a very healthy place at the moment, even if we are not at war."

"My orders are not clear on that, but Charles sent a covering letter with them. It is all rather mysterious cloak-and-dagger stuff, but I gather they are to extract a member of the French aristocracy from the country and, if I know Charles, to sow discord and mayhem as well. Yes?" - this in response to a knock on the door, which opened to reveal a spotty-faced Midshipman. "What is it, Mr. Crocker?"

"Master's compliments, Sir, and the wind has veered a point and strengthened. He wants to know if you would like to take in a reef."

"Thank you, Mr. Crocker. I shall be on deck presently."

The door closed. Johnston finished his brandy. Kirton said suddenly, "Young Crocker is coming along well. I think it is about time he started to think about sitting his examination for Lieutenant."

"Oh," said Johnston, momentarily taken aback, "Yes, he has the makings of a good seaman. I think he has the necessary sea-time, but does he have the book-knowledge? I rather fear we have been neglecting our obligations to him in the matter of encouraging him towards the examination. How old is he now?"

"Twenty, I think," replied Kirton. "Yes, he has done very well. He is a good practical seaman, and I am perfectly happy for him to stand a watch alone. The hands like him, they respect him, and Mr. Owen, at least, has certainly not been neglecting our obligations to him. I do believe he will not require much encouragement. I have seen his books in the gun-room, and not long ago, he left a set of workings lying around. I looked at them. They were neat and accurate, as far as I could tell. He has been studying, though he thinks I don't know it, and he may be almost ready. A pity about the spots, though."

"You are forgetting your own appearance at his age. 'Florid' would have been somewhere near."

"Only in places, and I seem to recall you saying at the time it would serve to terrify the enemy." Kirton drained his glass and stood up.

"It terrified the hands, anyway. I remember the occasion when they were convinced you had contracted some obnoxious disease, and they would all catch it and die horrible deaths."

"Oh, yes. You summoned Doctor Russell. He laughed and made me smear goose-grease all over my face. It did no good. In fact, I fancy it made matters worse."

"And you stank the gun-room out," said Johnston, turning back to his desk. "But we did not know Russell well then. I now suspect it was some sort of revenge, or that he was practising on us." He picked up the pen, wiped it, put it away, glanced over the letter which he had been trying to write to his father, shook his head, put the letter in a drawer of the desk and fished out his watch. "It will be dark soon, and we still have a fair way to go. We shall press on as quickly as we may. Double the lookouts, if you please. We should be there by noon, if this wind holds. I think we shall dispense with washing the decks in the morning, and make sure the men have a good cooked breakfast so they are ready for whatever tomorrow may bring."

❦

Tomorrow brought yet more rain. The wind had become fitful during the night, and around dawn it died altogether. Going on deck to take the forenoon watch, Kirton found *Vixen* merely ghosting along with all her canvas set. A light drizzle soaked everything, dripping from the sails and veiling the land. Kirton walked to the sodden little group of men by the wheel. Hearing his footfall, Owen turned. "Morning, Sir. Not a good one, but it should clear soon. Then we'll get some sunshine and a steady breeze from the nor'west."

"Thank you, Mr. Owen." Kirton smiled. How the Master knew that, he had no idea, but he had known him for several years now and the man was never wrong. Kirton turned to the Royal Marine on duty, "Turn the glass and strike the bell."

"Aye, aye, Sir."

As the watch was being changed and the men going off watch clattered below for their breakfast, Johnston appeared on deck, a mug of coffee in his hand. Spotting Crocker, who was just about to go below after his watch, he called sternly, "Mr. Crocker, a word with you in my cabin, if you please!" turned swiftly on his heel and disappeared.

Crocker made his way nervously toward the Captain's quarters, trying to ignore the nudges and winks and the mutter of, "Oh, watch out. Mr. Crocker's going to cop it something cruel. The Old Man's in a foul mood." He glanced at Kirton as he passed the wheel, receiving a frosty scowl in return. What have I done or not done now? he wondered. Oh, well, for what we are about to receive… Crocker glared at the smirking marine sentry, who crashed to attention, thumped the butt of his musket on the deck and announced, "Mr. Crocker, Sah!"

"Send him in!" To Crocker's fevered imagination, the Captain's voice had a sepulchral tone. He tugged at his coat, licked his lips, knocked and pushed open the door.

By the wheel, Kirton nudged Owen, who had remained

on deck, and the two men tilted their heads to catch any sounds from the cabin. After a minute or so, they heard Johnston's roar of laughter. The men at the wheel chuckled. They were all familiar with the Skipper's strange sense of humour and penchant for practical jokes. It seemed good that Mr. Crocker, who was a quiet and serious young man, should be the butt of that humour this morning. A moment later, the cabin door opened and Johnston, red in the face and still chuckling, poked his head out. "Mr. Owen, would you care to join us for breakfast?"

Owen found Crocker sitting at the table, surrounded by dishes. He was looking a little pale, but cheerful. Owen grinned at him. Johnston closed the door and said, "Mr Owen, I should like to seek your opinion on whether Mr. Crocker here is ready to sit his Lieutenant's examination. Under torture, he has just confessed to the crime of studying, which is a disgraceful admission for a Midshipman to make. They are supposed to have it thrashed into them, the way it had to be thrashed into me. Am I to take it that you have been abetting his felony by giving him tuition in the black arts of mathematics and navigation?"

"Aye, Sir, guilty as charged. I reckon he could probably pass tomorrow."

"I sometimes wonder who commands this vessel. I am told nothing, and my own officers conspire against me! Well, so be it. That is very good. Do you feel ready, Mr. Crocker?"

"I hope so, Sir."

"Excellent. In that case, with your permission, I shall put your name forward when we have finished this little voyage. Now, gentlemen…"

Johnston sat down and began removing the covers from

the dishes. "Hmm, what have we here? Oh, bacon, eggs, and beefsteak and – ah, kidneys. I do so much like a kidney. Pray help yourselves, gentlemen. Where is my steward? Wilby! Wilby, where are you, damn' you? Oh, there you are. You may bring the coffee now."

# CHAPTER TEN

Hugo reined in his horse and gazed at the scene to the left of the road. The party was now a few miles from the inn at Blackboys and they had passed the site of construction of the tower. There had not been much to see. The tower was still more or less at foundation level. They had paused briefly, and there Goodrich had left them. He had continued east towards Rye, while the rest of them had turned south towards Pevensey. Now, there was an obstruction in the road ahead. Another of the large gun-wagons was attempting to negotiate its way on to the road from a narrow entrance. Fletcher rode up beside Hugo. "I think this is as good a place as any to stop and let the lads have a brew," he said. He and Hugo dismounted. Fletcher moved over to his men while Hugo watched as the carters expertly manoeuvred their vehicle into the road and set off.

Hugo stared over the hedge. What he saw seemed to him like a scene from hell. There were some buildings away to his left. Smoke, and occasionally sparks, drifted from them, and the interior of one was lit by a lurid glow. In front of him was another building at the side of which turned a huge water-wheel. The air was full of fumes which assailed his nose, and the sound of hammering combined with the screech of metal to assail his ears. He turned and watched, shaking his head, as a cartload of charcoal turned into the entrance and headed for the buildings to the left. Fletcher returned. "They are brewing up. It will be ready soon."

"What is this place?" asked Hugo.

"This is one of the gun-foundries. That building over there" – he indicated the one to the left – "is the furnace, where the metal is cast, and that one is the boring-house, where the barrels are bored."

"What are they doing? Sir Charles said they only made guns in the winter."

"Oh, they don't just make guns. They are probably making more mundane things now – small parts, brackets and the like. Even pots and pans. Let us go and see."

Fletcher led Hugo through the gates and across the yard to the building which he had described as the 'boring house'. As they approached the large double doors, a man emerged. He was wearing a heavy leather apron and heavy leather gauntlets. He greeted Fletcher and Hugo with a nod and Fletcher shouted something at him over the din which was coming from the other building. In reply, he shouted something in return and waved a gauntleted hand towards the doors. Fletcher entered, Hugo following a few paces behind. Hugo became aware of a whining, whirring sound. Fletcher shouted something at him, but, unable to hear, he cupped his hand behind his ear. Fletcher leaned close to him and shouted again, "We are in luck. The last one of the batch." He gestured towards Hugo's right. Hugo turned and goggled in amazement. A huge machine occupied a good part of the length of the building. On one end of it sat a large chunk of metal which Hugo recognized as the barrel of a twelve-pounder gun. The metal was glowing, a dark cherry-red colour. The other end of the machine seemed to consist of wheels, gears and levers. From the centre of the assembly protruded a long metal bar which disappeared into the muzzle of the gun. The gun barrel was rotating, and slivers of hot gunmetal curled out of the muzzle to fall sizzling on to the wet floor. Two men, both dressed in the same protective leather aprons and gloves, were operating the machine, while a boy, also wearing a leather apron, was raking the bright, spiralling swarf away from its moving parts. Hugo could feel the heat radiating from the nascent gun, even though he was standing about fifteen feet away from it. Another man was leaning over the barrel, intently watching something on the shaft of the machine. As Fletcher and Hugo watched, he suddenly threw up his hand and shouted something. The two men at the controls continued to bore for another inch or so, one of them carefully watching a scale engraved on the bed of the machine, then they heaved on a wheel and the shaft was withdrawn from the still rotating barrel. They examined their work, and the foreman finally turned towards Fletcher and Hugo. He nodded in greeting, removed his gauntlets, and the boy pulled a lever. The noise stopped as the machine came to a halt. The foreman examined his work again, turned to Fletcher and Hugo, grinned and announced, "It's a good 'un. Last one for a few months." Then he walked to a doorway at the end of the room and called through it. The other man and the boy quickly removed the leather drive-belt from the drive of the water-wheel and attached another one, which ran through a hole in the end wall. Fletcher studied the machine, peering at the cutting-head of the boring shaft. The foreman patted the bed of the monster. "Good machine, this. Invented by a Mr. Wilkinson." He had to shout the last few words as the boy engaged the drive of the water-wheel and the gears began to whine and grind. The foreman gestured to Fletcher and Hugo to go through the doorway, shouting, "That's a trip-hammer. Have a look." He followed them into the next workshop. The boy ran after them.

The machine in the next room was less spectacular than the boring-machine, thought Hugo, as it consisted of a large hammer-head which was pivoted over an anvil. The head had been surrounded with pieces of red-hot metal. The foreman engaged the drive and the hammer head was raised slowly from the anvil, while the boy pushed the pieces of metal off the anvil. One of the foundrymen gave a shout, and suddenly two more men appeared, dragging a small trolley on which rested a billet of iron, almost white-hot. Using long tongs, the two deftly picked up the incandescent metal and positioned it beneath the hammer head. The foreman pulled a lever and the hammer began to rise and fall, beating the billet flat. Showers of yellow sparks rose and fell around the machine. The noise was incredible, the heat and fumes overpowering. In a few minutes the billet had been beaten into a slab about an inch thick. Almost casually, the two foundrymen tossed the heavy, now red-hot, metal back on to the trolley and trundled it back towards the furnace. The foreman stopped the hammer, wiped the sweat from his face and grinned at his visitors. "That's too cool now. Needs heating up again," he said. The boy started clearing up the scrap metal that had surrounded the hammer-head, throwing the pieces into a bucket.

"Do you not need that again?" enquired Fletcher.

"Oh, no, Sir. She's warm now. We have to warm her up before using her, or she could split and shatter. She'll stay warm for hours now, and we have quite a few of these billets to do. They have to be eventually rolled into plates a quarter of an inch thick, to make a boiler for a steam-engine. He gestured at another machine which was standing at the other side of the workshop. It resembled a giant laundry mangle. We'll do a few now, and after our dinner-break the gun will be cool enough for us to finish it – bore the touch-hole and so on."

Shouts from outside indicated that another billet was on its way. Fletcher and Hugo thanked the foreman, and Fletcher handed him a half-guinea, indicating that he should buy all his men some beer with it. All of the foundrymen grinned and waved at the two as they made their way out of the workshop, and after a few seconds the din began again.

"My God," said Fletcher as they walked out through the gates, "I have never seen anything like that. How on earth do they stand it?"

"It is like something out of hell," said Hugo.

"Some say it is the future. I think I have to agree with them, but it is not pleasant. There are places like this all over the area, and some men are becoming very rich on their proceeds. All this lot belongs to 'Mad Jack' Fuller."

"Mad Jack?"

"Yes, the Squire of Brightling, not far away." He gestured eastwards. "His name is John Fuller. His family have been ironmasters for a long time. He is a very wealthy man. I don't think he is really mad. In fact, it is said that he is something of a philanthropist. He is quite young, but it would appear that he is becoming somewhat eccentric, from what I have heard. I have never met the gentleman. I should like to. He sounds interesting."

Hugo shook his head in wonder and both men turned towards Fletcher's men as someone called "Brew's up." Costa waved a mug in their direction.

Hugo gratefully accepted the tin mug of bitter tea. Strange, he thought, he was already developing a taste for it, and had actually found himself looking forward to the brew-stop for the last couple of miles. He smiled ruefully to himself. He was becoming English. He turned to Fletcher. "How much further?"

Fletcher considered for a moment. "It is not very far now. We have made good time. Another mile or so to Herstmonceux, then on to Wartling, where we can rest and eat at the Lamb Inn. This afternoon we shall cross Pevensey Levels. It's marshy, but there is a road of sorts, and we should not have any difficulty. Then we arrive at Pevensey, where we shall meet our 'Naval Party' who will join us for our voyage for France. As I understand it, a lugger will take us out to a Royal Navy ship which will take us across the Channel and deposit us somewhere quiet on the French coast, or maybe transfer us to a fishing-boat for the last few miles. I do not know what is supposed to happen on the other side of the Channel. My instructions are simply to get us to Pevensey, and to expect further orders on board the ship."

"What about Sir Charles?"

"Well, it will take him another day to reach Rye. He told me he has a 'little business', as he put it, to see to first. He should cross tomorrow or the day after. More than that, I do not know."

❧

A little after mid-day, Sir Charles Goodrich eased himself from his mount in the yard of a coaching-inn in Battle. As a stable-boy led the horse away, Goodrich headed for the parlour, where he was greeted by the landlord. He sometimes stayed at the inn and was quite well-known in the little town. Looking round the room, he noticed a small, rather plump man hunched over his meal at a table in the corner of the room. Goodrich approached him and said quietly, "Good day, Blount. I trust I find you well."

The man looked up from his plate and peered myopically at Goodrich through a pair of gold-rimmed spectacles. Recognizing him, he laid down his knife, jumped to his feet and seized Goodrich's hand. "Jack! It is good to see you again. Do join me." He waved Goodrich to a chair and sat down again. "I have not seen you for some months. How is life with you?"

"Oh, I am keeping busy – very busy, in matter of fact. I am presently on my way to France." Goodrich summoned the serving-maid and requested a bottle of wine, then turned his attention back to his companion. He regarded the little man for a few moments. The Reverend James Blount was a churchman, Rector of several benefices surrounding Battle. His was a rich living, and Blount lived well – rather too well, thought Goodrich. The man seemed to have expanded further in the few months since he had last set eyes on him. Blount was a highly intelligent man who also acted as a magistrate. He was a fount of information, much of it inconsequential, about local affairs. He could also be relied upon to be very discreet. He knew of Goodrich's activities, but never mentioned them. Blount returned Goodrich's gaze for a moment, grunted, nodded, wiped his plate clean with a piece of bread, sat back on his chair and undid a couple of buttons of his waistcoat. "I suppose you have heard of the events a few miles away? Dreadful business."

"I have heard nothing," replied Goodrich, "but I have no doubt you are going to tell me."

Blount grinned at him, then became serious. "A vile murder. In Northiam." He paused, waiting for a reaction. "Do go on," said Goodrich.

"It happened at an oast, a couple of weeks ago. The owner, a Mr. Pelham, was away, leaving his wife in charge. It would seem that someone entered the house. A young man in Pelham's employment challenged the intruder, who attacked him and stabbed him. He then proceeded to ransack the place. Mrs. Pelham heard the disturbance and went to investigate. She also challenged the intruder, and was also stabbed for her pains, but Mrs Pelham is made of stern stuff and she beat her assailant off. She had been bleeding a pig at the time, and she threw a jug of hog's blood all over him, then smashed the jug over his head. She was not badly hurt, but the Pelham's young man died the next day. A very sad affair." He shook his head slowly.

"The culprit was not apprehended, then?"

"No, he escaped. He is being hunted. Mrs. Pelham identified him and a neighbour saw him running away. It is possible that you know of him. He is, or was, in service at the place at Rolvenden which that French count, Poitiers, took a year or two ago."

"Pelham. Hmm. I wonder if they are related to the Pelhams of Pevensey."

"Quite possibly, though Mrs. Pelham obviously is not. Just as well. She evidently has more spirit than her namesake, the one whom Richard the Second's men killed."

"Richard the Second?" asked Goodrich.

"Yes. Lady Joan Pelham was left at home while her

husband Sir John was away on a campaign. He was one of Bolingbroke's men. According to the story, Richard's men overran the castle and killed her. Her fetch still wanders around the battlements, wringing her hands and wailing for her husband to protect her. Our Mrs Pelham seems to be quite capable of managing without the protection of *her* husband." Blount chuckled at Goodrich's raised eyebrow. "Of course," he went on, "I don't believe a word of it, but I am told that some strange things happen in the old castle."

"Probably as a result of the effects of over-indulgence in un-customed brandy!" rejoined Goodrich.

"Quite so. Some of the rot-gut they smuggle in there is more than enough to make one see very strange things after only a glass or two." Blount shook his head sadly and broke off a piece of bread. Goodrich laughed.

A pretty serving-maid arrived with a bottle of wine and two glasses, which she placed, rather nervously, before Goodrich. "Thank you, my dear," he said. She blushed and fled. Goodrich stared after her for a few seconds, then turned his head to find Blount looking at him severely. He pulled himself together. "Er – yes. We digressed. You were saying? Do you have a name for this murderer?"

"I do. His name is Louis Vallon."

"Ah! Are you aware of any motive for this attack?"

Blount looked at Goodrich steadily for several seconds. Instead of giving Goodrich a direct answer, he asked, "May I enquire if this has any bearing on your current business? I have heard a rumour that the Count of Poitiers has disappeared."

Goodrich did not immediately reply, as the serving-maid had re-appeared bearing a dish containing a large beefsteak and kidney pudding. This she set before Goodrich, and fled once more, blushing even redder at his thanks. Blount turned to watch her as she disappeared into the kitchen, then turned his attention back to Goodrich, or rather to the pudding, into which Goodrich had just cut. An appetizing, sinful, aroma drifted from it towards Blount. He had just eaten two pork chops. Goodrich lifted a spoonful of the pudding and held it towards Blount, an interrogative expression on his face. Blount gazed at it for a moment. *O Lord, deliver me from temptation. But the sin of gluttony is not so great, and I am but mortal, and weak...*He held out his plate and Goodrich spooned a generous helping on to it. The girl re–appeared with a dish of vegetables and a loaf of bread.

It was several minutes before either man spoke again. Goodrich finally broke the silence. "I trust, James, that you are not digging yourself an early grave with your teeth."

"You are too perspicacious by half, Jack. I fear that my sins have found me out, and that I am probably far too fond of my victuals. I confess to weakness, particularly when confronted with a temptation such as this pudding."

"I shall pray for your salvation, James. Now, where were we? Oh I remember. To answer your question: yes, it certainly does have a bearing on my current business, as you put it."

"Very well. I shall tell you all that I have managed to discover. Mr. Pelham, naturally, was quite distressed at the attack. He was also somewhat reluctant to say very much, but I eventually persuaded him to tell me all he knew. It became clear that he was more in fear of my condemnation as a clergyman than as a magistrate. It would seem that his daughter had been 'carrying on', as he put it, with this Vallon, and even giving him money, for several months. The Pelhams were not particularly worried. They were aware that the lass had 'an eye for the men', as Mrs. Pelham put it, but neither of them liked or approved of Vallon. Anyway, about a month ago, the daughter gave Vallon his marching orders."

"Ah." Goodrich laid down his fork and picked up his wine-glass. "Anything more you can tell me?"

"Yes. Vallon stole money before he fled – not a great sum, and certainly not enough to warrant murdering for it. He apparently knew where the Pelhams kept some of it. The daughter suggested that he must have observed her when she went to get money for him. Pelham said that he and his wife had discussed Vallon with their daughter after she broke with him. She had told him that the man had revolutionary ideas. He apparently boasted to her that he would soon be in a position of power, and that he would no longer have to serve an 'aristo' because there would be no aristos, not in France, not in England, not anywhere, because the revolution would have swept them all away."

"Hmm. Most interesting."

"It sounds to me like madness. I think the Pelhams both considered it to be some sort of a joke," continued Blount.

"Some joke. It ended in murder!"

"I suppose that Vallon wanted money, knew the Pelhams had it, and simply went to steal it. When challenged, he panicked."

"Possibly, but I think it more likely that he is completely ruthless, and will stop at nothing to achieve his revolutionary aims."

"Indeed, and I would very much like to see him brought to justice. We are still searching for him, but I fear he must be many miles from here by now."

"I think you are correct in that assumption, but that is

very useful information. I thank you. There is something I have to tell you. More pudding?"

Blount sighed, looked at his plate, then at the pudding. "Well, if you insist." He held out his plate. Goodrich spooned more pudding on to it and continued, "Have you heard about the murder of an Excise man near Hastings?"

"I have heard rumours. Nothing more."

"It happened about the same time. I suspect that it was Vallon who committed that one as well."

Both men ate in silence for a few minutes more. Blount finally pushed his plate away and said, "I fear I have eaten too much again. I shall suffer for it later."

Goodrich grinned at him. "The wages of gluttony is dyspepsia, James. You have brought it upon yourself. Do not look to me for sympathy." He grinned again as Blount undid two more buttons of his waistcoat. "Something ironical has just occurred to me."

"What, pray, is that?"

"It is odd, is it not, that our murdering little revolutionary should share a Christian name with the King whom he is trying to do away with?"

"Most whimsical, Jack, most whimsical."

❦

Hugo, riding a little ahead of the rest of the company, reined in and gazed at the scenery of the Pevensey Levels. The party had descended from the woods around Wartling into a landscape which Hugo found strange and fascinating. It was very flat and marshy, and parts of it were criss-crossed by ditches which were lined with tall reeds. A few parts had been completely drained, leaving areas of wet pasture where cattle and sheep grazed, but there were still large areas of standing water. The road wound along a rough causeway from one drier part to the next. Strange, unseen birds called across the marshes. The birds he could see were small. They frequented the reed beds, flitting amongst the remains of last year's old feathery seed heads. About half-way across, the party stopped for a few minutes. Hugo was struck by the silence, which was almost tangible, broken only by the calls of the marsh birds. Occasionally, a breeze would stir the reed-beds, producing a faint whispering, hissing sound, and the small birds would take to the air briefly before settling once more on the seed-heads. Hugo could see no sign of habitation. He turned in his saddle as Fletcher caught up with him. "How much further? There seems to be nothing for miles."

Fletcher indicated an indistinct dark line in the distance. "That is Pevensey ahead. We shall be able to see the castle walls presently."

Eventually, the dark line in the distance to the south resolved itself through the haze into a line of trees, above which poked the stubby steeple of a church, and a high curtain wall. Fletcher, who had been riding some distance ahead, reined in his mount and waited for Hugo to catch up with him. "Nearly there. There's a good inn, the Royal Oak, by the castle walls. It will be most welcome after this bleak wasteland."

"Wasteland?" replied Hugo, "There are interesting birds."

Fletcher regarded him in surprise for a moment. "You had best tell Jack about those. Then you can both come here together and spend your days grubbing about in the marshes." He pulled a face and laughed.

Half an hour later, Hugo found himself riding towards a

high wall, built of a mellow yellow stone, the severity of which was relieved by occasional courses of red tiles or bricks. Every so often, a circular tower projected from the wall. Hugo gazed up at the wall as they drew nearer to it. "Pevensey Castle," said Fletcher. "Quite some edifice, is it not? They say it was begun by the Romans. Ah, there is the Royal Oak." He gestured with his crop at the inn, hard by the curtain wall. "We can stay there until the Navy arrives."

An hour later, Hugo had been introduced to three men who made up 'the naval party', as Fletcher had put it. They were evidently smugglers. The kit had all been stowed aboard the lugger which was to take them out to meet the ship, but of the ship there had been no sign. As evening fell, the party had retired to the inn. A man was detailed to watch for the ship from first light in the morning and, after a meal, the men retired to bivouac in a field across the road, leaving Hugo and Fletcher sitting in the parlour, a backgammon board on the table between them. After a few games, it became evident that the two were evenly matched and equally lucky. Fletcher sat back on his chair and poured himself a second glass of brandy. "This is uncommonly good," he remarked, looking at the light of a lamp through the amber liquid. "I hope it has been properly customed, but I fear that it probably has not." He pulled a face at Hugo's puzzled expression and added, "In these parts, there is not much for sale that isn't contraband. It does not do to enquire too closely into the origins of many of the goods which are to be had in Pevensey."

"I suspect it may be from one of my father's estates," said Hugo. "He has several vineyards, some in the Cognac area. Or rather, he had them.. I wonder what is going to happen to them, and I wonder where he is now."

"I think we may learn more of his whereabouts when this damn' ship arrives. She is apparently carrying our orders," said Fletcher. "Anyway, wherever he may be, I am confident that we shall be able to extract him. Goodrich's intelligence is always accurate, and our lads are very good at this sort of work. I surmise that he cannot be far from the coast, wherever he is, because we are travelling light. Let's hope the ship arrives tomorrow." He unbuttoned his coat. "It is stuffy in here. Shall we take a turn outside?"

Fletcher and Hugo strolled along the curtain wall. The last remnants of the evening light were fading in the west. By the main gateway they paused and gazed up at the walls, then they turned and walked through the gateway. "What a huge place," said Fletcher. "I wonder why it was abandoned."

"What is that noise?" said Hugo, suddenly. "It sounds like a woman weeping. It is coming from over there." He gestured to the right. Both men walked towards one of the gate towers. "There – there is a woman. What on earth is she doing?" said Hugo, pointing into the shadows. Fletcher peered into the gathering gloom. Suddenly, he saw, or thought he saw, the figure of a woman, dressed in an old-fashioned robe, standing by the wall near the tower. The figure was very pale. Both men strode towards her, Fletcher calling, "Madam, what is wrong?"

When they were about twenty feet from her, the woman vanished.

Fletcher and Hugo looked at each other for several seconds. Hugo felt the hairs on the back of his neck prickle. Then Fletcher said, "I am suddenly very cold. I think it must be time to return to the inn, even if it is stuffy." Both of them turned and walked quickly out of the gate. After fifty yards or so, they encountered Sergeant-Major Lloyd on the path.

"Where did she go, Sir," he demanded.

Fletcher pulled himself together. "Who, Sergeant-Major?"

"The woman, Sir. The one that went in the gate, just before you came out. I stepped out for a minute, and she walked past me. She seemed to be upset about something, so I followed her. You must have seen her. She must have walked straight past you." Hugo felt the hairs on his neck rise even further. Fletcher looked steadily at Lloyd. "There was no-one there, Sergeant-Major. It must have been a trick of the light."

"If you say so, Sir."

"I do say so, Sergeant-Major."

"Very good, Sir." Lloyd about-turned and fell into step with Fletcher and Hugo. The three men marched rapidly back to the inn. Not one of them glanced behind.

The landlord took one look at them as they entered. He smiled to himself, turned to a shelf behind him and picked up a bottle of brandy and three glasses. "Gentlemen, you all look as if you have seen a ghost. You will need some of this."

A few minutes later, Fletcher leaned across the table and said quietly to Lloyd, "I don't know what you saw, and I don't know what we saw, or thought we saw, but not a word to the men. You know how superstitious they are. If they think there is a fetch wandering around, they'll all desert on the spot."

Lloyd picked up his glass. "Of course not, Sir. But it was bloody odd, though, wasn't it?" Fletcher grunted and picked up his own glass. "Bloody odd," he agreed.

❧

The next morning dawned dank and misty. There was scarcely a chance of spotting the vessel through the murk even if she had been close to, so the party remained at the inn for the morning. Hugo and Fletcher wandered around the village and down to the beach, but there was little to see, so they returned to the inn and sat in the parlour. Fletcher, watched by Hugo, stripped and carefully cleaned his Girandoni, describing each part and explaining its function as he did so. When he had finished, he wrapped the weapon in oiled silk and finally stowed it away in his knapsack.

"What are we to do if the ship fails to appear?" asked Hugo.

"I am not sure," replied Fletcher. "Jack left no instructions for that eventuality. I suppose we must sit and wait for a couple of days at least. The problem is that he is probably already on his way to France, so how we are to contact him I do not know."

The door to the parlour opened and Lloyd poked his head round it. "Lookout reports a brig in sight, Sir. She's flying the signal."

"Excellent. Muster the men on the beach, please."

"Sir." Lloyd disappeared.

Fletcher stood and picked up his knapsack. "Good. It seems we can finally get going. Better late than never, I suppose." Hugo closed his notebook, which had been on the table before him, stuffed it into his pocket and picked up his own knapsack. The two men made their way to the beach, where they found Lloyd talking to the lugger-men while Hankins checked equipment. A small boat from the lugger was drawn up on the waterline. Lloyd turned as Fletcher approached him. It was obvious to Hugo that there were only eight men present. There should have been twelve, including the lugger-men.

"Usual two missing, Sir. Gibbs and Holden. I've sent Costa and Good to find them."

"Very well. Carry on, Sergeant-Major." Fletcher grinned at Hugo. "They will not be far away – Costa will try the tap-room at the inn. It is an unfortunate trait of the English soldier that, although he is an excellent fighter, he has a weakness for drink. In fact, he will take any opportunity that may present itself to get drunk. Those two are our most regular offenders. Costa does not drink much. He says he does not like our good English ale, and Good has recently become a Methodist, so he has 'renounced all spirituous liquors', as he put it."

A few minutes later, Good appeared, accompanied by Gibbs, who seemed relatively sober. He was followed soon afterwards by Costa. The Italian was carrying Holden, who was draped across his shoulders like a sack of potatoes. He dumped the insensible Holden in front of Lloyd, who turned to Fletcher and announced, "All present, Sir, but not necessarily sober." He nodded at Costa, who walked to the boat, pulled a canvas bucket out from beneath a thwart and filled it with seawater, which he then dashed into Holden's face. Holden groaned, opened his eyes, spluttered feebly and began to curse. Fletcher turned to Gibbs. "What the hell do you think you were doing, man?"

Gibbs swayed slightly. "Well, Sir, erm…"

"Out with it, man!"

"Well, Sir, it's like this. We heard this place is haunted, Sir, and we thought we could do with some, um…"

"Dutch courage, is that it, Gibbs?"

"Er, yessir, if you like." Gibbs swayed again.

"I do not like, Gibbs, and I have never heard such rubbish, or a more feeble excuse for being drunk, in my life. Of course this place isn't haunted. What a load of superstitious nonsense! Get into the boat." Gibbs shuffled off and Fletcher turned to Holden, who was being supported by Costa. "You are a disgrace, Holden. Consider yourself on a charge. I will deal with you when we return. There is not time now. Get him into the boat." Costa, ignoring the slurred protests, picked up Holden and threw him, none too gently, into the boat. Fletcher turned to Lloyd and Hugo. "How the hell did they know?" He pulled a face and turned to watch as Costa tried to make Holden comfortable. "Put his head over the side," ordered Fletcher. "I don't want him throwing up in the boat." He turned to Hugo and raised his eyes to the heavens, then smiled. "He'll be right as rain very soon – an hour or two at the most. He has a very small capacity for alcohol. He will only have had about three or four pints, a quantity which would leave most men unaffected. I don't know why he bothers. Gibbs will have drunk three times as much, and I would not consider him particularly drunk, at least, not by Army standards. The problem is that he leads Holden on. Still, they are grown men. They are responsible for their own actions. I cannot be a nursemaid to them all the time. Even so," he turned and looked back at the castle walls, "I shall be quite glad to get away from here myself." He shook his head and picked his knapsack up off the pebbles. Twenty minutes later, the lugger set sail and headed towards the brig, which was invisible from the beach, being well out to sea.

❦

Mid-day had found *Vixen* hove-to about three miles off Beachy Head, far enough from shore to discourage prying eyes. The drizzle and mist had, as the Master predicted, cleared and there was a gentle breeze from the north-west. Johnston sat at his desk, still trying to find the right words for his letter to his father. Odd noises and thumps sounded from on deck. They had arrived at the rendezvous, but there was no sign of the lugger which was to bring the party off, which was hardly surprising since they were almost a day late. It would be at least a couple of hours until the landing-party would be able to board, and Kirton and Owen between them had decided to use the spare time to do some 'housekeeping' as Kirton put it. Equipment, particularly the gun carriages and tackles, was being checked and greased. Simms, the sailmaker, had hauled every stitch of canvas out of the sail locker and he and his mates were carefully going over every sail, checking every seam, every reef point, every eye and every bolt-rope. Johnston stared at the paper and rubbed his nose with the feather of the pen. He had a suggestion to make concerning his brother, but he did not know how to word it. He did not know if his father had calmed down after his last outburst, and he could not think of suitably diplomatic language to use in case he had not. It was a pity that events had happened quite so quickly. He had hoped to have word from his mother that the 'coast was clear', as it were, before making his suggestion, but *Vixen's* sudden re-commissioning had meant that he was at sea before any further contact was possible. He fiddled with his pen and sighed.

His thoughts were rudely interrupted by a shout of alarm, followed swiftly by a crash as the heavy sheave-pin of a block smashed through his cabin skylight, showering him in glass and making him jump violently, upsetting the ink-well over his letter. Through the broken pane he could hear Owen's voice raised in anger. "You dozy lubber! What the hell do you think you're playing at?" He sighed again and stood up, brushing the glass from his coat. He was trying to mop up the ink when the marine sentry announced the arrival of Kirton, who looked at the sheave-pin lying on the cabin sole.

"What the hell is going on?" demanded Johnston.

"Sorry about that, Sir. That was a new block. The pin was loose. It just flew out, according to the bosun. You are not hurt?"

"No. That is very bad. Was it one of those supplied by the yard in Plymouth?"

"Aye, Sir. Fortunately, it was the first one we have tried to use. I shall have to have all of them checked before we try again. We'll put the old one back for the present."

Johnston screwed his letter into a ball and threw it out of the open window. "Don't bother to check them. Just don't use them. The dockyard can have the whole damn' lot back." He regarded the mess. "Better send for the carpenter."

By way of an answer, Kirton looked upwards. Johnston followed his gaze as the carpenter's round moon-face appeared in the broken skylight. He grinned at his captain, knuckled his forehead, reached in and delicately removed a piece of glass which still somehow clung to the frame. Several smaller fragments tinkled on to the table.

"I think it would be safer on deck," said Johnston. "Hicks!"

"Sir?"

"Get Wilby to clear this lot up."

"Aye, aye, Sir – and the lookout reports a lugger approaching, Sir."

"That will be our guests." To Kirton, "You'd better get everything shipshape."

"Aye. We were pretty much finished, anyway. They are just re-stowing the last of the sails, and Mr. Owen is happy with the guns now."

"Well, that's something, at any rate." He looked at his hands. "I'd better try to get this damned ink off. Let us go on deck."

Half an hour later, the lugger was alongside *Vixen*. Bundles of equipment were being swung aboard and men were scrambling up the side. Kirton had welcomed the officers on deck. There was no sign of Johnston, so Kirton began some introductions. Owen looked at the two 'officers'. They did not, he thought, look very much like officers. They were dressed in civilian clothes. The elder, and obviously senior, one was tall and well-groomed, but he was wearing a worn and patched old coat that would have been more suited to a tramp, and he carried a pack. He was evidently known to Kirton, who greeted him as a friend. The younger was already moving about with the ease of a seaman. Owen wondered who he could be.

Kirton turned as the door to the captain's cabin opened and Johnston strode out. He glanced round the ship and his eye fell on his guests.

"Fletcher, you scoundrel!"

Fletcher turned, gaped for a moment, then strode towards Johnston, his hand outstretched. "Johnston! Well, I suppose it had to be you, really. It is good to see that you are upholding the Navy's tradition of being late. How are you?"

"I am well, I thank you." Johnston ignored the jibe and beamed at his guests. "Mr. Kirton, if you will please to introduce the other gentleman, we shall repair below."

❦

Aboard the lugger, Holden had been positioned with his head over the side and was being guarded by Costa. Gibbs had turned a delicate shade of green and he was being pushed by Good toward the side as well. The remainder of the men had arranged themselves in the waist and were talking quietly amongst themselves. Hugo turned his attention away from the two casualties to watch the two lugger-men. He admired the economy of effort with which they, with the help of a single boy, handled their little vessel. There were no shouted orders. All three seemed to communicate without even speaking. He was still watching, fascinated, when Fletcher joined him.

"I am admiring the way they handle this vessel," said Hugo. "No orders, no shouting. It is very unlike the French navy."

"Well, it is very unlike the English navy, too," replied Fletcher. "But this is not strictly a navy vessel. She is merely hired for occasional special operations. The rest of the time, the nature of her business is such that it is an advantage for her to operate in as near as possible complete silence. After all, fish have excellent hearing." He winked at Hugo. "Do you see what I mean?"

"Oh yes, of course." Hugo grinned. It was obvious that the lugger did very little in the way of fishing. In fact, she did not smell even faintly of fish. True, there were some fish-boxes stacked on her little half-deck, and what looked like a net and some cork floats stuffed underneath it, but there was no sign that any of the equipment had seen any use. The little vessel moved easily, rolling gently. Groans sounded from the rail. Fletcher and Hugo moved forward and stared ahead. After a few minutes, Fletcher produced a small telescope from his pocket, extended the tubes and peered through it. "There she is." He passed the instrument to Hugo.

In the circle of vision, Hugo saw a trim little brig, painted black with a broad buff band through her gunports. There seemed to be considerable activity on deck, but she was still too far away and the telescope was not powerful enough to see what was going on in any detail. He and Fletcher discussed her for some minutes, and when Hugo trained the telescope on her again, the activity had ceased. Fletcher turned to his men. "Check equipment and get ready to transfer. He glanced to the rail, where Holden, though looking pale, had recovered sufficiently to stand up. Gibbs had already joined the other men and was enduring their jibes. He and Hugo moved aft to join them and checked their own equipment, and by the time Hugo looked up again the side of the brig was above them. Challenge and reply were made, a whip appeared from the brig's mainyard and the kit was hoisted aboard as the men made their way up the side of the ship to her entry-port, Hugo and Fletcher going last.

As Hugo gained the deck, he found himself immediately at home, unfamiliar though the vessel was to him. He began to look around him, taking in the familiar sights, smells and sounds – the neatly flaked and coiled ropes, the gleaming, blacked guns, the smell of paint and Stockholm tar, the tapping of a flag-halyard, the creaks of ropes and timbers, the squeak from a gun – carriage as it moved slightly in spite of its lashings. He pulled himself together just in time to be introduced to the First Lieutenant and the Sailing Master. His attention had already wandered back to an examination of the rigging when a voice suddenly boomed, "Fletcher, you scoundrel!" The owner of the booming voice, evidently the Captain, was a man of a little above average height, but heavily built. He had light brown hair, tied in a clubbed queue with a black ribbon. His face looked stern until he smiled, when it underwent a transformation, the expression becoming almost mischievous. He was smiling at Fletcher now, pumping his hand, which he had seized in one of his own massive paws. A moment later, Hugo found his own hand seized by the same paw and vigorously pumped up and down, while he looked into a pair of twinkling eyes of almost the same startling shade of blue as his own and the booming voice was declaring its owner delighted to make his acquaintance.

# CHAPTER ELEVEN

His Britannic Majesty's Brig *Vixen* ghosted gently towards the coast of France. She had set off from the rendezvous south of Beachy Head in a steady breeze, but by mid-channel she had been virtually becalmed. In the Captain's cabin, Fletcher and Johnston were huddled over a chart and a sketch-map. Fletcher's orders were open on the table between them, and the two men were discussing the finer points of the operation. Hugo was standing on the little foredeck with Kirton. The two of them were discussing the finer points of the little brig, and a friendship was developing rapidly, even though they had met only a few hours previously. The French coast was just discernable through a bank of haze to the south. Kirton examined it with a telescope, which he then handed to Hugo.

"You'll be landing just to the right of the small headland there. There is a cove with a hidden beach. The derelict farm that is mentioned in your orders is about half a mile inland. There is no sign of the lugger yet, though." Hugo swept the horizon again and handed the telescope back to Kirton.

"I am not sure why we have to keep changing vessels. Surely we could be landed by *Vixen's* boats?"

Before replying, Kirton extended the telescope's tubes again and swept the horizon once more. He lowered the glass and said, "I believe that the general idea is that secrecy is of the utmost importance. The lugger that brought you off from Pevensey cannot cross to France without raising suspicion. The one that will take you ashore is known in France, and can come and go as she pleases. The two of them are pretty much identical, so could pass for each other at a pinch, but we are not taking the risk. Neither lugger ventures far from its home port - at least, no further than she would on a day's fishing-trip. Of course, since we are not at war with France, the Royal Navy cannot be seen to be involved in clandestine operations, so we cannot go much closer than this to the French coast without attracting unwelcome attention. Hence all this cloak-and-dagger stuff."

They both looked up at a shout from the foremast lookout, "On deck there! Sail two points to starboard! Lugger, by the looks of her"

"That will be her." Kirton snapped the telescope open again and trained it in the direction of the lookout's pointing arm. "It *is* her. Mr. Crocker!"

"Aye, Sir?"

"My compliments to the Captain, and please to inform him that *Marie* is in sight."

"Aye, aye, Sir."

A few moments later, Johnston and Fletcher appeared by the wheel. Both moved to the starboard side and gazed in the direction of the lugger for a few seconds. Kirton and Hugo walked aft to join them. "Well, gentlemen," said Johnston. "Time for us to part company. We shall patrol between here and Boulogne as Sir Charles requests, returning here in two days' time, then every day thereafter. I wish you good luck." He shook hands with Fletcher and Hugo, then started bellowing orders. "Mr. Owen! Heave to, if you please!"

Pierre Chabot lounged in his chair behind the magnificently carved walnut desk in his office in Paris. He had had the desk 'liberated' from one of the Bourbon residences. He leant back and admired it. The grain of the wood was beautiful. He ran a pudgy finger over the tooled leather which covered the top, then stood up and walked to the window, from where he gazed down on the street. It was teeming with traffic of all kinds. He watched for a few minutes. There was a heady atmosphere in the French capital, an atmosphere that was, to Chabot at least, almost tangible. He considered the possibilities for the future, his imagination running away to picture himself in very high office, even President of the new Republic. He turned as his secretary gave a perfunctory knock on the door and entered, bearing an envelope. This he laid on the otherwise empty desk. "A message for you, citizen."

"Thank you, citizen." Chabot waited until the man had left the room and closed the door. Then he sat down again, lifted the envelope from his desk, examined the seal, opened a drawer of the desk, extracted a silver paper-knife and slid it under the seal. He read the letter carefully, then laid it on the desk. A slow smile spread across his features. He picked the letter up and read it again, folded it and placed it in a drawer. He rose and crossed the room to an elaborately-carved and gilded cabinet (also liberated from the royal residence). From this the took a crystal goblet and a finely – cut decanter, from which he poured a generous measure of the finest brandy into the goblet. Taking the glass to the window, he gazed out again at the bustle in the street. He nodded to himself and smiled again, then returned to the desk, opened another drawer and took from it a small hand-bell. He rang it, then replaced it in the drawer. After a pause of several seconds, the door opened.

"Yes, citizen?"

"Send citizen Dubois to me."

"Yes, citizen."

The door closed. Chabot sat down once more, opened the first drawer again and took out the letter. He opened it out, smoothed the creases out on the top of the desk and sat back on the chair, glass in hand. After a few moments came another perfunctory knock and Dubois entered the room. The secretary to the Committee was, unlike Chabot, an academic; a small, dusty looking man with a pinched, mean-looking face, scarred by smallpox, dressed in black. He regarded Chabot enquiringly.

"Dubois, we are going to Boulogne," announced Chabot. Dubois did not reply, but merely inclined his head slightly. "It would seem the Comtesse" – he almost spat the word – "de Poitiers has come to look for her husband. She was caught, naturally, and is being held in Boulogne." He pushed the letter across the desk. Dubois picked it up, pushed his small half-moon spectacles from the end to the bridge of his beak-like nose, and read it carefully. He laid it down on the desk.

"Very obliging of her," he said quietly. "It should be fairly easy to persuade her to reveal to us the whereabouts of her husband. She must have arranged his escape. When she has led us to him, the two of them can accompany each other to the Guillotine, after a suitable trial, of course, to demonstrate their guilt."

"Accompany each other to the what?" asked Chabot.

"The Guillotine. It is the new name for the Louisette."

"Oh. Why?"

Dubois shrugged by way of reply.

"Ah. Well, as long as it does not blunt its effectiveness, I suppose it does not matter what it is called." Chabot laughed at his own joke. Dubois regarded him with distaste, but smiled obligingly. He had found that the best way to deal with Chabot was to humour him.

"I think not," he replied. "The tests have proved that the machine is most effective. They are to be set up in all major towns."

Chabot grunted, picked up the letter and put it back in the drawer. "How soon can we be in Boulogne?"

Dubois considered for a moment. "Two days. The roads are bad, as you know. If we set off now, we could be there tomorrow evening, with luck."

"Then let us go. Have the carriage readied, and we shall need an escort."

Hugo cursed under his breath. It was now almost completely dark. There was no moon, and he could see virtually nothing. He took a few steps up the beach and tripped on something, barking his shins on a rock. He cursed again. A voice behind him hissed, "Stay there. Hankins will lead." Fletcher turned to watch the rest of his men filing up the beach. Hugo wondered how he could see anything. Hankins walked past and went ahead, leading the way up a narrow defile between the rocks. After a few minutes' stumbling behind him, Hugo found that he could just make out the man's whereabouts by the faint gleam of a white handkerchief which he had tied to his knapsack. Fletcher followed behind Hugo, and the rest of the party followed Fletcher, with Fensom bringing up the rear. Hugo desperately tried to remember how to move quietly, as he had been taught in the wood in Sussex. He was not always successful, and some of his more clumsy movements were greeted by a chorus of "Ssh!"

After about a quarter of an hour of what seemed like purgatory, the dark form of the abandoned farm loomed even darker than the surrounding darkness. The party halted while Lloyd, Hankins and Fensom checked the building, and then Hugo was relieved to find himself inside. The shutters were closed and someone lit a candle. Hugo heaved a sigh of relief and heaved his knapsack off his shoulders, depositing it on a rickety table in the corner of the room. Fletcher dumped his own knapsack on the table and grinned at Hugo. "So far, so good."

"How far to where my father is?"

"Only two or three miles. We'll leave tomorrow at dawn. With luck, we'll be back here by dawn the next day, then back to the beach in the evening and away." Fletcher turned to Lloyd. "Better get someone on guard. Will two be sufficient?"

"Yes, Sir. Costa and Good can take the first watch, Williams and Murrell the second. The rest of us had better try and get some rest."

"Very good. Make sure they have an air-rifle apiece. All other weapons to be loaded and ready as well. Wake me at midnight."

❧

Hugo stared into the grey pre-dawn light. He was standing in the doorway of the farmhouse, looking south and east towards a line of low hills as the lightening sky threw them into silhouette. Behind him, muffled sounds indicated that the party was preparing to leave. He glanced over his shoulder as a clinking noise was followed by a muffled curse and a snort of suppressed laughter. He turned his gaze back to the hills and stiffened. Something had suddenly appeared on the top of one of the hills. Two things, in fact. Hugo strained his eyes trying to make the objects out, then turned and hissed urgently, retreating from the doorway as he did so. A moment later, Fletcher appeared beside him, dragging his telescope from his pocket. He opened it, pulled the hood out as far as it would go, looked briefly through it and snapped it shut again. "Two men, armed, on horseback. Patrol. One of them is pointing this way," he whispered. "Well spotted, Hugo." He turned to his men and began giving orders in a fierce whisper, while Hugo watched as the two riders left the hilltop and began to make their way slowly down the hill towards the farm. Fletcher joined him after a moment and said, "We shall make our way out of the back door, then to the wood to the west. It is not far, and it looks fairly dense. Horsemen won't be able to follow there. Ready?"

Half an hour later, the party had taken up position in the wood. It had been coppiced, and the thick coppice-growth provided excellent cover. Hugo had not found the way to the wood pleasant. He had been terrified of making a noise, and at one stage the men had had to crawl on their bellies to avoid being seen against the brightening skyline. It was during that crawl that Hugo had discovered that a thorn driven slowly into the flesh is considerably more painful than one driven in quickly. He was now sitting on a fresh coppice-stool, attempting to remove several such thorns. Fletcher and Hankins were hidden under some scrubby bushes at the edge of the wood; the rest of the men were sitting amongst the coppice, similarly picking thorns from their persons. Hugo was joined by Lloyd, who sat down beside him on the stool and picked a thorn from his thigh. He examined it. "Wicked little buggers," he whispered. Hugo grinned ruefully at him and held up one of his own. "Did you recognize those men?" asked Lloyd.

"They are militia, I think," replied Hugo. A faint rustling announced the arrival of Fletcher and Hankins. "Those two are not alone. There is a foot-party with them. They appear to be Militia of some sort. They are heading for the farm," said Fletcher. "We should go while they are examining it and before they decide to search this wood."

The far side of the wood was delineated by a stream which ran between steep banks. Into this waded Fletcher's party. They walked upstream for several hundred yards before disappearing into another wood on the other side of the stream. In the midst of a dense thicket they made camp. Fletcher had a few words with Hankins and Fensom, who vanished silently in the direction of a nearby hill. The rest settled down to wait. After about half an hour a mist, accompanied by a thin drizzle, descended on the wood, blotting out the hill. The mist grew steadily thicker, and Fletcher decided that it would be safe to light a small fire to brew tea. In seconds, Costa had conjured up a blaze from damp wood, using gunpowder to start it, and not long after Hugo sat on a fallen log and felt the hot, bitter brew seem to seep into his limbs, replacing the cold and aches. He looked up as the sentry whispered a challenge, and was relieved to see that Hankins and Fensom had returned. They squatted down by the remains of the fire and gratefully accepted mugs of tea. Hankins took a deep pull at his tea, then turned to Fletcher.

"We got to the top of the 'ill, Sir, and yer can see the place from there. It's not very far. There's a little lane that runs from just a few yards up that way," he gestured with his mug, "an' goes straight there. No sign of any Frenchies, Sir. The lot at the farm," he jerked a thumb in the direction from whence they had come, "seem to 'ave settled in. They've lit a fire, an' all. We couldn't see much more before this bleedin' fog came down."

"Good," grunted Fletcher. "If the fog lifts, we'll move to the hill, so we can have a good look to see if the coast is clear before we go in. The keeper of the house is called 'Rameau'. He should be expecting us, but we don't want to cause alarm. Here is what we shall do. We shall need a guard on the drive, to warn if anyone approaches. The rest will remain hidden among the outbuildings. I will approach the house, as I am the only one whom Rameau has met before. The rest of you stay hidden until I call you. Then we must decide what to do. I fear we shall not be able to leave the way we came.

❧

Henri, Comte de Poitiers, was bored. His health had improved considerably since his arrival at the safe-house, but there was nothing much to do. He had been there for nearly a month now, but it was not safe for him to stray far from the house. He seemed to spend each day just waiting for the next meal, occasionally wandering around the yard, or just staring out of the window. He was staring out of the window now, watching the light fade in the west and wondering how much longer he could put up with this. In his youth, he had been very much a man of action, and he was sure that this enforced inaction was doing him no good. He wondered about his family. How was he to get word to them? They would be worried. He hoped Hugo had managed to see the specialist in London. He sighed. It must have been six weeks or more since they had parted on the quay at Dieppe. Hugo had boarded the channel packet, and Henri had turned to walk back to the inn where he was staying. He had arrived there to find himself under arrest. He sighed again. If only there were something he could do!

He sat bolt upright at the sound of the coded knock on the door – the same knock that he had himself used to gain entry. He listened as Rameau went to the door and made the challenge. After a few seconds, the chain rattled and the hinges creaked slightly. Whoever it was had been let in. Poitiers turned and placed his finger to his lips as Gaston entered the room. Gaston silently closed the door. Both men listened, and after a minute or so there was the now familiar creak of the loose tread on the staircase and a knock on the door.

"Come in," hissed Poitiers.

The door opened and Rameau peered round it. "You have a visitor, M'sieu." Poitiers did not move, but raised an eyebrow. Rameau went on, "It is the English Gentleman. He wishes to see 'Chasseur'." Poitiers gestured to Gaston to wait and followed Rameau down the stairs. He found himself face to face with a tall gentleman in travel stained clothes. "Good evening, Chasseur." He spoke impeccable French. "I have to say I am both grieved and relieved to find you still here. My men should have had you out of here last night. Something must have gone amiss, but it is fortunate that it has. I trust your stay has been comfortable?"

"Indeed, M'sieu. I thank you for all you have done, and Rameau and his good lady have been very kind to us."

"Good." The English Gentleman beamed at Rameau.

"We had better decide what to do. Shall we sit?" Rameau gestured toward the parlour.

The three had barely sat down at the parlour table before the coded knock sounded again. All three froze, then the English Gentleman got quietly to his feet, beckoned Rameau and signed to Poitiers to remain where he was. Rameau approached the door, while the English Gentleman stood behind it, one hand beneath his cape. He nodded at Rameau, who hooked the chain on and opened the door a crack. "*Qui vive?*"

"*Flêche.*" Rameau glanced at the English Gentleman, who nodded.

"*Mot de passe?*"

"*Oriflamme.*"

The English Gentleman let out the breath that he had been holding, grinned at Rameau, stepped beside him and nodded again. Rameau closed the door, removed the chain, and opened it again to reveal the grinning features of Major the Lord Augustus Fletcher.

"Taffy! You are a whole day late, damn' you, but I am very glad that you are!"

✤

Fletcher's men crouched uncomfortably behind a hedge about a hundred yards from the farm. Their initial progress towards the farm had been slow, but after about half an hour a breeze had sprung up from the direction of the sea, and the fog had thinned to no more than a light mist, enabling them to reach the hill. Soon after, the breeze had freshened, blowing away the remnants of the mist, and the party had rapidly moved to a position close to the farm. Williams and Good had been despatched to mount guard over the lane which formed the drive to the buildings, but they were not yet in position when a horseman appeared, trotting his mount swiftly towards the farm. Williams saw him first, and desperately signalled towards the hedge. Lloyd, who was peering out from the bottom of the hedge to check on the men's' progress, suddenly hissed, "Problem, Sir!" Fletcher rolled over and crawled over to him. The rest tried to flatten themselves into the ditch as much as possible. Hugo cursed as yet another thorn pierced his breeches.

"Ssh!"

Williams was still flagging with a hand as Fletcher gained Lloyd's side. Swiftly, he whipped the telescope from his pocket, extended it and trained it on the lane. A few seconds later, the head and shoulders of the horseman came into view. Fletcher examined him carefully. There was something vaguely familiar about the way the man sat his mount. Fletcher adjusted the focus on the telescope, and the rider slowed his horse to a walk. As he reached the open gate to the farm, he reined in and looked about him. Fletcher's glass was by this time trained on his face. "What the hell?" he hissed, then, as Lloyd shot an enquiring glance at him, "It's Jack! What - what the bloody hell is he doing here?"

Sir Charles Goodrich looked carefully around him, spotted nothing amiss, clicked his tongue and walked his mount gently into the farmyard, where he dismounted and looped the reins around a fence-rail. Then he crossed the yard to the farmhouse and rapped the coded knock on the door.

Fletcher and Lloyd, to the surprise of the rest of the party, stood up and walked the few yards along the hedge to the huddle in the ditch. "That," announced Fletcher, not even whispering, "was Jack. What the hell he is doing here, I have no idea. We shall go in. Take up your positions while I go and endeavour to find out exactly what the bloody hell is going on. Cover the doors and windows."

Fletcher strode off towards the house while the rest of the party ran to the outbuildings, where they got into cover. There was a series of faint metallic clicks as weapons were moved from half to full cock. As Fletcher approached the door, he turned and waited for a moment. Lloyd signalled to him. Confident that everyone was in position, Lloyd waved. Fletcher turned and knocked at the door. Hugo found himself holding his breath and forced himself to release it and to try to breathe normally. After a few moments, the door was opened and Fletcher stepped inside.

About a minute later, Fletcher emerged again and waved. Hugo was aware of a faint hissing sound, and realized that he had not been the only one to be holding his breath. Pistol hammers were eased off from full cock, and Lloyd stood up and walked across the yard. A few seconds later, he returned and beckoned Hugo. Hugo rose from his hiding - place behind a heap of straw and walked across the yard, feeling suddenly exposed and vulnerable as he did so. Fletcher stood in the doorway. Just behind him was Goodrich, and behind him was a little plump man whom Hugo assumed must be the owner of the house. Goodrich nodded at Hugo, then turned and pointed at the door to the parlour. "In there." Hugo walked into the room. A man stood at the window, peering out of it and craning his neck in an attempt to see what was happening in the yard. He did not hear Hugo enter. Hugo looked at his father for a moment. He appeared to have lost weight since he had last seen him, and his hair seemed greyer, but he seemed otherwise well. "Good evening, father," said Hugo, quietly.

❧

"Well, I have to say," said Henri Poitiers to his son, "that you seem to have disobeyed my instructions again. I left you with strict orders to go to the specialist in London, whom I had engaged at great expense. After that I fully expected you to return and sit for your Lieutenant's examination, but what did you do? You seem to have spent your time swanning around England, associating with some extremely disreputable characters." He glared at Goodrich, who grinned at him and winked. Feigning to ignore him, Poitiers continued in an admonitory tone, "And, instead of pacing a quarterdeck in a fine uniform, furthering your career, you suddenly appear here, dressed as a vagabond, in the company of what I can only describe as a bunch of bandits and highwaymen." He shook his head. "But I am extremely pleased to see you, all of you." He became serious, "This is very bad news about your mother. What on earth could have possessed her? But then, she was always somewhat headstrong, and you evidently take after her. Just who is this Doctor Russell, and…"

Goodrich interrupted, "He is a very eminent physician. I have intelligence that the Comtesse was arrested in Boulogne, and is being held there, I assume until the authorities in Paris decide what to do about her. It may be that they will try to hold her to ransom against your recapture, in which case we must whisk you out of the country as quickly as possible and trumpet your escape. It would not make much sense to continue to hold her after that, and doing so could well create a diplomatic incident, which I am sure is something that Paris would prefer to avoid at this stage, having just unwisely invaded Austria." The Count nodded. Goodrich went on, "The problem is that we could have had you away from here by tomorrow morning, but the presence of the militia is a confounded nuisance."

"What is it all about?" asked Fletcher. "We only just avoided them."

"Well, from what I could gather, it was decided that there should be an exercise aimed at reducing the numbers of people escaping the country in small boats, and also at combating smuggling, which has increased considerably over the past few months. There is supposed to be a French frigate off the coast here by morning. It is all most unfortunate that it was decided that the exercise should take place here. I do not think that was accidental. I suspect that Lessard has had a hunch. He is good, and when one has spent some years in this business, one tends to develop almost a sixth sense. I came to warn Rameau as soon as I heard. Not that he is in any danger as long as we are not here if a search party should arrive, and that is most unlikely to happen before morning. The exercise was supposed to begin yesterday, and I fully expected to hear that you had all been captured, or worse. It would seem that the fog delayed the start, or perhaps it was just inefficiency and confusion, which seem to be rife here now."

"So what do we do now?" asked Fletcher.

"The *Marie* will have returned to Dieppe to avoid the French frigate. She will remain there, ostensibly for repairs, for three days. I am beginning to see a plan that means we could all leave from Dieppe, while the authorities' attention is turned elsewhere. As you know," he glanced at Fletcher, "Our second escape route, should this one be blocked, was to have been to skirt round to the east of Dieppe, while *Vixen* patrolled between Dieppe and Boulogne, so she could take us off. If we could persuade Lessard and his men that that is indeed where we have gone, they would not be in Dieppe to obstruct our departure. Furthermore, I know exactly how to get that false information to Lessard." He turned to Henri Poitiers. "Sir, do you recall a man called Louis Vallon, in your service?"

"Why yes, of course. He is my under-butler. He is quite attentive to his duties, but a bit sly. I am not sure he is totally trustworthy, which is why he is at my house in Kent, where the butler can keep an eye on him."

"I am sorry to inform you that he is not in Kent. He ran away. In the process of escaping, he killed an innocent youth and an excise man. He is wanted in England for murder. I know where he is."

Henri Poitiers spent some seconds gazing at his hands, which he had placed palms down on the table in front of him. "The little bastard! Do go on," he said bleakly.

"Our men in Dieppe inform me that he has reported to Lessard. It would seem that Vallon is, in some way, in Lessard's employ. However, they have both made a mistake. They both frequent a certain establishment in Dieppe. An establishment which is actually the cover for our operations there."

"How on earth can that be? How can they not know?" demanded Poitiers.

"Because it is a brothel, that is how."

"It is a *what*?" cried a startled Fletcher.

"A brothel, man, a whorehouse, a bordello, a stew. How else would you like me to describe it?" Goodrich suddenly roared with laughter at the astonishment he had caused. After a few seconds, Fletcher joined in, followed by Hugo and, finally, the Count. "Well, bless me!" said Fletcher after a few minutes. "Do you mind if I ask how on earth…"

Goodrich held up a hand to stop him. "It is better that you do not know. It is the brothel I mentioned at the meeting in Markham's library. It is a very safe house. It is run, ostensibly, by a pimp, who is actually a Lieutenant of Royal Marines. His name is Martin. Should anything happen to him, he will simply be replaced by another suitable man. The brothel is actually run by a Madame, as usual. We have another house, just on the outskirts of Dieppe, which is also safe." He turned to Fletcher. "Right, here are your orders. Leave here before dawn. Take the carts and the donkey from the yard. You are farmers going to Dieppe. Hide our guests in the cart. Go to this house." He passed over a scrap of paper. "The next evening, go to the brothel, in twos and threes, so you look as if you are clients. I have written its address on there as well. The following morning, split into two or three parties and make your way to the harbour. *Marie* will be waiting. Meanwhile, I shall return to Dieppe and spend the night at our brothel, where I shall be careful to inform the 'pimp' of your impending departure from the village up the coast, and of your actual impending arrival at his premises. Being, of course, a good revolutionary, he will pass the false information to Vallon, who will, in turn, inform his boss. I shall then leave by one of my normal routes, and see you in England in a few days' time. Martin may wish to accompany you. He is overdue to be relieved. Any questions?"

"No, Jack. It seems pretty straightforward. I just hope we don't run into too many militia."

"Well, approximately half of them are about four miles from here, on exercise." Goodrich gestured out of the window. "And, with even only a little luck, most of the rest should be chasing wild chickens towards Boulogne by this time tomorrow. Now, I must have a word with Rameau, and settle for our board for the night. Then I shall away to Dieppe. Gentlemen, I bid you good night and good luck."

# CHAPTER TWELVE

Sir Charles Goodrich settled himself more comfortably into a high-backed chair in the back parlour of the brothel. The room served as an office. Books and papers were scattered about the room. An ornate ormulu clock, in the form of a shepherd boy and shepherdess supporting a drum in which was mounted the dial, sat under a glass dome on the mantelpiece, and on the walls were oil paintings of bucolic scenes. The room was comfortably furnished and smelled faintly of beeswax and turpentine. The brothel keeper was taking glasses and a decanter from a wine-cabinet. After a moment he turned to Goodrich. "Madeira, Sir?"

"Yes, please, Martin. That will be most welcome." Goodrich took the proffered glass and raised it to look at the light through its contents. "Verdelho, Sir," said Martin, lowering himself onto a chair opposite Goodrich, who took a sip of the wine. "It's excellent," he announced. "It is," agreed Martin, "Quite a bit lighter than the usual Malmsey."

"Hmm. I must see if I can obtain some. How is business?" Martin grinned. "Surprisingly good. I have to tell you that Lessard has sought other lodgings, though. He is now at the inn in the square."

"Any particular reason?"

"Let us say that we found ourselves unable to cater for his tastes for the present. The whore he particularly liked has gone to visit her aunt in Paris, and the inn can accommodate him more cheaply. He also seemed to think he could use his position to attempt to bully me over the matter of payment, and I was forced to disabuse him of that notion."

"Ah, quite so. Well, as long as we know of his movements, it is probably better if he is not under your feet all the time. Still, it's a shame. I was hoping we could take him to England, but if he is no longer staying here we probably cannot do so. What about Vallon?"

"A particularly oily, nasty piece of work. He is a raving revolutionary, with a chip on his shoulder concerning 'aristos', and a particular taste for young girls. He creeps to Lessard, like some sort of lap-dog, though I don't think Lessard likes him any more than I do."

"Excellent. Would he pass on information, do you think?"

"Oh, within minutes, I am sure. He is always interested in the activities of his fellow revolutionaries, and a sponge for the more salacious information. I have him believing that I am an even more avid supporter of the revolutionary cause than he is."

"When are you next likely to see him?"

"Oh, he will be here in about a hour's time, give or take a few minutes. He is as regular as... clockwork." Martin was interrupted by the ormulu clock, which began to announce the hour on a light, silvery bell. When it had finished striking, Goodrich said, "That is a fine clock. What is it?"

"It is a Brocot, made in Paris. It is an excellent timekeeper, but a little temperamental if disturbed. It has to be set up just so. I hate having to wind it. I am terrified of dropping that glass dome."

"Hmm. It is a trifle florid and ornate for my taste, but I suppose it is in the latest fashionable style."

"I believe it to be modelled on one at Versailles. More Madeira?"

"Just a drop, if you please." Goodrich frowned and placed the tips of his fingers together, deep in thought. Martin filled his glass and waited expectantly. After a few moments, Goodrich sat up straight, looked at the clock again and picked up his glass. "A change of plan."

"Yes, Sir."

"Right, this is what you do. We shall need this establishment to be closed. We don't want to be tripping over clients, and, more especially, we don't want clients asking awkward questions. Send the women away, or as many of them as you can. Give whatever reason you like. My men will arrive in twos and threes. Usual arrangements. Any questions?"

"No, Sir. You will be staying in your usual room?"

"No. I am going to Boulogne, or, rather, to near Boulogne. I will leave the country from there."

Martin gaped at him. "Boulogne? Why?"

"To see if I can find the Comtesse." He glanced once more at the clock. "It is a long way, but if I set off now and wear out several horses, there is a chance, just a chance, that I might be able to take her with me. Inform Fletcher when he arrives. Any questions?"

"No, Sir."

Goodrich glanced yet again at the clock. "Then we are done. I must away." He stood up.

"Very good, Sir. I suggest you leave by the back door."

⁂

Next morning, before dawn, the donkey was hitched to the

cart and the party prepared to set off. The vehicle boasted a canvas cover. Rameau searched the outbuildings and unearthed a couple of boxes of rough pottery, some stone jars of locally-made cider and various items of peasant's clothing. The boxes and jars were loaded on to the cart, together with several sacks of turnips. Poitiers, dressed as an artisan, sat on one of the boxes. Gaston, similarly attired, sat on another. The rest of the party wore an assortment of smocks and old coats. Weapons were concealed. To all intents and purposes, the party would pass a cursory inspection as simply a group of peasants going to Dieppe to sell their wares at a street market. The donkey plodded stolidly along the road. The cart creaked and its poorly-greased axles squeaked. Costa drove. The rest of the party took turns to ride on the cart. Those who were not riding trudged alongside or behind them, trying to avoid marching in step, occasionally pausing to drink from wineskins and chattering amongst themselves. They looked as if they would arrive at market quite merry, a bunch of men released from their labours and nagging wives for a couple of days, and enjoying themselves. The wineskins contained nothing stronger than water, and the men were all keeping a sharp lookout for potential trouble.

In the event, they encountered very little traffic on the road, and even stopped near an inn at midday. Fletcher and Hugo bought bread and cheese and the men made a leisurely meal at the roadside. The few other travellers they did meet simply called greetings and passed on, and by early evening the party had reached the safe-house, another small farm on the outskirts of Dieppe. The men made themselves as comfortable as possible in one of the outbuildings and prepared to spend the night and the following day there. The owner of the house, a 'business associate' of Goodrich's, was a wealthy wool-merchant who lived in Paris. He had purchased the farm some years before, using the substantial outbuildings as warehouses to store the wool which he imported from England, renting the land out to neighbouring farmers and occasionally using the house as a hunting-lodge. The house was normally kept shut up. There were no other houses in the immediate vicinity and Goodrich came and went more or less as he pleased. Hunting-parties of the owner's friends would periodically stay for a few days, so the presence of just another armed group would arouse no suspicions, if they were noticed at all.

❦

Henri Lessard laid down his pen, stretched his arms and rubbed at a sore spot in the small of his back. He had been writing for some time, and the desk which he had improvised from a table was a little low for his comfort. He was a tall man, and was beginning to feel some twinges of rheumatism. He sighed and reflected that he was now the wrong side of fifty years of age. Perhaps he was getting too old for *espionage*, as his business had recently been termed. It was a game for younger men. Maybe he should retire and take up – what? The sound of sawing and hammering came faintly from the rear of the inn, where workmen had made a start on repairing the stables. Lessard sighed again and rubbed his eyes, then looked out of the window. The view across the square was hardly inspiring, just the Louisette, shrouded in a canvas cover, and the front of the town offices behind it. He had recently shifted to the inn, partly because it was cheaper, partly because Chabot had left and returned to Paris, and partly because of his falling-out with the brothel-keeper, who had proved to be made of much sterner stuff than Lessard had expected. In the course of their slightly heated, but polite exchange, Lessard had discovered that the man was not the least bit frightened of him, and was perfectly prepared to use some of Lessard's own methods against him. He wondered where the man had learned them. The two had parted in an uneasy state of truce. Lessard disliked the pimp, but had learned to respect him in those few minutes. He grunted and stood up. He would have to arrange to find a proper desk. He opened the door and looked along the landing toward the staircase. It could not be a very large desk – a large one would not fit up the stairs. He turned and looked at the window. That was also small, so there was no way anything of any size could be pulled in through it. He would have to get one of those military campaign desks, the sort whose legs were removable. That was it. He would visit the cabinet-maker in town later and see what could be done. Satisfied with his decision, he turned back to the door and walked along the landing and down the stairs. After ordering coffee to be served at his favourite table outside, he returned to his room and put his papers away, then made his way downstairs again. He sat at the table and gazed at the shrouded form of the Louisette across the square. Dufay brought a pot of coffee and the two men passed the time of day for a few minutes before Dufay went back indoors. Lessard sipped at his coffee and stared into space until a sudden crash of breaking crockery behind him made him turn his head sharply. As he did so, a twinge of pain shot up his spine. He cursed quietly. Laughter came from within the inn and Lessard picked up his cup again. He was just bringing it to his lips when he spied the figure of Vallon over its rim. Lessard felt his heart sink. He detested the oily little man, and he was one of the last people with whom Lessard wished to have to make polite conversation this morning. Vallon, rapidly approaching, waved at him. Lessard sighed and put his cup down.

Vallon's "Good morning, citizen," made Lessard suddenly doubt that he really wanted to have anything to do with the revolution. He decided that he did not, after all, like being addressed as 'citizen', particularly by individuals such as Vallon, whom he would normally do his best to avoid. With an effort, he returned Vallon's greeting and gestured at a chair. Vallon sat down and immediately leaned conspiratorially across the table. "I have some information for you, citizen. Important information."

*I bet you do*, thought Lessard, *you nasty, greasy, creeping little toad*. He forced himself to look interested. "And what is that, citizen?"

"A group of men has been sent from England to rescue Poitiers. It is commanded by a Major Fletcher. Poitiers has been hiding at a farmhouse near Morlay, between here and Boulogne, near the mouth of the Somme," he gestured eastwards. "The English are planning to get him out tonight at midnight and escape in a boat."

"Where, pray, did you discover this?"

"Citizen Martin told me. One of his women 'entertained' one of the Englishmen yesterday, apparently. She told Martin and he, being a good revolutionary, passed the information on to me."

Lessard, prepared to dismiss whatever Vallon had to say as a waste of time, was suddenly interested. He found it made sense. It would explain Poitiers' mysterious disappearance and the convenient fire. Though he disliked Martin, he trusted him.

If Martin had come by this information, it was very likely to be reliable. He had passed it to the authorities, as represented by Lessard, and it was for Lessard to act upon it. He stared at his coffee-cup and considered further. If he could recapture Poitiers and take him to Paris, together with some English spies for good measure, the standing of Henri Lessard would be considerably enhanced, and Chabot would not be able to claim any credit for the successful operation. Lessard raised his head and fished his watch from his waistcoat pocket. Ten o'clock. He closed it and put it away. It would take about eight hours to get to Morlay. Plenty of time to gather his men. It was a pity that so many of them were away on the exercise. A dozen would have to be enough, leaving six or seven here in Dieppe to watch the harbour. No matter – Dieppe was quiet, they should have little to do, and Lessard should be back by tomorrow evening. He would bring his prisoners here and question them himself first, before taking them to Paris. A faint smile spread slowly over his craggy features. He turned it on Vallon.

"Do you have a description of this Major Fletcher?"

"No, but I am told he is tall, and has fair hair. He speaks French, but with an accent. He is said to be quite ruthless."

"Thank you, citizen. I am sure the committee will be most obliged to you. Some coffee?"

⚜

"Aloysius! It is good to see you again." Markham's booming voice seemed to echo around the library. Russell turned from the bookcase into which he had been peering and removed his spectacles. Markham strode to him and shook him warmly by the hand. "I trust you are well?"

"Indeed I am, thank you, Horace. Have you heard anything?"

"Not much. Let us sit." Markham waved towards two armchairs and nodded at Taylor, who retired from the room. "They got away a day late, due to *Vixen* being delayed. She was forced to put into Portsmouth for emergency repairs – something apparently overlooked by Plymouth dockyard. I have received no reports of any progress, or lack of it, since. I did, however, receive an interesting communication from Goodrich." Markham paused as Taylor entered the room, bearing a tray containing a decanter and two glasses. He placed the tray on the table and withdrew. Markham went on, "It would appear that Vallon, the count's servant who disappeared, not only killed the excise man, but also murdered another man in the course of his disappearance."

"Ah."

"Yes. He is therefore wanted for murder."

"Hmmm. Interesting. I wonder if it has any bearing on one of the two reasons for my calling upon you this morning."

Markham looked at Russell, who appeared deep in thought for a few moments, then picked up his glass and said, "A stranger has appeared in Horsham in the last few days. He is foreign. He claims to be an Italian merchant, and calls himself 'Gianni Marcelli'.

"And you are suspicious of him?"

"I am, particularly since I am sure his accent is not Italian. I think he is French. He has been asking questions. He seems particularly interested in this place, and in you."

"Oh, does he, now?"

"Indeed. He is staying at Mr. Fisher's guest house, near Carfax."

"Hmm. I think we should have a word with this gentleman. Perhaps we should get our good Captain Hughes of the Militia to bring him here so that he can have a good look for himself. He can do it on the way while he is escorting him to London."

Russell looked at his friend. The sinister smile had appeared. Markham chuckled to himself and went on, "I would welcome the opportunity to seek Gianni Marcelli's - or should that be Jean Marcel's? - opinion on recent events in France. Thank you for the information, Aloysius. I am greatly indebted to you."

"Which brings me to the other matter," said Russell. Markham waited while he pulled a pair of steel-rimmed spectacles from his pocket and scrubbed at them with his handkerchief. He hooked the legs over his ears, pushed the spectacles up to the bridge of his nose and continued, "Would you sell me Bluebell?"

"No, Aloysius, I would not. You may have her, as a gift."

"My dear fellow, I could not possibly…"

"A gift, or not at all. That is my final word."

"Then I gratefully accept. Thank you, Horace. I do not know what to say."

"Then say nothing. You have thanked me. That is sufficient." Markham raised his glass and beamed at his old friend.

Outside the door, his ear pressed to the panel, Taylor silently cursed his employer. No-one had thought of the possibility of Markham making a present of the damned nag to Russell. The sweepstake lay in ruins. Muttering under his breath, he headed for the kitchen to break the bad news.

❧

Hugo and Fletcher left the brothel by the discreet rear entrance and headed once more for the safe-house. They had already, that morning, conducted Henri Poitiers and Gaston safely to the brothel, where Martin had installed the Count and his valet in a comfortable sitting-room upstairs at the rear of the building. A few of the men had followed about mid-day, and Martin had quartered them in the kitchen for the time being, leaving Hankins, Costa, Gibbs, Good and Holden to secure the safe house. All that remained to be done was to collect the remaining five men from the safe-house, check that the *Marie* was in harbour and to wait until an hour before dawn. Then the party, in two groups, would make its way to the harbour.

The two men walked slowly towards the little square, past buildings which were evidently storehouses. They were shuttered and locked. It was late afternoon, and the narrow little street was deserted. Fletcher peered through one or two dusty windows. Finally, he stopped at a warehouse about half-way along the street, peered through its window, and knocked at the door. He knocked again, harder, then tried it. It was locked. Fletcher examined the lock for a moment or two, then motioned to Hugo to keep a look-out. He produced from his pocket a small piece of bent metal and inserted it into the simple lock. After a few seconds, Hugo heard a faint metallic scraping sound, followed by a click. Fletcher straightened up, replaced the lock-pick in his pocket, lifted the latch, opened the door and peered into the dusty gloom. After a moment, he closed the door again, turned and grinned at Hugo. "Not been used for years, by the look of it. I'll leave it unlocked. It might be useful. The harbour is just over there." He gestured in the general direction. "We are going straight through the square to get back to the safe-house. Tomorrow, we cross the square diagonally, effectively turning left, and the harbour is just yards away from the far corner." Hugo nodded. He did not know Dieppe at all well, having been there only once or twice. Fletcher knew it far better. As they continued to walk towards the square, Hugo asked, "Where did you learn to do that?" Fletcher looked at him, then tapped the side of his nose with a finger. "I may decide to tell you, one day," he replied, mysteriously. Then he held up his hand, "What on earth is going on?"

They were almost in the little square now, and a hubbub of voices grew louder as they approached. A few moments later, they were peering cautiously out of the little alley-way towards the steps of the municipal building near which, on their way to the brothel, they had noticed a tall object shrouded in a tarpaulin. During the hour or so they had been in the brothel, a sizeable crowd had gathered around this object. As the two watched, the crowd fell quiet, and a man mounted a step-ladder next to the object. He untied something, and the cover was drawn off. Something like a gasp came from the crowd, and the hubbub of voices increased once more. "What is it?" whispered Hugo. "I think it's a Louisette," replied Fletcher. He made way for Hugo to get a proper look. After a glance, Hugo ducked back into the alley. "Yes, it is. It is just like the picture in the *Moniteur,* the one that Russell showed us. I have a feeling it is about to be used."

"Damn'! That is inconvenient."

The crowd fell silent again, then there came a series of catcalls, boos and jeers. Fletcher craned his head around the corner. "They have just brought the victim to the machine, and…"

"Ssh!" interrupted Hugo. "Someone's coming."

Fletcher straightened up slowly. "We shall have to cross the square. There is no way round that I know of. We would risk getting lost, and anyway, to turn round and go back now would look suspicious to whoever it is who is coming. Let us just walk slowly across the square."

As the two men stepped out into the square, all eyes were turned on the Louisette. The jeering and booing increased, and, suddenly, the footsteps behind them broke into a run. Hugo glanced at the Louisette across the heads of the crowd. The blade was at the top of the frame. The footsteps behind them quickened still further as their maker began to sprint. Then the blade dropped. The crowd roared, and the footsteps slowed to a walk. Hugo glanced round as a small, slightly portly man caught up with them, gasping from his exertions. "Have I missed it?" he gasped. "I fear so," replied Hugo. The man's shoulders sagged. "*Merde!*"

"I think there will be another one in a minute," said Fletcher, gesturing towards the Louisette. "They seem to be bringing another victim up." The little man brightened visibly. "Oh, good." He trotted off to join the crowd. Fletcher and Hugo walked slowly across the square. When they were about two-thirds of the way across, there was another roar from the crowd. Both of them paused and turned to look for a moment, but the crowd hid the scene from them. They turned away and continued across the square.

In Lessard's room in the inn at the side of the square, a telescope glinted dully in the light. Louis Vallon had taken a small glass upstairs to watch the executions. However, as the blade fell for the second of the three scheduled executions and the blood spattered the pavement, his telescope was trained, not on the Louisette, but on the two men who were crossing the square. They eventually disappeared from his view, and he closed the glass. The tall man he had not seen before, but he recognized the younger of the two as Hugo Poitiers. The other must be Fletcher... He slipped out of the room and made for the stairs.

Fletcher and Hugo turned out of the square on to the street that led to the safe-house. They walked in silence for several minutes, then Hugo suddenly said quietly, "How barbaric! What is my country coming to?" Fletcher looked at him thoughtfully. Though their view of the execution had been obscured by the crowd, Hugo had turned very pale. "Surely you have encountered death in battle?" he said. "Oh, yes," said Hugo, "But that - that was different. This was just cold-blooded slaughter. What upsets me is that the victims were probably innocent, and the crowd..."

"People turn out in hundreds for public hangings in England," interrupted Fletcher.

"I know, but..." Hugo's voice trailed off into silence and he shook his head sadly.

Fletcher suddenly reflected that they had both just witnessed Hugo's likely fate, should he be caught. He was probably safe enough himself – France would be unlikely to provoke a diplomatic incident with England under the current circumstances. The two countries were not at war, so he could not be tried as a spy and executed. Probably the worst that could happen to himself was imprisonment, but Hugo would probably be dragged to a Louisette in front of a screaming crowd, baying for blood, there to be publicly humiliated and decapitated. He changed the subject.

"Martin said, just before we left, that one of his friends

has reported that *Marie* is in the harbour. She is moored at the outer end of the quay, not far from the entrance. It saves us having to go and check for ourselves."

"That is good to hear. I hope there is some wind by the morning, or we shall not get out. There is not a breath at the moment."

"No," agreed Fletcher. "I don't fancy having to row." There was, indeed, no wind at all. The air was still; the atmosphere heavy, warm and oppressive. The sky was hazed with a veil of thin cloud, through which the sun shone weakly, a pale yellow disc. The two men walked on, taking the left hand road at a fork, and, after another half mile, the farm came into view on the left of the road. Before they turned into the gateway, Fletcher glanced back they way they had come. There was no-one in sight: they had not been followed.

A quarter of a mile back up the road, the sunlight once more shone dully off the telescope's unpolished brass tubes. Vallon, crouched behind a bush, watched as the two men entered the farmhouse, then collapsed the tubes of the telescope, put it in his pocket and began to walk rapidly back towards Dieppe. He was feeling very pleased with himself. Thanks to the telescope, he had managed to trail the two men without them seeing him, at a safe distance. As he walked, his thoughts turned to the rewards he imagined would be his after the capture of the Poitiers boy. He, Louis Vallon, would be hailed as a hero of the revolution. He would have fame and money. He quickened his pace as he approached the militia guard-room.

❦

Fletcher removed his hat and tossed it on to the table in the parlour of the farmhouse. He nodded at Hankins, who silently handed him a wineskin. Fletcher took a pull at it and passed it to Hugo. "All well?" he asked Hankins.

"Yes, Sir. There's no-one about. A few people passed on the road earlier, heading for town, but it's very quiet."

Fletcher grunted. "They've all gone to see an execution." He took out his watch. "We'll wait until dusk. That should be long enough for the crowd to disperse. We may as well have a bite to eat." I'll see what we've got left, Sir", said Hankins, and clattered off to the kitchen. Fletcher sat down on one of the chairs by the table and looked around the room. After a few moments his eye caught Hugo's, and the two grinned at each other. "It is – a trifle oppressive, perhaps?" ventured Hugo. The room was comfortably, if sparsely, furnished, but the walls were covered in trophies. There were old matchlock hunting-guns, swords and mounted heads of animals - lots of mounted heads of animals. Foxes, wild boar, deer and even the head of a bear all seemed to jostle for space among the ancient weapons, their metalwork dulled by the passage of years. Everywhere were beady glass eyes. "A display of this size is a little overpowering," agreed Fletcher, looking up at the bear, which seemed to dominate the room. "It is the sort of thing one encounters in large houses in England. I think it would be better in a much larger room. One would not get quite such an impression of being watched!" He sniffed. "And they lend a certain something to the atmosphere." He sniffed again. "A certain, *musty*, something. Perhaps this weather has something to do with it." He stood up and crossed the room to the bear, sniffed at it more closely, wrinkled his nose and said, "I think it's mostly coming from that." He glared at the bear and turned away. "Let us open a window. We can eat in the kitchen, Perhaps this room will be better for some fresh air."

⁂

The Militia Sergeant drummed his fingers on the table and looked long and hard at Vallon. He was not at all sure what to do. He had listened to Vallon's story. He had no orders which covered this sort of eventuality, and he wished that Lessard was around to give some. He was a simple sergeant, and was not used to having to act on his own initiative. But Lessard had taken the majority of his men away with him a couple of hours ago, and the responsibility now lay with the sergeant. He sighed and shook his head. "I don't know." Vallon was impatient. When he had arrived at the guard-room, he had found just one man left on duty. Everyone else had gone to see the executions. It had been some time before the Sergeant and the rest of his men had finally turned up. The Sergeant smelled of cheap wine. Vallon tried again. "Citizen, it is our duty to the revolution, and besides, think of the reward."

Slowly, the idea that he might become rich dawned on the Sergeant. If he did this, and did it right, he could become an officer. Yes, surely the committee would promote him. He would be showered with honours, and gold too. He would have gold lace on his uniform, and a medal on a sash. He straightened his shoulders. "Well, citizen. I think we must act on your information. I will fetch my men. Wait here."

The Sergeant was not a man to be rushed, and the sun was setting when Vallon eventually found himself standing nervously a few yards from the gate to the farm. There was no sign of activity in the house or in the outbuildings. The militia

198

sergeant and his men were arguing over the best way to approach the house. It was decided that three men should go to the back and check the yard, while the Sergeant and the other two should remain at the front. One of the men sent to the back would then return to report the coast clear, and the Sergeant would then simply knock at the door and ask for Hugo Poitiers. As the two men detailed to check the yard began to walk cautiously round the corner, Vallon began to retreat. He did not like the idea of being caught up in a potentially violent situation, and he did not want to be recognized by the Poitiers boy. He silently crept off back up the road, back to a safe distance. The Sergeant did not notice his going.

# CHAPTER THIRTEEN

Fletcher, Hugo and Hankins sat round the table in the parlour of the farmhouse, checking their weapons. Costa and Good were keeping watch, Good at the front door and Costa at the back. Gibbs was keeping watch from an upstairs window which looked along the road to the town, to give advance warning of anyone approaching. Each was armed with a Girandoni. Fletcher finished checking his pistol, loaded it carefully, stood up and tucked it into his belt. After a moment or two, he asked, "Where is Holden?" Hankins looked up from loading his own pistol, frowned, and replied, "Don't rightly know, Sir. Come ter think of it, I ain't seen 'im for a good while." He finished loading the pistol and rose to his feet. "I'll 'ave a look for 'im, Sir."

Hugo tucked his own pistol into his belt and checked his knapsack. "How long until we go?" he asked Fletcher. Fletcher consulted his watch. "About half an hour." He glanced out of the window. "It's nearly sunset." He swung round as Hankins appeared in the doorway. "I found 'Olden, Sir. 'E's in the barn, but I'm afraid I 'ave to report that 'e's drunk."

"Drunk?"

"As a lord, Sir, beggin' yer pardon."

"How? Where did he get it from?"

"Seems 'e picked the lock to a wine cabinet in the kitchen, Sir." Hankins jerked his thumb backwards over his shoulder. In his other hand was a brandy-bottle. He held it up for inspection. "'E's 'ad about a third of it, Sir."

"Damn and blast the bloody man!" Fletcher stomped out of the room, followed by Hankins and Hugo. Across the yard, in the outbuilding where the men had spent the night, was Holden. He was slumped on an old chair. His head was on a pile of woolsacks, and his arms hung limply at his sides. Fletcher took one look and called, "Costa!"

"Sir?" the Italian appeared silently. His eyes lit on Holden, then turned to look heavenwards. Holden groaned gently and muttered something. Costa marched over to him, dragged him from the chair and slapped him around the face a couple of times. The only reaction he provoked was another groan. Fletcher glared at Holden. "Get him outside. Pour water over him." He nodded at Hankins, turned on his heel and strode back across the yard. Hankins and Costa seized the limp form of Holden under the armpits, dragged him into the yard and dumped him beside the well. Hugo went back into the kitchen and closed the door. After a few seconds he heard the clank of a bucket, and Hankins growling something at Holden. He shook his head and followed Fletcher back to the parlour.

As Hugo entered the room, Fletcher looked up and announced, "That man is a liability. I shall dismiss him when we get home. He will get us all killed if he is allowed to carry on like that. He can go and make a bloody nuisance of himself in the ranks of a foot-regiment. The are used to dealing with his sort there." He shook his head sadly and went on, "I don't know what has happened to him. He has only started drinking recently. He was a good stalker, and an excellent shot. It is a shame."

"Perhaps Doctor Russell could do something for him?"

ventured Hugo. Fletcher looked at him steadily for a moment, then shook his head again. "Possibly, but I am afraid we cannot have him with us while there is any risk of a repetition of this sort of behaviour." He broke off and stared moodily out of the window for a few moments. "God, it's hot in here, and that damn' thing stinks!" He gestured at the bear. This weather is appalling. I suppose Holden's state may have something to do with it." He picked up a cork mat from the side table and fanned himself with it. "If Holden is not fit, I suppose we shall have to carry him. Damn him!"

At that moment, Hankins appeared. "We've got 'im 'alf sensible, Sir. Costa's still flushing 'im out." Fletcher grunted and picked up his pack. "We leave in half a hour."

"Sir." Hankins disappeared.

Fletcher opened the door to the passageway and called "Gibbs!"

"Sir?" The man appeared at the top of the stairs. "Have you been drinking?"

"No, Sir."

"Are you sure?"

"Yes, Sir!"

"Well, Holden has. Do you know anything about it?"

"Oh, Sir! I told him not to even think about it. The silly bugger! How is he?"

"Not well. Fetch his kit and check it, will you?"

"Good's doing it now, Sir."

A minute or two later, Good appeared in the parlour, carrying his own kit and Holden's. He dumped Holden's kit on the table and undid the canvas roll which contained the parts of Holden's Girandoni. He proceeded to check the weapon while Fletcher stared out of the window. A few moments later,

Hankins appeared again. Fletcher turned to him and raised an interrogative eyebrow. "'E's quite a bit better, Sir. We've flushed most of it out of 'im, I think. 'E's in the jakes at the back o' the yard. Costa's still with 'im, in case 'e still needs an 'and ter walk."

"Well, that's something, at any rate." Fletcher fished in his pocket and produced some coins. "Leave these on the kitchen table to pay for the brandy. Will he be fit to travel in about fifteen minutes, do you think?"

Hankins took the coins. "I should think so, Sir. 'E might be a bit wobbly, but the walk will do 'im good." Hankins grinned at his commanding officer, who relaxed slightly. "Good. Well done, Hankins. Let us…" Fletcher's voice trailed off at the sudden sound of a shout, followed by a shot. It had come from the rear of the building, the direction of the yard.

❧

Jean Marcel sat at the table in his room in the guest-house in Horsham. He had dined quite well, though the food was not up to the standard of French cooking, he thought. Even so, it had been a good meal. He had had quite a successful day so far, having, by discreet questioning, established that the Park was indeed the residence of Horace Markham. Citizen Chabot would be very interested in the news. Marcel made some careful notes in code in his diary. It was fortunate that he should have stumbled on this information. Markham's place of abode was not known to Chabot, though he had been trying to discover it for some time. Had it not been for the problems finding the highwaymen, it would have remained undiscovered, but luck was on Marcel's side, for once. He twiddled his pencil between his fingers and smiled to himself. Citizen Chabot *would* be pleased! He poured himself another glass of wine, walked to the window and looked out of it. A few more days, and he would have made a detailed reconnaissance of the Park. In a month or so, he should be able to compile a list of all of Markham's visitors and all the comings and goings at the house. He would encode his observations and send them to Paris. He took a sip of wine and put the glass down, walked over to the window and pulled a small telescope from his pocket. He opened the casement and peered up the street with the telescope, wondering if it were possible to see the main road. It was not, but as he lowered the telescope two horsemen came into view in the lens. They were Militia officers. Behind them marched a party of a dozen men, red coats bright in the sunlight. Marcel watched them as they turned off into a side street, then picked up his wine-glass and moved back to the table. He put his pencil away and read through his notes. His ears registered the knock at the front door, but he took no notice until he heard a voice demanding to know if 'Gianni Marcelli' was staying at the house. He froze for a moment, then picked up his notebook, thrust it into his pocket and ran to the window. Peering cautiously out, he could see one of the Militia officers at the front porch. He was accompanied by three of the men. Marcel backed away from the window, crossed the room and opened the door. On the landing, he cautiously opened another window and peeped out. There was no-one in sight around the back. Marcel headed for the back stairs as footsteps sounded on the treads of the main staircase. A few moments later, he slipped out into the yard at the back of the building. He listened for a few moments, then began to run as quietly as he could. He ran to the corner where a passageway communicated with a lane behind the house. He waited at the corner and listened again. He could hear nothing. He poked his head round the corner. There was no-one in sight. He paused and listened again. He could hear voices from the open windows of the house, prominent amongst them being that of the officer who had knocked at the front door. Heavy footsteps sounded along the landing corridor, then someone hammered on a door and a voice called, "Signor Marcelli!" Again the hammering, then more voices, lower now. Marcel licked his dry lips and peered into the lane again. The lane along the rear of several properties before giving on to a side-road which joined the main street at right angles. Half-way along it, an alleyway led away from the lane and ran away from the main street where it joined a maze of other little alleys which led eventually to the other side of the town. All Marcel needed to do was to get into this system of alleys and they would not be able to find him. He licked his lips again, crept into the lane and headed along it. Just before he reached the junction with the alley he paused and listened again. Sounds still came faintly from the house, but from the alleyway there was no sound. He made up his mind. Obviously, no-one had thought to watch the rear of the house. The English were so stupid! He strode purposefully into the alley and began to walk quickly but quietly down it. After a few yards he came to the first junction, where he turned left and began to run.

Straight into a grinning Lieutenant of Militia.

"Signor Marcelli?" enquired the officer, "Or should that be 'Monsieur Marcel?'"

The Lieutenant was still several feet away. Marcel turned round quickly and began to run back the way he had come.

He had not covered more than a few yards before a militiaman stepped out of the gateway to a back yard in front of him. Another one appeared a few yards behind the first. Marcel, in desperation, glanced back towards the Lieutenant.. Perhaps he could barge past him. He turned again, and as he did so, a third militiaman appeared behind the officer. The lieutenant drew his sword and from behind Marcel came two metallic clicks as the militiamen cocked their muskets. The Lieutenant walked slowly up to Marcel. "Monsieur Marcel?" he repeated.

Marcel glared at him and did not reply.

"I must ask you to come with us. You are under arrest."

❧

Costa cursed and fumbled with the hammer of his Girandoni. He was crouched behind the small cover provided by the low wall around the well. He glanced towards Holden's body, then back at the entrance to the yard. A few seconds before, Holden had emerged from the jakes, buttoning his breeches. Costa had taken him by the arm and was steering him towards the house when there was a sudden shout of "*Halte-là*!" Costa immediately moved to his left, unslinging his Girandoni as he did so and shouting at Holden. But Holden was still too befuddled to realize what was happening, and the next moment there was a shot. Holden's head jerked backwards. Blood splashed the cobbles and, as Holden fell, Costa could see that the ball had taken him in the throat. An instant later, Costa felt the wind of another musket ball as it passed within an inch of his right ear, smacked into the wall behind him and ricocheted off into the sky. The third ball hit the wall of the well. With no time to aim properly, Costa simply pointed the

Girandoni at the three blue-coated figures who had appeared in the yard and pulled the trigger. The metallic smack of the weapon's discharge was followed immediately by a scream of pain and a clatter as a musket fell to the cobbles as Costa, not waiting to see the results of his shot, dived behind the well.

It took him another second or so to finally get the weapon cocked and he cautiously poked his head above the top of the wall. One of the two uninjured men was trying to drag his comrade out of harm's way, while the other was re-loading. They knew that it would take Costa at least twenty seconds to re-load, so they were not hurrying. Costa levelled his Girandoni at the man who was reloading. The man was not even looking at him, but concentrating on his musket. Costa aimed carefully and squeezed the trigger. The man span round, a surprised expression on his face, and his musket also clattered to the cobbles, the dropped ramrod making a musical ring on the stones. Costa thumbed the bolt of his Girandoni and pulled the hammer to full-cock. His second shot missed the third man as he suddenly threw himself flat. Before Costa had time to charge his weapon again, the man had jumped to his feet and run from the yard, screaming at someone outside. Costa raised his head and waited as the sound of boots came from the entrance. Costa put a ball at the wall of the entrance passage. It ricocheted off the stone and there was a yelp of alarm. The boots retreated. Keeping low, Costa ran for the open back door, which by now framed the figure of Hankins who, Girandoni levelled at the yard entrance, was covering him. As Costa gained the doorway, Hankins put the weapon up, stepped aside to let him in, slammed the door behind him and bolted it. Fletcher appeared in the kitchen. "Where is Holden?"

"Shot, Sir." Costa jerked his thumb at the back door.

"Dead?"

"I don't know, Sir. Bad, anyway."

"Damn and blast!"

"It's 'is own fault, Sir. Shouldn't 'ave got drunk," said Hankins. Fletcher grunted in reply. At the first shot, He and Hugo had slammed and locked the shutters on the windows in the downstairs front rooms, and Good had raced back up the stairs to join Gibbs. The sound of breaking glass now came from the parlour, together with a warning shout from Hugo. Fletcher turned on his heel and he and Hankins ran for the parlour. The sound of a shot came from upstairs, followed by Good's voice shouting derision. His boots sounded on the landing as he took up position at another window. More shouts came from outside, followed by blows on the front door. Costa edged to the kitchen window, which was small and had no shutters. He could see no-one in the yard. Although the Girandonis which the party was carrying had all been shortened to carbine length, they were still somewhat unwieldy in a close fight, so Costa propped his against the table while he drew his pistol from his belt, cocked it and checked the priming. The hammering on the door had stopped, and, after a brief attack through the broken window on the shutters of the parlour, there was silence from outside. Hugo appeared, carrying his pistol and a sword which had, until a few minutes before, been one of a pair which, crossed, formed an ornament on the wall above the parlour fireplace. Both he and Costa looked upwards as a scraping sound came from the lean-to roof of the kitchen, which was a single-storey extension on the rear of the house. Costa realized that someone had climbed up there from the end by using a pile of crates and barrels that had been stacked near the entrance to the yard. Costa moved to the back door and silently unbolted it. Next moment came the sound of breaking glass and a pistol shot from upstairs, followed by a louder report as Hugo fired his weapon up through the ceiling. There was a shriek from the kitchen roof. Costa wrenched the door open. A slithering noise, followed by a thump, announced the sudden descent of the man from the roof. He landed just outside the back door and began to roll about on the cobbles, clutching his right leg. Blood began to spread on his trousers.

Costa poked his head out of the door, levelled the pistol, fired and ducked back in again, slamming the door. Now there were two men screaming in the yard. Before he had time to bolt the door, there was a loud crash from the front of the house and the front door suddenly burst open.

The burly Militia Sergeant was well used to this sort of fighting. He had spent many years apprehending smugglers and desperate criminals, and was well versed in making sudden violent entries into buildings where armed criminals were holed up. In addition, he was angry. He was angry with the jumpy idiot of his who had started this by shooting at the two men in the yard. The idiot was now dead, but violence could probably have been avoided had he not been so eager to use his weapon. He was angry that the criminals in the house had reacted by killing two of his men and wounding a third. He was angry that Lessard had taken most of his men on what was probably a wild-goose chase, and he was angry because he had just hurt his shoulder charging the door. He had burst through rather more rapidly than he had anticipated, and managed to pull up only when he was several feet down the hallway. His two remaining men followed him. The Sergeant motioned one of them towards the parlour, the other to the staircase. He himself walked cautiously down the hall towards the kitchen. The next moment, he spun round as the parlour door was slammed. From within the room came a muffled shriek which turned to a gurgle, a thump, then silence. The Sergeant found himself looking into the horrified eyes of the man he had directed to the foot of the stairs. The next moment, those eyes widened in alarm and the Sergeant noticed they were looking not at him, but over his shoulder. The next moment, his world turned black.

As the Sergeant slumped to the floor, Hugo reversed the pistol, which he had used as a club. The man at the foot of the stairs slowly raised his hands, staring intently at the muzzle of Costa's Girandoni, which was pointing at his chest. Hugo moved to one side to give Costa a better view and tucked the pistol into his belt as Hankins clattered down the stairs, followed by Gibbs. Hankins disarmed the man. Costa turned and vanished. The parlour door opened and Fletcher appeared, carrying the other sword of the pair which had adorned the parlour wall. Blood dripped from its tip. He gestured at the militiaman with it and pointed to the kitchen, then called up the stairs, "Good?"

"Sir?"

"Any more of the buggers?"

"Not that I can see, Sir. Road's clear."

"Costa?"

"Sir?"

"Clear out the back?"

"Yes, Sir. Three dead in the yard, one wounded."

"Holden?"

"Dead, Sir. Ball broke his neck."

"Damn, damn, damn! Very well. Come back in. Bring the wounded one with you."

Fletcher pointed to the kitchen door. "In there," to the militiaman. He kicked the Sergeant. "Bring him, too."

Hankins and Gibbs dragged the inert form of the Sergeant into the kitchen and dumped him by the fireplace. "What about the one in the parlour?" asked Hugo.

"Dead," replied Fletcher curtly. He looked at the sword in his hand with an expression of sudden distaste and propped it against the wall. "Damn' thing's blunt. Could have ridden to York on it. I did remember your advice about using the point, but I would probably have done better to bludgeon him with it. You must give me more fencing lessons when we get home." He pulled a grim face at Hugo and turned his attention to the wounded man, who had a pistol ball in his left thigh and another in his right buttock. He had also sustained a sprained ankle in falling from the roof. The wounds were not serious, but the man would not be walking very far. Fletcher tore some towels which had been hanging on a rail into strips and roughly bandaged the wounds. Then he checked the Sergeant. "Who hit him?"

"I did," replied Hugo. Fletcher grinned at him. "You did a thorough job. He'll be unconscious for some time. Gentlemen, it is nearly dark. Time for us to go. We shall have to leave poor Holden for the Frogs. Make sure he has nothing on him that could identify him." Costa disappeared into the yard. "What about this one," asked Hugo. "He will have to sleep for a while," said Fletcher, looking directly at Hankins, who moved silently behind the man. Fletcher continued, "As long as they cannot follow us, we are safe. They will be found soon enough, but they won't know where we have gone."

There was a thump and a sigh. The militiaman folded up and gently slid to the floor, Hankins supporting him under the armpits. Fletcher continued, "We must just hope they didn't leave anyone outside to watch, in which case we may be in trouble, but there is not much in the way of cover out there, so it's unlikely, but keep a good look-out as we leave." He gestured at the unconscious men on the floor. "Better tie these two up, just in case, then take them out to the shed. Get that one out of the parlour, as well. Dump him in the yard with the others." Costa returned. "Holden had nothing on him, Sir."

"Very well. Take his kit. Don't forget his air rifle, for God's sake, or Markham will have us all strung up."

Costa slung Holden's Girandoni on his shoulder. "The bugger owed me three shillings," he growled. Good grinned at him and picked up Holden's pack.

Ten minutes later, the seven men slipped out of the house and cautiously began to walk towards the town, their path illuminated by a pale, hazy moon. An owl hooted at the gathering darkness. In the distant west, lightning flickered and played on the gathering clouds.

There was no-one to watch them go. At the sound of the first shot, Vallon had taken off back to Dieppe as fast as his legs could carry him.

In the woolshed, the Sergeant snored. The wounded man lay on his belly and waited for help to come, occasionally groaning softly at the pain. In the yard lay the dead. A second owl, perched on the roof of an outbuilding, hooted its reply to the first. A rat, whiskers quivering, sniffed at Holdens' corpse. The owl launched itself on silent wings and stooped…

Henri Lessard hunched his shoulders and muttered under his breath. His men poked around in the burned-out and weed-covered ruins of a remote house and its outbuildings near to a small beach. Fletcher and his men were not there. There was no-one there. There had not been anyone there for a long time. Lessard had been sent on a wild-goose chase. He cursed fluently for several seconds, then turned to Lemaire, his second-in-command. "We are wasting our time here." He pulled out his watch. "We must return to Dieppe immediately. I fear we have been hoodwinked, and I fear trouble. The men can follow as quickly as possible." Lemaire nodded, "I will give orders." He strode away while Lessard checked his mount's girth-strap. A few moments later, he returned. Both men mounted and watched the search party form up on the road. After a few moments, the horsemen galloped off and the search-party began its weary journey back towards Dieppe, the boots kicking up a cloud of whitish dust from the road into the sultry early-evening air.

From behind a clump of Marram grass in the dunes at the head of the beach, a figure rose and brushed the sand from his clothes. Sir Charles Goodrich put away his small telescope and turned towards the beach. He was very tired. His had also been a wasted journey. He had ridden straight from Dieppe to a village about fifteen miles from Boulogne in the hope that his men in Boulogne had been able to free the Comtesse, but they had reported that their enquiries revealed that she had escaped of her own accord the previous day. It was suspected that she had boarded a vessel in the harbour, and was probably back in England by now. Goodrich had missed his rendezvous with the lugger that was to take him back to England, but his men had assured him that he would be met at this beach two hours before dusk and taken out to the fishing-fleet, which the lugger would have joined. He checked his watch. It was time. He grinned to himself as he walked the few yards to the water's edge. There was one compensation for his failure to find the Comtesse and missing his boat. He had thoroughly enjoyed watching Lessard's men trudging disconsolately back off up the road. If all had gone according to plan, he would have been nowhere near here and unable to witness the sight. Obviously, Lessard had taken the bait. Barring unforeseen events, Fletcher and his men should get out tonight, and the operation would be at least a partial success. A pity that they would probably not be able to take Lessard with them, but never mind. He looked up as the sound of a gentle splash of oars reached his ears, and a boat appeared through the haze. A figure in the boat waved. Goodrich relaxed.

Ten miles from Boulogne, François Chabot sat on a travelling-chest at the side of the muddy, rutted road and mopped his brow with a silk handkerchief. Dubois sat slumped on another pile of luggage a few feet away, reading a book. Chabot sighed, stretched out his right leg and rubbed the knee. A wheel had come off the chaise, which had slewed alarmingly across the road before coming to rest in a ditch. In clambering out of the vehicle, Chabot had wrenched his knee, which now ached dully. Chabot's escort had ridden on to a nearby village to summon help, returning after about half an hour with half a dozen men. He watched, muttering, as the men attempted to jack the chaise up on to baulks of timber. It had already slipped off the teetering pile of blocks once, and Chabot feared it would do so again, but finally it was securely jacked up and a man offered the wheel back on to the axle. At this point, it became clear that all was not well. Chabot could not see exactly what was wrong as the chaise was now surrounded by the men, all of whom were talking at once and waving their arms around. After a moment or two, one of the escorts walked over to him. "Citizen, the axle is damaged. The wheel will not go back on. The chaise will have to be repaired by the blacksmith tomorrow. There is an inn at the village. I will send for a cart for the luggage." Chabot cursed. Dubois simply closed his book and stood up. "How far is the village?" he asked the escort. "About a mile, citizen." Dubois nodded, turned on his heel and began to walk.

# CHAPTER FOURTEEN

Margaret, Comtesse de Poitiers, sat at a table in a dingy room in a run-down house overlooking the harbour in Boulogne and cursed her own stupidity and impetuousness. She should never have come to France. She should have stayed at home and waited. Instead, on being told of her husband's disappearance, she had packed a small valise, gone straight to Dover and taken the packet to Boulogne, accompanied by her French maid. Now she had had time to reflect on her actions, she found several faults with them. Firstly, she could not now imagine how she, having arrived in France, would have found her husband. France was a big country. She had had some notion of going to the main family estate and waiting there for news of him. Thinking about it now, that was probably the last place he was likely to show up, especially if the republicans were involved in his disappearance. Secondly, she, being a poor sailor, had taken the shortest available passage from England to France. That was another mistake. She should have put up with being seasick and had herself smuggled into the country. Instead, she had landed from an official passage and been immediately arrested and cooped up in this poky little house a mere few dozen yards from her point of arrival, so she was now of no use at all to her husband. Her maid had disappeared on the second day, together with some of Margaret's jewellery. Thirdly, for some curious reason, she had omitted to bring anywhere near enough money with her, in spite of being fully aware just how far a substantial bribe would go in this now apparently Godforsaken country. As a further consequence of this lapse, she could not often afford to send out for decent food, and was forced to eat whatever her guards thought fit to provide her with – usually nothing more than stale bread, thin soup, an occasional piece of cheese and a little rough wine. There was a good hotel across the road: had she brought more money, she could have had meals sent round from the kitchens every day, a fact of which she was painfully reminded on the occasions when delicious smells were wafted in her direction by the breeze. On the first day of her incarceration, she had sewn some gold coins into the hems of her riding-jacket, together with a silver wimple-pin (a family heirloom which she carried everywhere with her) and one or two other potentially useful items, just in case she should get a chance to escape, but that had left her with precious little to be eked out over – she had no idea how long. In addition, she had some more cash, enough to pay her return passage, and some jewels, including a diamond pendant, in a little case in her pocket. Margaret liked her food; she was beginning to feel weak after several weeks of a poor and monotonous diet. She was also very bored. Twice a day, she was permitted to walk around the back yard of the house for about fifteen minutes. Once or twice a week, she was allowed to walk round the harbour with one of the guards. After walking for a while, she and the guard would repair to an inn on the quayside, where Margaret would take a cup of coffee and sit at a table reading whatever was to hand, while the guard spent an hour drinking with his cronies at another table. The rest of the time she was mostly confined to her room. She had demanded reading material. Occasionally, books would appear, but she usually ended up with an old copy of *Le Moniteur*, which she found extremely tedious. About once a week, she was visited by a strange, gnome-like, dusty little man who was obviously some sort of minor official. He looked frightened, she thought. Whenever she demanded to know what was going to happen to her, he would shrug his shoulders and say, "It depends on Paris." She sighed and looked at the valise she had brought with her. She hadn't even packed any decent clothes, just a couple of old gowns and the riding habit which she was wearing now in anticipation of one of her visits to the harbour. She sighed and shook her head sadly. Her father had been right when he had described her as 'wayward' and 'hot-headed'. She had been something of a tomboy as a child, preferring riding, hunting and shooting to the pursuits thought more suitable for a young lady. Now she was suffering the consequences. She stared out of the window. It was chilly for May, and a dank mist hung over Boulogne. It smelled of smoke and fish.

She turned her head as boots clumped towards the door to her room. There was a perfunctory knock and the door opened to reveal the guard who called himself Verlais. She quite liked Verlais. He was getting on a bit – older than herself, and he had manners, unlike some of the others, who seemed to think that revolutionary 'equality' meant treating everyone with equal disrespect.

"*Bonjour, Madame.*"

"*Bonjour, Verlais.*"

Verlais held the door open for her, then closed it and followed her down the stairs and out of the house.

An hour later, Margaret was sitting at her usual table in the inn, leafing through some pamphlets. She read one, about a new machine for beheading people, thought "How barbaric!", wrinkled her nose with distaste and looked over to where Verlais was sitting, a bottle of wine in front of him. He had his back to her and was talking to his friends at the next table. He had not been his usual chatty self during their walk, and she had thought that he did not look at all well. His face was grey, and he had seemed to be having some difficulty breathing. She had had to stop and wait for him to catch up with her on several occasions. When she had enquired after his health, he had merely shrugged and muttered something about oysters, so she had not pursued the matter further. She picked up another pamphlet.

She was half-way through reading it – another dismal tract calling for all spies and traitors to the revolution to be executed, when she was startled by a crash from across the room. She looked up. Verlais was slumped over his table, the wine bottle broken on the floor. Within seconds, his friends had surrounded him. One of them lifted Verlais' head. Margaret saw that his face was now a more livid shade of grey – almost blue. She pretended to study the pamphlet again and watched as Verlais' friends lowered him from his chair and carried him to another room, one of them shouting for someone to send for a doctor. No-one was paying her any attention: she had been forgotten. Quietly, she slipped out of the inn.

A few minutes later, she was standing on the quayside beside a moored cutter which she had noticed on her previous walk. She was moored a little way away from all the other vessels and looked very similar to the couriers she had seen at Dover, which is why Margaret had made for her now. There were three men on deck. Margaret guessed she was some sort of courier vessel. She called out, "*Messieurs!*"

219

Armand Boutin, owner and master of the cutter *Fayette*, was sitting on a coil of rope on the deck of his vessel. He was, ostensibly, a businessman, and *Fayette* plied for small, often high value, cargoes for rapid delivery around the channel coast of France. He would occasionally venture further afield, to England or Holland. In spite of the war, business was quite brisk and *Fayette's* strongbox held a substantial sum in gold, but Boutin was a greedy man, and his latest venture had met with near-disaster. About ten days ago, *Fayette* had set sail from Cherbourg, her home base, heading for a meeting with one of her English counterparts about fifteen miles off Beachy Head. When the two vessels met, just before dawn, they were to exchange cargoes, swapping *Fayette's* barrels of brandy for bales of wool and silk, boxes of spices and some other luxury goods which had become difficult to obtain in France since the demise of the French East India Company. She would then make her way back to somewhere quiet on the Normandy coast and unload her goods. Half-way through the cargo transfer, they had been surprised by a revenue cutter. A running fight had ensued. Attracted by the sound of gunfire, a Royal Navy frigate had appeared on the scene as well. The cutter had seized *Fayette's* English counterpart and *Fayette* had fled the scene as the frigate opened fire on her with grapeshot, damaging her steering and rigging and killing one of her crew. Unable to beat back down the channel, Boutin had been forced to run for Boulogne, where he had put in for repairs. He had hoped he might be able to offload his cargo somewhere quietly, but there were too many customs officials and too many prying eyes. He would have to slip out of Boulogne, return to Cherbourg and lick his wounds before trying again. The rigging had been repaired, and the rudder had been jury-rigged, but some people were beginning to take a rather unhealthy interest in *Fayette* and Boutin had decided to head for home without further ado. He had sent two men into town to buy a few supplies. The wind was from the north-east, fair for Cherbourg. *Fayette* could jog home easily, keeping fairly close to the coast, but far enough out to sea to avoid trouble from some of the lugger-men, who were known to be not above a spot of piracy. When his men returned he would unmoor and quietly leave.

He looked up at the sound of the woman's voice, and recognized her. He had seen her a day or two ago, walking round the harbour. There had been an armed guard with her. She was evidently under arrest - probably someone trying to enter the country illegally. Now she was standing there on the quayside, calling to him. He stood up and returned her greeting. Then she asked, "Are you the captain?"

A few minutes later, Margaret found herself sitting at the table in *Fayette's* tiny hutch-like cabin. Boutin sat opposite her. He had, she decided, a certain charm. He also had some old-fashioned manners, which she found refreshing after the way she had been treated for the last few weeks.

Boutin smiled at her, showing blackened, broken teeth. Perhaps it was not so much charm as a certain oiliness, she decided. "I have just returned from England," he was saying. "We had some, er, difficulty due to the nature of our business." Margaret nodded. So, he was a smuggler. Boutin continued, "I will do it, at least as close as I can get until we can transfer you to a fishing-boat. There are always fishing-boats. But it will be expensive."

"I can pay you this," said Margaret. She laid the standard packet fare on the table. Boutin regarded it impassively.

Margaret doubled the amount. There was still no response. Finally, she took the little jewel-case from her pocket, opened it and laid the diamond pendant in front of Boutin, watching his face as she did so. His eyes widened perceptibly, but the rest of his features remained impassive. "I have nothing more," said Margaret.

"Oh, it is enough."

It is more than enough, thought Margaret. That jewel is probably worth as much as this vessel.

She looked up to find Boutin staring at her. "You are an 'aristo'," he said, flatly.

"It is better if you do not know who I am," she replied, her heart in her mouth.

Boutin regarded her for a few seconds more, then shrugged and smiled. "I do not care," he said simply, "I am not a revolutionary." He took a bunch of keys from his pocket, unlocked the strongbox which was bolted to the top of his desk, dropped the pendant into it, locked it, and stood up as thumps from the deck announced the return of his men. "Please, make yourself as comfortable as possible. We are sailing very soon. I hope it will be a quick passage."

Two hours later, Boutin was cursing his luck. Minutes after *Fayette* had left Boulogne, the wind had backed to the north and strengthened considerably, turning what should have been an easy reach to the English coast into a nightmare of tacking. He was short-handed, thanks to the English frigate, and *Fayette* was making heavy weather of it. They had made only about five miles out to sea from Boulogne, and no northing to speak of. He was beginning to think of turning back when a heavy wave struck the cutter's counter. There was a crack and a yell of alarm, and *Fayette* suddenly began to swing into the wind, her canvas flapping and flogging. Boutin turned to see the helmsman sprawled on the deck. The tiller had sheared off at the rudder-head, the result of unseen damage caused by the frigate. That decided things for him. *Fayette* would have to reduce sail, turn and run before the wind until they could rig jury-steering again. He walked over to the rail, over which the woman was hanging in misery. He had better break the bad news to her.

The next hours were purgatory to Margaret. She was still in the grip of sea-sickness and could only huddle on a chair in an out-of-the-way area of the deck as the men struggled and cursed and *Fayette* left England further astern with each passing minute. She was cold, wet and miserable. How had she managed to get herself into this predicament, and at her age, too? She cursed herself for a fool, a damn' fool. Her hopes had risen slightly when Boutin had told her that they had finally managed to rig a jury-tiller, only to be dashed minutes later when a crunching sound announced another problem as one of the rudder-pintles gave way. They had tried to heave-to during the night, but *Fayette* had drifted inexorably southwards and westwards, carried by the wind and the tide, away from England.

Dawn found the little cutter a mile or so south of the mouth of the Somme. During the night, the crew had managed to fashion a steering-board out of some planks, and she now had some limited steering. Boutin and another man were still working on the repairs. The other man was working under the counter, a safety-line tied round him. He was frequently submerged as *Fayette* pitched in the swell. Margaret was feeling a little better. The wind had eased in the last hour or two, she had become more used to the motion, and the member of the crew who acted as the ship's 'surgeon' had persuaded her to take a few sips of brandy. She leant on the larboard rail and looked towards the coast of France, occasionally visible through the mist which persisted in spite of the wind. A sudden shout caused her to turn round. One of the crew was pointing out over the starboard quarter. After a few seconds, all the crew seemed to be running hither and thither. Amid much shouting, the little swivel guns mounted on the bulwarks were loaded, and Boutin was staring through a telescope. Margaret followed his gaze. Looming out of the thinning mist was a ship, about a mile away and running fast towards them. She caught snippets of a muttered conversation between Boutin and his mate, during which she thought she heard the word '*Anglais*'.

Boutin was worried. *Fayette* was now known to the English as a smuggler. He still had a good deal of contraband on board, and if the approaching brig were to order him to heave-to and submit to a search he was doomed, ruined, possibly even facing a death sentence. He looked at the brig again. She was now only about half a mile away, and her profile had not changed, which meant she was heading directly for *Fayette*. With a heavy heart, Boutin ordered his men to start jettisoning the cargo over the larboard side, out of view of the brig. Although there would not be time to get rid of all of it, it might help if it could be reduced. Within moments, the hatch cover was off and some of the more valuable cargo, of greatest interest to the authorities, was splashing into the sea.

A few minutes of frenetic activity had got rid of most of the bales of silk and some of the boxes of spices, when the mate glanced up and announced, "She *is* English." Boutin looked up. He could now see the ensign. Damn'! Seconds later, a call, distorted by a speaking-trumpet, floated across the rapidly-closing gap between the two vessels, "This is His Britannic Majesty's brig *Vixen*. I order you to heave-to and be examined!" After a moment, the call was repeated in French.

Boutin looked from side-to-side. He was trapped. *Fayette* was caught between a lee shore, only a mile or so away, and *Vixen's* guns to seaward. Had *Fayette's* steering been serviceable, he could have made a run for it. She would have been faster than the brig and could point much closer to the wind. As it was, there was nothing he could do. He looked at the brig again. Her gunports were partly open, though her guns had not been run out, and she was already preparing to lower a boat. Then he suddenly remembered the woman.

⚜

Rupert Kirton leaned on the taffrail and gazed out towards the coast of France. He could not see very much. After the stiff blow of yesterday, the air was heavy and sultry, although there was a light breeze from the north-west. *Vixen* was about ten miles off the coast, which was hidden in a haze, and she was making three or four knots, heading south-west. He glanced behind him, looking up at the set of the sails, then back at the wake. She was making the best progress possible under the circumstances. He straightened up. It was not his watch, and he was not being useful leaning on the taffrail, surmising and fretting about their progress. He turned about and headed for the Captain's quarters.

Johnston was sitting at his desk, worrying. He was worrying about Goodrich. *Vixen* had been on station at the appointed time, about half-way between Boulogne and

Dieppe. The lugger which was supposed to be bringing Goodrich off had kept the rendezvous, but there was no Goodrich. The skipper of the lugger had reported that she had waited for an hour beyond the appointed time, but his orders were to sail if Goodrich had not appeared. All he could say was that he had a message that *Vixen* was to continue to Dieppe, and that Goodrich would make other arrangements. There was no hint as to what those arrangements could be, and nothing in his orders to cover this eventuality. He stood up, crossed to the little chart-room and leaned over the chart on the table, drumming his fingers on it. He was staring at the chart without really seeing it when the sentry's announcement of the arrival of the First Lieutenant cut through his thoughts.

"Ah, Rupert. Any ideas?"

Kirton joined Johnston at the chart-table, and both men gazed at the chart for some seconds. "Nothing springs immediately to mind, Sir. I gather our orders are of no help?"

"None at all. I suppose we just carry on. There must have been some change of plan, but if there has been, there is no way of telling us."

"Indeed, so Sir Charles will know that. He will make his other arrangements to fit in with our known itinerary, so I suggest that no special action is required of us, at least until we know otherwise."

"Yes, of course. Thank you, Rupert. I have been worrying unnecessarily. You have just pointed out the obvious, which for some reason has been eluding me." Johnston slapped his hand on the chart and strode out of the chart-room. He walked to the drinks cabinet, opened it and peered inside. Then he closed it again and said, "By God, it's hot! I don't like the feel of this weather at all. I feel parched, and I don't fancy anything in there." He opened the cabinet again. "Would you like something?"

"No, thank you, Simon. I think we may need clear heads for the next few hours."

Johnston grunted, closed the cabinet once more, then said, "Ah! I have it! Wilby!"

"Sir?"

"Have we any fresh lemons?"

"No, Sir, but there are some oranges."

"Ah, then a jug of orangeade, if you please, as cool as you can get it."

"Aye, aye, Sir." Wilby clattered off in the direction of the galley. Johnston sat down on the bench under the windows and stared out of them. Kirton perched on the table. Both men watched *Vixen's* wake. The surface of the sea appeared almost oily, and there was a yellowish quality to the light. "I don't know," said Johnston after a minute or two, "but if we were in the Caribbean I would say we were in for a hurricane. However, I don't think that either the Master or you can be that far adrift in your calculations, so I assume we are still off the coast of France, where hurricanes do not occur." He grinned at Kirton, who bowed with mock modesty. "Ah! Wilby! Good man. Put it on the table, will you? Mr. Kirton will be mother."

A shout from on deck was followed by the sound of feet approaching the door, which the sentry opened to reveal the Master. "Lookout reports a boat in sight to larboard, Sir. Can't see it from the deck, but he says it's probably a gig. Also, a fishing-fleet in sight to starboard. Boat appears to be heading for the fishermen." Owen's gaze settled on the jug of orangeade.

"Thank you, Mr. Owen. I'll come up. Have a glass of orangeade, " replied Johnston. Kirton poured a glass and handed it to Owen, who lowered it in one go, smacked his lips and said, "Thank you, Sir. Most welcome." Kirton swung his legs off the table and all three went on deck.

A few minutes later, the boat was visible from the deck as she appeared out of the haze. It became evident that she spotted the *Vixen* at about that moment, as the oarsmen stopped pulling and she appeared to be about to sheer off. In the stern of the boat, a figure stood up. Johnston took the signals telescope from the binnacle drawer and trained it on the boat. "There is someone having a good look at us," he announced. Then, "Dammit, it's Goodrich!" He lowered the telescope and waved. The figure in the stern of the boat waved back. The oars dipped once more and the boat shot towards *Vixen*. Goodrich sat down hurriedly.

Ten minutes later, Goodrich was sitting in Johnston's cabin, a glass of orangeade in his hand. *Vixen* was under way again, and the boat was pulling back to the shore. Goodrich leaned back against the cushions of the bench and said, "Well, what a spot of luck! I was not looking forward to another crossing in a small boat, particularly as the weather is beginning to look threatening. I cursed a bit when I missed our rendezvous yesterday. The thought of a crossing in relative luxury was most attractive, but I had to make other arrangements in a hurry." In response to Johnston's raised eyebrow he continued, "The Comtesse de Poitiers was, as you know, missing. It appears she travelled to France to try to find her husband. She got no further than Boulogne. I suspected that she might not have done, which is why I asked you to meet me yesterday. Had I been able to find her, I would have brought her out. However, it would seem that she escaped on her own two days ago. God only knows where she is now. I just hope she had the sense to head straight back to England. This is excellent orangeade."

Johnston re-filled his glass, then added a shot of brandy. "What of the others?"

"That nearly went wrong as well, due to their late arrival – no," he held up a hand, "I know you cannot control the weather, and it is just as well they were late. The Frogs decided to stage some sort of exercise right off the beach where it was planned to take the party off. *Marie* would have run into a frigate, no less. There would have been some very awkward questions to answer. Thankfully, she spotted the frigate in good time and ran away. There were also Frog militia crawling all over the place. Anyway, I know the shore party have taken Poitiers to Dieppe. All that part appears to be going to plan, eventually. The *Marie* is in the harbour. She should be at the rendezvous at dawn." Goodrich looked around the cabin. "I am dead tired. Is there anywhere I can rest for a while?"

"Use my cot," said Johnston. "I am going on deck."

# CHAPTER FIFTEEN

Margaret fingered the wimple-pin through the hem of her jacket. Boutin was gripping her right arm tightly with his left hand, while his right held a knife within inches of her throat. In an instant, he had changed from his slightly oily charm to a savage, calculating monster. Margaret glanced sideways at him. His eyes showed desperation. He was, she decided, capable of anything. He was shouting across the thirty yards or so of water which separated the two vessels, "Stand away, or I will kill her!" She glanced around to see where the rest of the crew were. Two were by the jury-helm, the one who had been trying to repair the rudder had vanished, the mate was by the mast, and two were at the forward swivel gun. Of the 'surgeon' there was no sign. He must be below. She licked her lips and realized that she suddenly no longer felt sea-sick. The other swivel-gun was about seven feet away, its trigger-lanyard snaking across the deck towards her. She fingered the wimple-pin again and grasped its round head between her fingers. It was a pity she had not removed it from its place of concealment, but…

Boutin was shouting again. Margaret watched him from the corner of her eye, waiting for a chance. It came as he took the knife away from her throat to gesture at the other vessel. With all her might, she drove the wimple-pin through her jacket and into Boutin's midriff. Boutin screamed in pain and alarm and the knife shot from his hand and clattered across the deck as he sank to his knees. Everyone else seemed frozen to the spot as Margaret lunged forward, seized the trigger line and pulled hard. She scarcely noticed the report from the gun or the mate's bellow of shock and rage as she ran for the hatch leading to Boutin's cabin and slithered down the ladder, slamming the hatch behind her and shooting the bolt into place.

The mate ran forward and picked up an axe. As he ran aft again, Boutin staggered to his feet, screaming "The bitch, the bitch!" He picked up his knife and, holding his side where the blood was spreading over his shirt, staggered over to the hatch. The mate joined him, pushed him to one side and swung the axe. Thud! The mate changed his stance and delivered a second blow. The area of timber around the bolt keeper shattered and the mate stooped and opened the hatch.

*Vixen's* first six-pounder ball picked the mate up like a rag doll and hurled him, axe and all, straight through the larboard bulwark. The hatch-cover vanished, as did the helmsman and a large part of *Fayette's* counter, the skylight over Boutin's cabin, most of the starboard bulwark and her bowsprit. Vicious splinters whined through the air and screams came from the two men at the forward swivel-gun. Boutin glanced round to see one of them struggling to release himself from underneath the gun, which had been blasted from its mountings and was pinning him to what was left of the deck. An ominous creaking made him look up. The mast, shot half-through and with its shrouds smashed from the chain-plates, tottered, seemed to hover for a moment, swivelled slightly and plunged over the side, its foot ripping a large gash in the deck planking and catapulting the trapped man and the swivel-gun overboard in the process. Screaming incoherently with rage and frustration, Boutin rushed to the hatch. It lay under a pile of tangled rigging. Boutin started to hack at the mass of rope.

After a few moments, he was able to pull aside the tangled mass sufficiently to gain access to the hatchway. He launched himself down the ladder and came to a halt. The door to his cabin was shut. He pushed at it, but it did not move. The bitch had barricaded herself in there! He listened for a few seconds, but he could hear nothing. He would have to break in. He turned, climbed back on deck and looked for something he could use to break down the door. Oblivious to the shouts from the brig, and to the boat, bristling with men armed to the teeth, which was now rapidly approaching, he picked up a piece of broken timber, went back down the ladder and began to beat at his cabin door with it.

After about a dozen frenzied blows, the door began to disintegrate. Boutin noticed neither the thump of the boat as it ground alongside, nor the thud of the grapnels as they bit. He stood back from the door. One more, heavy blow should do it, then he would destroy that damned woman...

Crash! The door gave way, and Boutin charged into his cabin, his feet crunching on the broken glass from the skylight. Feet thudded on the deck above him and there was a shout of "Down there, lads!" A moment later, something struck him sharply behind the knee. The pain was agonising, and he dropped to the sole, clutching his leg. He looked up to see the woman standing over him, the blunt old sword which had adorned his quarters as an ornament raised in her hands. She struck again as a figure appeared through the doorway. There was a yelp of pain, and the man crumpled. Margaret, recognizing an officer's uniform, froze. Boutin rolled over and was trying to get to his feet when a second man appeared, a pistol in one hand, a cutlass in the other. The man's eyes took in the whole scene in a flash. He merely glanced at the officer on the sole, stepped over him and pointed his pistol at Boutin. Boutin screamed. The ball took him in the heart.

Two seamen clattered down the ladder. One of them helped the officer to his feet. The latter, grunting with pain, sheathed his sword, picked up his hat, jammed it back on his head and bowed stiffly to Margaret. She placed the sword on the table and looked at Boutin's body. Then she shifted her gaze to the man who had pistolled Boutin. "Thank you," she said quietly.

The officer looked round as a shout came from the deck. "Sir! Sir! She's on fire!". He nodded to Margaret and disappeared, together with one of the men. Margaret looked at the sailor with the pistol. he tucked the weapon into his belt. "Hicks, Ma'am, at your service, and that was Mister Kirton." He gestured towards the door. Crashes and shouts sounded from somewhere forrard. Hicks moved to the ladder and mounted it far enough to poke his head out of the hatch. Thick smoke, already accompanied by flames, was billowing from a hole in the foredeck. Hicks surmised that the galley stove must have been overset. He squinted along the deck. Surely it was beginning to tilt. Kirton turned and spotted him, limped a few paces towards him and waved his sword at the chaos. "She's holed," called Hicks, "That lot over the side has stove her in." A shout came from forward. Kirton turned in time to see what he had taken to be a corpse lying in the scuppers leap to its feet and jump over the side. He ran to the side, but the man was already swimming strongly for the cutter's boat, which had been towing astern as part of the rudder repair operation, and had been cut free when the ball had smashed into *Fayette's* counter. The man who had been trying to repair the rudder had dropped into the boat and was trying to ship the oars. A crash came from below. *Fayette* lurched and the deck took on a steeper angle. Kirton turned away. "Abandon!"

Hicks jumped back down the ladder. The woman was bending over Boutin's body. "Time to go, Ma'am. This lot's going to the bottom." She straightened up and Hicks saw that she had a bunch of keys in her hand. "One moment," she said. She moved to the little built-in desk and began trying the keys in the strongbox. There was another crash, and the deck lurched once more. "Here, Ma'am, let us do that." The woman stepped back. Hicks and the seaman inserted the points of their cutlasses under the top of the desk and levered sharply. There was a splintering sound and the top came off, complete with the strongbox. The seaman picked it up, his eyes widening as he discovered the weight. Margaret pocketed the keys. As she turned towards Hicks, he noticed blood running down her arm. "Are you hurt, Ma'am?" "Glass," she replied curtly, gesturing at the remains of the skylight.

"Come on! She's going!" Kirton's voice sounded down the hatch. Hicks caught hold of the woman and almost threw her up and out of the hatch, then scrambled up the ladder. The seaman pushed the strongbox up and Hicks took it from him while he climbed up out of the hatch. The cutter was well down by the head, and the deck was awash as far as midships. The vessel rolled heavily as Hicks and Kirton propelled the woman over the side and into the waiting boat. Hicks jumped in after her and turned to give Kirton a hand. At that moment, *Fayette* gave a lurch, knocking Kirton off his feet, and rolled sickeningly towards the boat. "Pole off, pole off!" shouted

Kirton, and scrabbled up the steeply tilting deck to the far rail. As the gap between the cutter and the boat widened rapidly, *Fayette* slowly turned on her side, Kirton climbing over the rail as she did so. Hearing Margaret gasp in dismay, Hicks turned to her and said, "Never fear for him, Ma'am. He's a good swimmer." Kirton waved the jolly-boat towards *Vixen*, then elaborately stood to attention on the sinking hull, doffed his hat, removed his coat and his shoes, jammed the shoes into the coat pockets, draped the coat over his arm and stepped off into the sea as the cutter sank beneath him. Various items bobbed to the surface around him. One of them was a small barrel of brandy. He seized hold of it and struck out painfully for the boat. Hicks threw him a line. He caught it and hauled himself to the boat, which was already pulling towards *Vixen*, grabbed hold of the transom and looked up to find the woman watching him anxiously. Kirton winced at the pain from his leg, then, finding he was still wearing his hat, he raised it to her and said gravely, "Rupert Kirton, at your service, Ma'am." "Margaret Poitiers at yours, Sir," she replied, with equal gravity.

❦

Sir Charles Goodrich lay on Johnston's hanging cot. He ached in every limb. Strange, he thought, that he did not feel even a little queasy. Perhaps it was the rum, and the fact that he had not eaten for some time. He fell into an exhausted sleep.

About half an hour later, something woke him. He lay there for a few moments, listening to the water sluicing past the hull, then heaved his legs out of the cot and stood up. The wind seemed to have increased a little, and *Vixen* was moving easily, heeling gently. Goodrich stood up. He still did not know what had woken him, but he suddenly felt wide awake. He groped his way out of the little cubby-hole which passed for Johnston's sleeping-cabin, walked slightly unsteadily to the door and went on deck. The light was fading. Johnston and Kirton were on the little quarterdeck, conferring over something. Goodrich glanced towards the coast. The haze had thinned somewhat. He joined the two naval officers.

"No need to come up." said Johnston. "We just altered course a little." "Ah." replied Goodrich. "Something woke me. It must have been that." He looked forwards to where a group of men were staring intently out over the larboard bow. Johnston followed his gaze. "There's a cutter over there. She seems to be in some sort of trouble. The rule of the sea requires us to render assistance, should she require it. She seems to be becalmed. This breeze will not reach her for a few minutes yet." He picked a telescope off the rack and called, "Can you make anything out, Mr. Owen?"

"No, Sir, I can't rightly say that I can. She has a boat under her counter, and they are doing something at her stern, but I can't see what."

Johnston put the telescope to his eye. "I think we should assume she is in some sort of trouble. Let us run down to her."

"Aye, aye, Sir."

Goodrich moved to the rail. After a moment, Johnston joined him. Goodrich indicated the telescope. "May I?" "By all means." Johnston passed it to him. He peered through it for a few moments, then passed it back with a shrug.

"Sir, she *is* in trouble. Seems to have lost her steering. They're trying to rig a jury-rudder."

"Thank you, Mr. Owen. Steer straight for her." Johnston

turned to Goodrich, who looked at him and said quietly, "You are not happy about her?"

"No, I confess I am not. I don't know why, but..."

"Sir!"

Johnston turned away and put the telescope to his eye. "What the devil is she up to? Mr. Crocker, you have the signals telescope. Can you see?"

"Yes, Sir. They seem to be throwing things overboard."

Johnston handed the telescope to Goodrich. "She's a smuggler, but I don't know why she is shy of us. She's up to no good. We'll investigate her. Mr Kirton?"

"Sir."

"I don't trust that cutter. Hands to quarters, but quietly, please. We don't want to alarm her any more than necessary. She may be quite innocent, though it don't look like that from here. And detail a boarding party, if you please. Get the jolly-boat over the starboard side."

"Aye, aye, Sir."

Two minutes later, Crocker announced, "They're manning a gun, Sir. They can't get her under way. The jury rudder's not rigged yet. They're still throwing things overboard. Looks like bales of something. They aren't sinking."

"Ah! She is a smuggler. Those are probably bales of silk. That means she's probably French. She probably thinks we're the Frog customs. Very good, Mr. Crocker. Thank you." Johnston turned back towards Goodrich.

"Sir?"

"What is it, Mr Crocker?"

"She's *Fayette*, Cherbourg, and there's a woman on board, Sir."

Johnston turned to look at him. "Are you sure?" "Quite sure, Sir. About midships." Crocker proffered the telescope. Johnston took it. "Damme, you're right. What is she doing there?"

"If I am not very much mistaken," said Goodrich quietly, his eye still to the telescope, "'She' is the Comtesse de Poitiers."

*Vixen* was now nearly abeam of the cutter, and about fifty yards away.

"Heave to. Give her a hail, Mr. Kirton."

Kirton seized a speaking trumpet and climbed a short way up the main shrouds. Goodrich watched the reaction on board the other vessel. Some sort of scuffle seemed to have broken out. Suddenly, the woman was dragged into view by a portly man who held a knife to her throat. Johnston swore.

"Sir, they've…"

"Yes, I can see, Mr. Crocker. Come down, Mr. Kirton."

"Now what the hell do we do?" muttered Goodrich.

Johnston strode to the rail. "Mr. Kirton, please tell that damned pirate that if he harms the woman I will blow his vessel out of the water." He trained his glass on the other vessel.

Kirton raised the speaking trumpet. The next moment a scream sounded from the deck of the cutter. It was followed an instant later by the flash of a gun. The grapeshot lashed into the rail between Johnston and Goodrich as the report reached the *Vixen*. Goodrich flinched as something stung his cheek. Johnston took the telescope from his eye and spun round. "Mr. Kirton! Belay that last command. Run out. Boarding party away."

"Aye, aye, Sir." Shouting orders, Kirton ran for the side and jumped down into the jolly-boat. *Vixen's* gun-ports creaked fully open and there was a rumble as her larboard guns were run out. Goodrich had to dodge as the gun nearest to him slammed against the side. He was roughly pushed out of the way by the gun captain. "Over there, please, Sir."

"What about the Comtesse, man?" Goodrich, aghast, shouted to Johnston.

"She fired the gun, and now she has fled below. Aim high! Sweep her decks! Reload with grape!"

Johnston watched as the jolly-boat cleared *Vixen's* stern, her crew pulling for the cutter with all their might. He waited a few seconds more.

"Fire!"

Goodrich clung to the rail, his ears ringing from the report of the broadside. Clouds of dirty yellow smoke obscured his vision for a few seconds and he closed his eyes. When he opened them again a few seconds later, he could not believe what he saw. The cutter was reduced to a shambles. Even as he watched, her mast crashed over the side. Already, the jolly boat had reached her and Johnston's men were swarming aboard. Johnston joined him at the rail. Both men stared towards the cutter. The sound of a pistol shot came from below and Goodrich stiffened. A few seconds later, Kirton appeared on deck. He waved towards *Vixen*. Johnston stepped back from the rail and grinned at Goodrich. "She's on fire, and holed. Down by the head already. Kirton had better hurry." He suddenly noticed Goodrich's cheek. "You're hurt. I'll send for the surgeon."

"What? Oh…" Goodrich remembered his cheek. "It's only a scratch."

"It is not. There is a splinter about two inches long sticking out of your face. Boyce will remove it and put a court plaster on for you. You will look ravishing."

Goodrich put his hand to his cheek, winced and withdrew his hand in surprise. He cursed and glared at Johnston, who roared with laughter. A cheer sounded from forward. Both men looked back at the cutter, which was now on the point of foundering. They were in time to see Margaret, Comtesse de Poitiers, being bundled rather unceremoniously into the jolly-boat.

Moments later, the boat bumped alongside *Vixen*. As Margaret Poitiers was being swung aboard in a bosun's chair, Kirton became aware of a row of grinning faces peering at him over the rail. The row parted and Johnston's face appeared. "Mr. Kirton, I would not have thought that losing your latest command after, let me see…" he pulled out his watch, "…all of eleven minutes, was really something to celebrate by indulging in swimming, but you obviously believe differently. However, if you have finished disporting yourself, I would be obliged if you would kindly report back on board so that we can get under way!" Kirton removed his hat again and flourished it at the bellow of laughter from the deck.

Johnston peered down into the boat. Strangely, it seemed to contain considerably more items than it had left with, including another brandy-barrel, several bolts of silk and a pile of boxes, including what looked suspiciously like *Fayette's* strongbox. "Mr. Kirton!"

"Aye, Sir?"

"Better bring your contraband with you."

"Aye, aye, Sir."

Hicks leaned over the transom. "Here, Sir, let me give you a hand with that there."

# CHAPTER SIXTEEN

About two miles away, on shore, two horsemen reined in their mounts, dismounted stiffly and hitched their reins to a convenient bush. One of them sat down heavily on a tussock and stretched his arms, flexing the fingers. At least they could enjoy an hour's break, have something to eat and enjoy the view out across the bay. The weather was already very warm and sultry, and the view out to sea was a little hazy. Above his head, a skylark soared, its bubbling, silvery song the only sound above the whispering hiss of a gentle breeze in the grass. Lessard felt tired and angry. He was angry with that fool Vallon for having given him false information. He was angry with himself for acting upon it so precipitately, and he was angry with Chabot for.. well, he was just angry with the fat incompetent idiot from Paris. He turned to his companion. "I need to stretch my legs for a few minutes." Lessard rose to his feet and rubbed his back. Then he set off at a gentle stroll along the path. Lemaire sat down on the tussock and stared out to sea. After a few minutes, he glanced along the path to see where Lessard had got to, then stood up, walked over to his horse, fished in a saddlebag and produced a flask of wine, a hunk of bread and some cheese. He sat down on the damp grass and began to eat.

Lessard, glad to have a few minutes away from his companion, sat down again. He fished his pocket-book out and spent a few minutes looking at his notes. After a short while, still unable to make sense of the situation and unable to glean any inspiration from his scribblings, he sighed, put the pocket-book away and gazed vacantly out to sea again. Quite soon, he noticed a small, single-masted vessel a mile or so off the shore. He watched it idly. It was moving slowly westwards. He pulled out a small telescope and trained it on the vessel. There seemed to be a fair amount of activity on deck, but he could not make out much through the haze and lost interest. He panned the telescope around a little, and presently spotted another, larger, vessel, a little further out to sea, also moving westwards. He trained the telescope on her. She appeared to be catching up rapidly with the first vessel. He watched for a few moments more, then became aware that his stomach was crying out for sustenance. He lost interest in events out at sea, closed the telescope, pushed it into his pocket, rose to his feet and made his way slowly back to join his companion.

Lemaire proffered a chunk of bread, a piece of cheese and the wine-flask. Lessard grunted his thanks, sat down, took a pull at the flask and began to eat. After a while, he became aware once more of the song of the skylark. Then he realized that there was not one, but two. He craned his neck, squinting against the light, trying to catch a glimpse of them. A flock of sparrows disturbed the peace, descending on a clump of bushes a few yards away. Here, they proceeded to squabble noisily for a few minutes before settling down, presumably to feed. Lessard searched for the larks again. He had just succeeded in spotting one, a tiny speck far overhead, still pouring out its song, when he was brought to earth by a grunt from Lemaire. He turned his attention to his companion, who was pointing out to sea. Following his pointing finger, Lessard could see that the two vessels were stationary a short distance apart. The smaller of them was closer to the shore and seemed to be in some difficulty. Lemaire said, "It looks as if one is rendering assistance to the other." Lessard grunted again by way of reply. Lemaire went on, "The little one must be in some sort of trouble. They have been throwing things over the side."

"Oh?" Lessard turned his head to stare at the vessels again. As he did so, faint shouting carried across the water to the two men. Lessard's mare snorted and pricked up her ears, turning to look to seaward. Lemaire's horse continued to munch stolidly at the grass. More shouts drifted to the ears on shore.

"What *is* going on out there?" said Lessard after a few minutes. He rose to his feet, pulling out his telescope. He looked through it for a few seconds, then passed it to Lemaire. Lemaire adjusted the focus, then said,

"They have been throwing barrels over the side. They are probably smugglers, and our gallant navy is apprehending them."

Lessard took back his telescope and peered through it for a few seconds, then lowered it and said quietly, "You may be right, but I think the larger vessel is English. Look at her flag."

"Perhaps they are English smugglers, and they have chased them all the way from England. It is not really all that far," volunteered Lemaire. "*Mon Dieu!* What was that?"

Lessard clapped the telescope back to his eye. "That, my friend, was gunfire." About a minute later, the sound of a rolling broadside echoed across the water. The flock of sparrows seemed to explode, screeching, from the bushes, gathered, wheeled, and flew away inland. Lessard watched through his telescope as the smaller vessel's single mast teetered, then crashed over the side in a mass of torn canvas and tangled rigging. Lessard watched for about another ten minutes, although he could see little of what was happening through the smoke and confusion. It seemed that the smaller vessel had caught fire. A minute or two later, it had disappeared. The other vessel stayed for a few minutes more, then hoisted in her boat, crowded on sail and headed off down the coast towards Dieppe. Lessard swept the area again with his telescope, and spotted a small boat. There were two men in it, pulling painfully towards the beach. Lessard snapped the telescope shut. "We had better go and see if they require assistance."

❧

Pierre Chabot sat at a table in the inn in Boulogne – the very same table in the corner which had been occupied by Margaret three days previously. He stared morosely into the middle distance, the fingers of his right hand drumming on the surface of the table. The village blacksmith had patched up the carriage sufficiently for it to reach Boulogne, but the wheel had come off again in the outskirts of the town, and Chabot had walked to the militia station. It had been a difficult journey, and he had not been in the best of tempers even before the unwelcome news of Margaret's escape had been broken to him. He had ranted and raved, threatened everyone in sight, but of course it was useless. Now here he was, stuck in yet another accursed fishing port – *God! That smell again!* – with no means of moving until the carriage had been properly repaired. He looked up as Dubois approached the table, and waved vaguely to a chair. Dubois settled himself.

"I have drawn a blank, I am afraid. Apparently, no-one saw the Comtesse leave. They were all concerned about Verlais. I have asked around the harbour, but no-one recalls seeing her. There was only one possible lead – a small cutter was moored at the end of the mole on the day in question. It left around the time the woman disappeared. I have made some enquiries. The cutter was basically a smuggler, and well-used to going to England. It would seem likely that the Comtesse persuaded the cutter's crew to give her a passage. She is probably in England by now. I have left orders for the cutter's crew to be questioned should they return."

Chabot sighed. "Thank you, citizen. We had better go and see the wheelwright. We need to get back to Paris as soon as possible. What a mess!"

❦

Louis Vallon scuttled up the steps to the front door of the brothel. He had not stopped running until he was well into the town, and he was still out of breath. He opened the door and crept into the hall. He must find Martin and tell him that things seemed to have gone wrong. He wondered what Lessard would have to say. He closed the door behind him and leaned his back against it, trying to get his breathing back to normal and praying that no-one, particularly one of the English, had followed him. After a moment, he raised he head to find Martin regarding him from beside the staircase. "Oh, citizen! Trouble!" He began to babble out his story. After a few moments, Martin took him by the arm and steered him into the small office at the back. Martin sat Vallon on a chair. "Calm yourself, citizen," he said. "You may hide in here. I will fetch some brandy." He slipped out of the room, closing the door and locking it all in one movement, which Vallon, in his distressed state, did not hear.

Vallon sat and looked around the room for several minutes. It was comfortably furnished and softly lit by two ornate oil lamps. He stood up and went to the window. It looked out on to the courtyard, but it was now dark and he could see nothing in the faint light from the windows of the house. He turned away and began to examine the desk, quietly opening the drawers one by one. In one, he found a quantity of English sovereigns, which he pocketed. At the sound of approaching footsteps, he quietly slipped back on to the chair. The footsteps went away again, and Vallon wondered why there should have been so much English money in the desk. He stood again, walked round the desk and opened another drawer. Nothing but papers. The footsteps approached again, and he heard voices. He stood up and pressed his ear to the door, but was unable to hear anything clearly. He returned to the chair, sat down again and gazed at the clock on the mantelpiece. After a few moments, it whirred and struck nine. Vallon shifted uncomfortably on the chair. More voices came from the hall, then there was the sound of the front door closing. He rose again and opened another drawer of the desk. In it he found a small pistol. He was not used to firearms, but he had, a couple of years ago, assisted Poitier's gamekeeper in the armoury at the house in England. He raised the frizzen and checked the pan. The weapon was primed, so it must be loaded. He lowered the frizzen again, tucked the pistol into his belt and pulled his coat around himself to conceal it, scrabbled in the drawer again and found a powder-flask and a small bag of shot. He stuffed these into his pockets and felt safer.

Fletcher, Hugo, Costa and Hankins stood in the hallway of the brothel. The party had split into two groups on the way. Fletcher, Costa and Hankins had tailed the others at a short distance in case of trouble, and were the last to arrive. They had been met by Martin, holding a finger to his lips. Williams and Murrell had remained in the kitchen and all the rest were in a room upstairs. Fletcher and Martin conversed in whispers.

"Your little rat Vallon is in the office," Martin indicated the door at the end of the hall. "I have locked him in."

"The office has a window?" Fletcher asked Martin.

"Yes, on to the yard." Fletcher turned to Hankins and Costa. "You two, round the back. Poitiers, watch the front door." He and Martin walked to the door to the office.

Vallon was beginning to think that Martin had forgotten him. He wandered around the office for a few minutes, then finally went to the door. He turned the handle and pulled. The door was locked! He pulled harder, then crossed the room to the window. He tried to heave it open, but it appeared to be stuck. Beginning to panic, he returned to the desk and tugged the pistol from his belt.

At that moment, the door was thrown open and he found himself staring into the face of the man he has seen crossing the square with Hugo Poitiers. He pointed the pistol and pulled the trigger as Fletcher slammed the door shut again and threw himself to one side. The ball passed through the door and down the hall. Hugo, standing by the front door, gasped and clutched at his left knee as the ball struck it a glancing blow, but most of its impetus had been spent in passing through the door, and it had simply bounced off Hugo's leg. It rolled across the marble tiles and came to rest against the panelling. Hugo, rubbing his knee, gave Fletcher a rueful grin.

Fletcher, still pressed back against the wall, nodded to him, grasped the doorknob and hurled the door open.

The recoil of the pistol hurt Vallon's wrist. He yelped, dropped the weapon and looked fearfully at the door. It remained closed. He looked desperately about him, then picked up the poker from the fireplace. A moment later, the door burst open again and Fletcher charged in. Vallon raised the poker to take a swing at Fletcher, but the poker caught the glass dome of the clock, which promptly shattered, showering shards of glass everywhere. Vallon, shocked, dropped the poker. The desk was between him and his assailant. He pushed the desk violently toward the other man, seized the chair and heaved it with all his might at the window. The chair crashed through the glass and delicate glazing – bars and Vallon scrambled out. Upstairs, a woman screamed. Vallon jumped from the low sill into the courtyard and began to run towards the back gate, looking over his shoulder. He never saw Hankins, who tripped him up, or Costa, who sat on him. He began to scream and Hankins tapped him behind the ear with a pistol-butt. Fletcher leaned out of the window. "Bring him in." The back door opened and Martin emerged into the courtyard. Hankins and Costa dragged Vallon through the door and dumped him on the kitchen floor.

Alarmed voices sounded from nearby. Someone called, "Citizen Martin! Is everything all right?"

"Yes, Yes. Do not be alarmed." called Martin, but the neighbour was not satisfied. "I will get help." Running footsteps faded into the distance. Martin looked at Fletcher, who had by now followed Vallon out of the window, and shook his head. "Damn!" said Fletcher and vanished back into the house, followed by Martin, who vanished upstairs to reassure the few women who remained. He re-appeared a few moments later, carrying a small leather satchel, and paused at the top of the stairs, rummaging through its contents.

At the front door Fletcher found Hugo still rubbing his knee. "Vallon raised the alarm with that shot, damn him. We cannot stay here. Go and get your father and Gaston. Then take Good, Gibbs, Williams and Murrell with you and go to the warehouse. I left it unlocked. You remember which one it was?"

Hugo nodded. "Third door on the left," said Martin, pointing to the landing. Hugo, limping slightly, vanished up the stairs. Moments later, he re-appeared with his father and the other men. Fletcher opened the front door and peered out. "No-one in sight. Go! Hurry! We will follow soon, but we will have to come the other way, so we'll join you in about twenty minutes."

Fletcher closed the front door and bolted it. Then he returned to the kitchen, where Hankins was going through Vallon's pockets, watched by Costa. Martin, having quieted the women upstairs and, presumably, found whatever it was he was looking for, had disappeared back into the office. He appeared a few moments later, carrying a bag. "I have rescued everything important, but I can't find my money. I'm sure I had some in the desk." Hankins silently handed him a handful of sovereigns. Martin glared at the inert Vallon, who was beginning to show signs of coming round. "Finish him off," he said.

"He's wanted for murder in England," replied Fletcher. "We'd better take him with us. There will be quite a few people who will enjoy watching him dance on a halter."

Martin grunted. Hankins turned Vallon over and slapped

his face a few times. "On yer feet!" Vallon groaned and put a hand to his head. Costa seized him and dragged him roughly to his feet. He swayed and staggered and groaned again. Costa and Hankins pushed and kicked him to the back door. The group crossed the yard and left quietly by the private entrance. Someone knocked on the front door. A few seconds later, the knock was answered by the Madame, who assured the militiaman and the neighbour that all was well, just a quarrel between a couple of the girls and an accident, and no, she regretted, the house was not open for business this evening.

# CHAPTER SEVENTEEN

In the small warehouse not far away, Hugo sat on a pile of old sacks and looked at his father in the dim light of a partially-shuttered lanthorn. He looked older than when he had last seen him, his aristocratic features somehow sharpened by the events of the last few weeks. He had lost some weight, and looked a little gaunt. Perhaps it was that, Hugo thought. He shifted his gaze to Gaston, who seemed little changed. He had been loyal and faithful to the Poitiers, as had his father and grandfather before him. The valet was sitting on a barrel. From somewhere or other he had produced a small roll of cloth which contained needles and hanks of thread, and he was busily sewing a torn pocket on his master's coat. Hugo turned his attention to his other companions. He had got to know them a lot better in the few days they had been on French soil. Fensom was standing guard by the door, which was barred and bolted from the inside. Williams and Costa were busy cleaning the group's equipment, Williams taking care of the pistols and Costa the blades. Hugo watched as Williams carefully stripped Fletcher's Girandoni, cleaned and oiled it, then methodically re-assembled it. He laid the weapon carefully aside and picked up one of the spare stocks. After examining it, he pushed his small screwdriver into the end and pressed something. There was a sharp 'psst' sound. Williams nodded in satisfaction and proceeded to clean the stock, wiping it gently with an oily rag which he had produced from his pack. Costa was using another oily rag to clean the blades, humming to himself as he did so.

Fensom suddenly stiffened and held up his hand. Costa reversed the blade he was cleaning and gripped it by the hilt. Williams twisted the stock on to the air gun, tilted the muzzle upwards, pressed and released the cross-bolt and pulled the cocking-hammer back in a single movement. He then pointed the weapon at the door. From outside came the sound of a footfall. There was a brief pause, then the coded knock at the door. Tap, tap-tap-tap. Fensom drew back the bolts and opened the door a crack.

"It's me," hissed Fletcher. "Open the door." There was another rumble of thunder, louder this time. Fletcher stepped in, followed by Martin. "It's brewing up out there. May be very useful."

There was a faint scraping sound, and Lloyd and Hankins entered the warehouse, dragging an inert form between them. They dumped it unceremoniously on the floor and Hankins rolled it over with his boot. The Comte gasped. Vallon groaned and tried to move. Hankins stepped back over to him, turned him on his side, wrenched his arms behind his back and bound his wrists together. Henri Poitiers looked up to find Fletcher grinning lop-sidedly at him.

"Yes, Sir. This is our little rat." He poked Vallon with his boot.

"How did you find him?" asked the Comte, faintly.

"Oh, that was easy. He went to the brothel, to see his friend and fellow-revolutionary Mr. Martin, who thoughtfully detained him for us."

"But Martin will now be in danger," said Poitiers. "What will happen if Lessard catches him?"

Fletcher grinned at him. "Not much chance of that. Mr. Martin is not really a pimp. Allow me to name Lieutenant Martin of the Royal Marines, who will be accompanying us to England."

"Ah, so this is the gentleman…" Martin bowed to Poitiers.

Thunder rumbled again. "It's beginning to get light, Sir," said Fensom.

"Right. Walters, Murrell, Good and Gibbs, you will escort the Comte and Gaston to the boat. Don't hurry, just walk. Conceal your weapons. You are just fishermen going to your boat. The rest of us will follow in about five minutes. If you are challenged, stall. We will be with you shortly." A peal of thunder drowned his last words. "Not that I think there will be anyone much about in this," he grinned. "Get ready, while we decide what to do with our little rat, here."

As the first group prepared to leave, Hugo could hear Fletcher and Lloyd muttering in the corner. Hugo heard Fletcher hiss, "He should stand trial in England," but he could not hear Lloyd's reply apart from "…damn' nuisance…suppose he escapes?"

Vallon lay and watched them, his shifty little eyes darting from one to the other, then to the wicked-looking knife which Hankins was holding a few inches from his throat. He made occasional whimpering noises.

Fensom unbarred the door again, stuck his head out and looked around. "All clear."

Fletcher turned away from Lloyd. "Go, gentlemen, and good luck."

Thunder pealed again as the five slipped out into the last of the night, the sky now noticeably paler in the east. As they turned the corner into the square, it began to rain gently. Fensom withdrew back inside, and Fletcher pulled out his watch. Vallon began to curse them, first in English, then in French. Fletcher did no more than glance down at him. "Shut him up," he said to Hankins. Hankins produced a rag from his pack.

⁂

A dim, grey light filtered across the little square. The bloodstains around the Louisette, the legacy of the previous day's 'experimental' executions, had been scrubbed away, and the device seemed to dominate its surroundings. It had been covered with a canvas tarpaulin to keep the worst of the weather off, and the shapeless bundle seemed to brood menacingly. A flash of lightning briefly illuminated the shrouded form and appeared momentarily to extinguish the two lanterns hanging from posts at its foot, which marked its presence and threw a feeble, flickering light on it. The ensuing peal of thunder was followed by the hissing of rain on the cobbles. The square was deserted, being mainly surrounded by offices, infrequently used warehouses and municipal buildings. There were no dwellings as such. The inn stood on one side, its doors bolted, its windows tightly shuttered and its few inhabitants asleep.

Out of a side-alley walked Fletcher, Lloyd, Hankins, Fensom, Williams, Costa and Hugo. Costa and Hankins were half dragging, half carrying Vallon between them. His wrists were still bound tightly behind his back and muffled protests and curses were audible from behind the gag. Hankins tried to silence them with a slap, but after a few moments they began again. Fletcher stopped and looked around the square, then at Vallon, who had begun to squirm and shout through the gag. Fletcher moved over to Lloyd. "I think you are right. He is a damn' nuisance, and he is slowing us up." After a moment, having observed that the square was deserted, he nodded at Lloyd and gestured towards the Louisette. Lloyd walked over to it, unhooked one of the lanterns, climbed the step-ladder and pulled the tarpaulin off. He directed the feeble light of the lantern at the mechanism at the top. After a few moments, Williams climbed the ladder behind him, reached out and investigated something. After a hurried, whispered conversation, the two men descended. They then examined the lower end of the device.

"This rope hauls the blade up," said Williams after a few moments. "There is some sort of catch at the top. This line is attached to it and must be what trips it. The victim is laid on this plank and this bar holds his head in the correct position. It should be quite swift and efficient. The blade looks heavy."

"Hmm," said Fletcher. Then he looked at Lloyd. "It would save us the trouble of getting him back to England, don't you think?" Lloyd, in answer, hauled on the rope. The blade rose between the uprights until there was a click. Lloyd gently released the tension on the rope. The blade stayed where it was. He grasped the line and tugged. There was a swishing sound and a thump.

"And it will save all the trouble of a trial. The blade *is* heavy." said Lloyd. He hauled the blade up again, ensured it was on the catch, lifted the locking-bar and prodded at the plank. It moved, and he swung it upright. "Oh, I see. That makes it easy, and there are straps attached, too." Fletcher grunted and walked over to where Vallon was being held by Hankins and Costa. A few moments later, the muffled protests became more urgent and shrill as Hankins and Costa frog-marched their captive to the plank. They held him, his back to the plank, while Lloyd strapped him to it. The nature of Vallon's fate had now dawned on him, and his eyes were terrified. He struggled. Hankins punched him sharply in the face. Blood ran from his nose and mouth and he gasped for breath as they tightened the straps. Fletcher stepped across to him, looked steadily at him for a few seconds, then said quietly, "This is for the English exciseman you helped to murder, for the lad you murdered in Sussex, for our friend Holden, and for what you tried to do to Poitiers. I hope you rot in hell."

As Lloyd and Hankins lowered the plank to the horizontal position, Vallon found himself staring up at the blade of the Louisette. It gleamed in the light from the lanterns, and droplets of water ran down its length. Vallon struggled and began to sob, "*Non, non!*" Lloyd dropped the locking-bar into place. Costa moved round to the head end of the plank, crouched down and put his face within inches of Vallon's. "*Mais oui, oui, citoyen,*" he murmured, then patted Vallon's cheek, snarled and spat at him. Costa stood back and Fletcher took hold of the line. As he did so, another flash of lightning was followed almost immediately by a crash of thunder. The sound of the rain changed from a hissing to a roar, through which Vallon's muffled voice could be heard screaming incontinently, "*Salauds! Salauds!*"

Fletcher took up the strain on the line.

"Mind your fingers," said Lloyd, in a conversational tone.

Another flash of lightning froze the scene for an instant, then Fletcher gave the line a tug. Just audible above the roar of the rain there came a click, followed by a swishing sound and a thump; then there was an enormous clap of thunder. "*Salaud* yourself," muttered Fletcher in the short silence which followed. The next flash of lightning briefly illuminated Vallon's head, now lying about three feet away from the Louisette, and his blood, glistening and bubbling as it mingled with the rainwater in the gutter.

"Well, it seems to work," announced Fletcher, to no-one in particular.

Costa, carrying the tarpaulin cover, climbed the ladder. He threw the cover over the Louisette and its attendant corpse, descended again and arranged it carefully over the machine. Hankins picked up the severed head by its hair and thrust it under the tarpaulin. Lloyd replaced the lantern on its hook. The rain would wash away the blood, and it would likely be some hours before the body was discovered. Fletcher glanced up at the sound of someone being violently sick. He gestured at Lloyd. "Get Poitiers away from here."

"Time we were all away from here, Sir. It'll be properly light in about another half-hour, and the storm will pass soon. The others should be aboard the boat by now." He beckoned at Fensom, who had been keeping a look-out from the middle of the square.

Fletcher glanced at the inn, where the windows remained shuttered. It was now scarcely visible through the torrential downpour. He nodded in agreement, and the little group melted into another side alley, heading in the direction of the harbour a couple of hundred yards away, their progress aided by frequent flashes of lightning, the sound of it masked by the roar of the thunder and the rain.

Johnston groaned. *Vixen* shuddered as she ground and

bumped across the reef. How had he managed to run her on to it? It was a bright, clear day, and very, very hot. He could see Antigua, only a few miles distant. Why was the reef not on his chart? Waves were breaking over the deck, soaking him to the skin. His crew, officers and men, had all deserted him and he was alone, alone with the doomed ship…

The shaking became more violent, and Johnston became dimly aware of a voice saying urgently, "Sir, Sir, wake up, Sir!" He groaned again, and Hicks stepped back from the side of his cot. "You said to wake you at first light, Sir."

"Oh, yes, I am awake now. Thank you, Hicks." Johnston discovered that he was drenched in sweat. It had still been a warm and sticky night when he had turned in. It was now even warmer and stickier, if that was possible. What on earth had possessed him to use three blankets? His tiny sleeping quarters were pretty airless. He had offered the little cubby-hole to Goodrich, but his offer had been declined. Goodrich had borrowed Kirton's little canvas-walled box instead. There would probably have been more air in there. Johnston sighed and swung his legs out of the cot. Hicks had disappeared. Johnston shook his head to clear it, and Hicks re-appeared, carrying a clean shirt. As he struggled out of the old one, Johnston asked "Anything happening?"

Nothing to speak of, Sir. It's very muggy, and we can see lightning over the coast. Someone's copping a big storm."

"Ah, hm. Who has the deck?"

"Mr. Kirton, Sir. He didn't turn in at all; sent the Master below. Said he wasn't tired."

"And our passengers?"

"The Comtesse was still a bit green around the gills last time I saw her, Sir, but I think she's more comfortable than she was."

"And Sir Charles?"

"Grumbling."

"About what?"

"Oh, everything in general and nothing in particular. He did manage to fall down a companion, though, and opened his wound again. Mr. Boyce is seeing to it."

"Good. He was very quiet when he came aboard. I have known him for a long time. On board a ship, he grumbles when he is happy. I was worried about him. If he is moaning, it means he is feeling better. The companion probably served him right – *Vixen's* revenge for grumbling about her. Well, it shouldn't be long now. Has Boyce seen to her Ladyship's arm?"

"Aye, Sir. He says it's a clean wound. He's bound it up. He gave her something to help her sleep."

"Excellent." Johnston pulled the clean shirt over his head and buttoned his breeches. "Is the galley stove alight?"

"Aye, Sir, one range of it, anyway, enough for a kettle. Your coffee is on its way." Hicks grinned at his Captain.

"Good fellow. I'll have the large mug, on deck. Better bring one for the First, as well. You know what he's like in the mornings, sleep or no."

"Aye, aye, Sir." Hicks grinned and vanished. Johnston tied his neck-cloth, dragged on his second-best coat, grimaced at his reflection in the tarnished mirror, jammed his hat athwartships on his head and went on deck, where he found Kirton studying the coastline through the large signals telescope. Thunder rumbled almost continuously and lightning played and flickered over the land to starboard. At the sound of Johnston's footfall, Kirton lowered the telescope, turned, touched his hat and said formally, "Good morning, Sir. All's well."

Johnston touched his own hat. "Thank you, Mr. Kirton. Carry on."

"Aye, aye, Sir." Kirton turned back to the rail.

"Anything about?" asked Johnston.

"Not a thing. No fishermen out yet. That's some storm going on over there. It will miss us, though. I've been watching it for the last hour. Thing is, it's about over the rendezvous area. It might delay the shore party."

"Oh, well, can't be helped. As long as we keep a good lookout, we should see them if they are there. Ah! Here is a sight to gladden the spirits! Not you, Jack – the coffee. How is your stomach?" Goodrich had spent a poor night, kept awake by his wound, which had only begun to sting some hours after it was inflicted. He had also begun to feel queasy in the few moments he had been on deck. He muttered something inaudible and growled before pulling himself together and replying, "Good morning, gentlemen." Johnston beamed at Hicks, who had appeared bearing two steaming mugs. "Thank you, Hicks." He nodded towards Goodrich. "Better fetch a another one. Put a shot of something in it." Goodrich brightened visibly. Johnston blew the steam from his coffee and took a sip. Hicks grinned, knuckled his forehead and disappeared once more in the direction of the galley. Johnston nodded towards the rail and said, "I see the carpenter has finished patching us up. How is your wound, Jack?" Goodrich gingerly touched the dressing on his cheek. "Damned painful, since you ask. Bloody silly, for such a little scratch." Hicks appeared, bearing another steaming mug.

"Never mind. Boyce says you will have a lovely scar there. The ladies will adore it. The rumour will get around that the dashing Sir Charles is a famous duellist, and they will be queuing for your favours."

"Bah! Thank you, Hicks. You are more civilized than your Captain, who used to be such a decent fellow, but is now a boor. The Navy has coarsened you, I find, Simon."

Johnston chuckled and turned to Kirton. "How is your leg?"

"Boyce says it's only bruised."

"I'd keep quiet about it, if I were you. You'll never live it down if it gets out that you were floored by her Ladyship."

Kirton grinned ruefully. "Oh, I don't know. I might be able to dine out on it. She has some spirit, though. I can see where young Hugo gets it from. See a grey goose at a mile yet?"

"I think so. Better pipe all hands and have the guns loaded, but don't clear for action. I think we'll stay as we are, at least for the present. Besides, I should like a decent cooked breakfast, so I don't want the galley stove put out without good cause. We can do it in minutes if need be. Better get some lookouts aloft, though, then we'll see about getting closer to shore."

"I've had lookouts aloft for the last hour, Sir. I thought they might be able to spot something. I was a little concerned in case that Frog frigate we heard about is hanging around."

A matter of seconds later, there was a shout from the mainmast. "On deck, there! Sail on the starboard beam!"

Johnston grabbed the telescope from Kirton, who peered up at the mainmast, waiting for details.

The mainmast again, "Fisherman, Sir!"

"Can't be them," said Kirton. "Too early."

"She's showing two lights – red over white. Now they're t'other ways round. Now back again."

"Dammit, it *is* them!"

"It is indeed them, Rupert." Johnston took the telescope from his eye. "Acknowledge the signal, though they must know who we are. We had better prepare for the landing party. Have a boat ready for lowering, if you please."

Half an hour later, the fishing boat was hove to about half a cable's length from the *Vixen*, with *Vixen* shielding her from any prying telescopes on shore. As the *Vixen's* jolly-boat was pulling across the short distance between the vessels, Johnston lowered his telescope, collapsed the tubes, handed it to Crocker, who was hovering nearby, and said to Kirton. "Prepare to receive our guests, Rupert."

"Aye, aye, Sir."

❦

Henri Lessard was plastered in mud. He had set off again for Dieppe as soon as he could after observing *Vixen's* interception and sinking of the cutter. He had assumed that the cutter was a smuggler. She must have had a valuable cargo aboard to have risked opening fire on the larger and much more heavily-armed brig. He was no seaman, but he knew enough to realize that the English Captain would regard the cutter's firing on his ship as an act of piracy, and would show no quarter thereafter. It mattered not what nationality the cutter was, or under whose flag, if any, she was sailing. Lessard knew that a French navy vessel would have reacted in the same way. It was only when the brig had crowded on sail and headed in the direction of Dieppe that he had begun to think there was something slightly odd about the affair. His mind had then connected the brig he had just seen with Lemaire's report about the English ship which had apparently been loitering off the coast between Boulogne and Dieppe, and he had become more suspicious. Only after questioning one of the cutter's surviving crew did he come to know the nature of the valuable cargo, and suddenly everything had become clear. With a sinking feeling that the situation was now out of control, he had ordered Lemaire straight to Paris to report to Chabot. They had ridden hard through the night, with only two brief stops for hurried refreshment and fresh horses, and Lemaire had already obtained a fresh mount and set off for the capital. Lessard was now standing outside the inn in the little square, trying to brush off some of the caked mud, which was slowly drying on him. A stable-boy had led his tired horse away. Lessard was looking forward to some breakfast, but first of all he must stir his men and get them to cover the harbour, then organize a search of the town. Fletcher could not be far away, and where Fletcher was, it was likely that Poitiers would be as well. Lessard could still recover something of his operation.

Twenty minutes later, he was sitting at one of the tables outside the inn. The sun was already hot: it would dry his still-damp clothes. He sipped at his coffee and watched as two men walked towards the Louisette. After last night's rain, they would need to check the mechanism. There would doubtless be some more executions within the next day or so. One of the two climbed wearily up the ladder, pausing half-way to call something to his companion, and seized hold of the tarpaulin cover. Lessard smiled grimly and began to pour himself more coffee.

He looked up quickly as a yell of alarm and horror came from the other side of the square, and froze. Even from where he was sitting, he could see what lay on the plank of the

Louisette. Unheeded by Lessard as he gaped at the sight, the coffee overflowed from the cup, ran across the table and splashed on to his breeches. He cursed, put the coffee-pot down, jumped to his feet and hurried over to the Louisette.

An hour later, he was sitting back at the table, picking half-heartedly at his belated breakfast. He had questioned a few people at the inn, but no-one had heard or seen anything. The storm had been terrible, they said. No-one had dared even to open the shutters. He had then gone to the militia's guard-room, but of the Sergeant and most of his men there had been no sign. The one man he found on duty was worried. Vallon had turned up and reported that Hugo Poitiers and an Englishman were at a farmhouse on the road south, and the Sergeant had taken a squad to arrest them. The squad had not returned, and the man had been left to fret at his post all night. Lessard had immediately despatched a squad to the farmhouse. After about half an hour, three of them had returned, bringing the injured and furious Sergeant with them, and Lessard had learned the full horror of the events of the previous evening. The Sergeant was unable to say who he thought the men at the farmhouse might have been. He had managed to escape from his bonds only minutes before the search-party had arrived, but had examined the member of the group whom he had found lying dead in the yard. He was sure the group had been smugglers, but he was unable to describe any of them, not having seen any of them before being put out of action. Lessard poked about at a piece of cheese on his plate. He still had no proof that this criminal gang were who the Sergeant had said Vallon had claimed they were. No-one, apart from Vallon, knew what Hugo Poitiers looked like, and it was perfectly possible that Vallon had been mistaken, or lying. Lessard looked up as one of the men he had sent to the harbour approached, and waved him to a chair.

"Well?" he demanded. "Any news from the harbour? Any sign of the 'English'?"

"No sign of them, but there is something…"

"What?"

"One of the fishing-boats set out during the storm. Before she left, two of the fishermen went to the baker's on the quayside. The baker thought it was unusual."

"In what way?"

"Well, he said that it was odd that they seemed in a bit of a hurry to set sail. He could not understand why they apparently did not want to wait until the storm had cleared. All the other fishermen did. Then again, he said he did not recognise them: thought they might be new and just wanting to get to the fishing-grounds before all the rest."

"A sound idea, as far as it goes." Lessard relaxed a little. "Which boat was it?"

"No-one knows, citizen. The baker was busy, and did not look. I asked around, but no-one saw her leave. They were all sheltering from the storm. All the boats are out now."

So, there was no way of knowing which one it was. "Go on," said Lessard.

"They bought a dozen loaves, the first batch straight from the oven. They were still hot."

"A dozen?"

"The baker was surprised. A boat will usually buy one, maybe two, but a dozen... They stuffed them into two haversacks. The baker said he thought there was something vaguely military about them."

"Did you ask him what they looked like?"

"Yes. He said one was tallish, fair-haired, dressed in a greeny-brown coat. The other was small: looked like a weasel. They both had blood on their trousers, he noticed."

Lessard drew his breath in and leaned towards the man. "Anything else?"

"Yes. The tall one did the ordering. The baker says he spoke French quite well, but with an English accent."

Lessard threw himself back on his chair and banged the table with his fist. "*Merde!*"

"*Merde, merde, merde!*"

Fletcher had been here after all: only he and his band of villains would have had the gall to have done that to Vallon, then walk into a bakery, bold as brass, and buy bread before coolly putting to sea in a storm. It was rapidly dawning on Lessard that the English had run rings around him and his men, then slipped out of the harbour, unnoticed, under cover of the storm, no doubt taking Poitiers with them. Lessard's plans lay in ruins; he had lost four good men, five if he included Vallon, who had certainly been useful. What Chabot would have to say about the whole sorry affair did not bear thinking about. With the state of turmoil in the country at the moment, there was no chance of turning the matter into a diplomatic incident. The new war with Austria was already enough, without stirring up the old enemy England again. Silently, he cursed Fletcher and Markham. Then he cursed Poitiers and his son. The boy had apparently disappeared after arriving in England, and Lessard could discover nothing of his whereabouts or of what the English had done with him. Never mind: Lessard had other fish to fry. He was a patient man, and he felt certain he would encounter Fletcher again. In the meantime, he would make a start with that greasy little pimp

Martin at the brothel. He should never have trusted him. He knew in his bones that it had been he who had betrayed Vallon. He also realized that it must have been he who had, through Vallon, fed him the false information about the whereabouts of the Englishmen, sending him off on his wild-goose chase around Morlay. The English must have subverted him somehow. Lessard wondered how much they had paid him. Anyway, with a little luck, the little rat would take Vallon's place on the Louisette in the very near future. All that was necessary in the case of the English *salauds* was to bide his time. He shrugged and picked up his coffee-cup.

⚘

Squeezed around the table in the small Captain's cabin of the *Vixen* were Goodrich, Johnston, Kirton, Fletcher, Martin and Henri and Hugo Poitiers. The table was piled with food: eggs, bacon, a sea pie, cheese, butter, marmalade, a large pot of coffee and another of cocoa. There was a basket of fresh bread, courtesy of Fletcher and his men. Johnston helped himself to more bacon. It was the last of his supplies, but they would shortly be back in England, so he had ordered this grand spread to welcome the others. Lloyd, Gaston and Hankins were being regaled by the Master in the gunroom, and the other ranks were no doubt by now embellishing the tale of their exploits further forward. He broke off another piece of bread and turned to Fletcher. "This bread is uncommon good. Just how did you get hold of it?"

Before Fletcher could reply, there was a tap at the door, which opened to reveal Margaret, Comtesse de Poitiers, still looking rather pale and with her arm in a sling. Confusion ensued as everyone tried to stand up at once and Johnston shouted for Wilby. Order restored and the lady seated beside him, he proffered eggs and bacon, which were refused. "Thank you, Captain. I am afraid my constitution is probably not up to that yet, but I should like a piece of bread and a cup of coffee, if I may." She beamed across the table at her husband and son, then turned to Kirton.

"Lieutenant Kirton, I believe I owe you an apology."

"Not at all, Ma'am. It was nothing, I assure you. The surgeon assures me it is but a scratch and a bruise." Kirton blushed and stared at his plate.

"What's all this, Kirton?" demanded Fletcher.

"Nothing, nothing," mumbled the unfortunate Lieutenant.

Johnston, grinning mischievously, broke off another piece of bread and said, "Well, if Rupert won't tell you, I will." Kirton glared at him across the table. Johnston pulled a face at his friend's discomfiture and went on, "Well now, it would seem our gallant First Lieutenant…"

By the wheel, Midshipman Crocker, Master's Mate and Officer of the Watch, looked again at the compass, glanced up at the set of the sails, took a pace toward the weather side of the deck and peered forward at the approaching white cliffs. He turned back as a roar of laughter floated up through the open skylight of the Captain's cabin, with Kirton's voice raised in over it in mild protest. Surprised, he looked quizzically at the bosun, who simply grinned at him and winked. He sighed and turned away. The bosun evidently knew something that he didn't. To judge from the merriment also audible from forrard, the whole ship's company seemed to know something he didn't. He sighed again. Whatever happened, he always

268

seemed to be the last to know. He was a lowly Midshipman: nobody ever told him anything. Oh, well, he would probably find out in due course. He turned to the men at the wheel. "Watch your steering, damn' you!" He strode to the weather rail, oblivious to the nudges and chuckles behind him.

# EPILOGUE

A week later, Jean Marcel sat uneasily on a chair on the Turkish carpet in front of Markham's desk. Behind him stood the Lieutenant of Militia who had arrested him. At the door to the library stood an armed Militiaman. Near the window sat Russell and Goodrich. Markham was looking steadily across his desk at Marcel. Marcel glared at him and began again, "I am an Italian subject. My government will not tolerate this treatment of me. I demand to see the Italian Ambassador!"

"You are in a position to demand nothing," said Markham, quietly. "We know who you are, and we know you work for Chabot's committee. How else do you explain your possession of this?" He picked Marcel's code-book off his desk and waved it in front of him.

"I don't know what it is! I have never seen it before! I demand to see the Italian Ambassador!"

Goodrich sighed, un-crossed his legs, stood up, walked to the guard at the door and whispered in his ear. The guard left the room and Goodrich took his place. Markham laid the code-book back on the table and sat back on his chair.

"Marcel, I am giving you one more opportunity to co-operate. Simply denying everything and screaming for an Ambassador will not avail you. What is his name, by the way? There, of course you do not know. I invite you to look at the matter from my point of view. There is a good deal of tension between France and Britain at present. Suddenly, in a small garrison town near my home appears a man who speaks English with a foreign accent. This man is seen watching people, poking his nose into matters, some of them sensitive matters, which should not concern him, making notes. When he is arrested, these notes, lots of them, are found in his rooms, together with a copy of the latest edition of the French naval code-book."

Marcel shook his head. Behind him, the door opened. The Militiaman quietly entered the room and handed something to Goodrich, who concealed it behind his back. Markham leaned across his desk towards Marcel, picked up the code-book again and waved it in front of his nose. "I know, Marcel, because I can read this code. I have read everything you have written." Marcel stared at him, aghast. So the English had broken the code. His shoulders sagged. Markham sat back again and nodded at Goodrich, who moved to stand behind the Lieutenant. Markham continued, "Spying is one thing. You will stand trial, and, if you are found guilty, we will shoot you. We will put you up against a wall and shoot you dead." He paused while that sunk in. "However, if you co-operate fully, that need not necessarily happen. There need not be a trial at all. On the other hand, if you persist in denying everything, you will certainly stand trial, not for spying, but for murder."

Marcel jerked upright. "Murder? I have not murdered anyone!"

Markham looked at him for several seconds, then replied quietly, "Shortly, very shortly, before you arrived here, two men were murdered in the east of this county and an attempt was made to have an innocent man executed. Your lack of co-operation seems to me to be indicative of your involvement. You will be tried for murder, attempted murder and conspiracy to murder, and I have no doubt that the court will find your story as unbelievable as I do. When, not if, you are found guilty," he paused and looked at Goodrich, who took from behind his back the halter that the Militiaman had fetched from the stables, "you will be hanged." Goodrich dropped the noose over Marcel's head and swiftly pulled it tight. Markham, the reptilian look on his features, leaned across the desk towards him.

Marcel fainted.

Five minutes later, Marcel, having been restored somewhat by Russell, was sitting in one of the easy chairs at the far end of the library, still guarded by the Lieutenant. Russell was with him, talking to him. Fletcher tossed the code-book back on to Markham's desk and said, "I didn't know you had read all his correspondence. What was it all about?"

Markham stood up. "I haven't the faintest idea, Taffy. The code is a recent one, and we have not yet managed to decipher it." He shot Fletcher a mischievous grin. Fletcher shook his head, laughed and said, "So what happens to our little frog now?"

"If he co-operates, and I think he will – he could be useful. We can use him to feed false information back to Chabot. Yes, Aloysius? Is your patient sufficiently recovered?"

"Not entirely, Horace. He has expressed a wish that he be kept away from Jack, but he is ready to talk to you, provided I am present also."

"Splendid, so some of the French do have some sense, after all."

✥

Across another desk, in Paris, two men faced each other. Both were standing. Chabot's face was bright red with fury. There were drops of spittle on the front of his waistcoat and he was screaming incontinently at Lessard, who regarded him impassively.

"You incompetent idiot! We had Poitiers within our grasp, and you let him go! Not only that, but you let the whole damn' lot get away. They murdered several citizens, while you were chasing shadows!"

Lessard drew himself up to his full stature and replied, quietly, "Citizen, I would remind you that you were the one who had the Comtesse in your charge, but your functionaries did not see fit to inform you of her arrest until she had been held for weeks, then they managed to let her escape!"

"Don't talk to me like that, citizen! I will report all of your miserable failures to the Committee. You are too old!"

Lessard reached into the inside pocket of his coat and extracted a folded sheet of paper. He opened it out and glanced at it, then said, "Marcel sent me a report about ten days ago. It is quite interesting. It contains some detailed information about Markham's headquarters." Chabot glared at him, "So what the hell has that got to do with your losing the English and Poitiers?"

"Nothing, citizen, except that it is written in code."

"Well?"

"I have good information that Marcel has been arrested." Chabot stared at Lessard, who went on, "so the English are now, presumably, in possession of his code-book. There are many codes that he could have been asked to use, but I think the Committee will want to know why he was issued with the latest naval one, don't you? That is, after all, the responsibility of your department."

Chabot sat down. After a few moments' silence, he opened the drawer of his desk and pulled out the little bell, which he rang. The door opened. "Send citizen Dubois to me."

After a minute or so, during which Chabot fiddled with a pencil and Lessard stared out of the window, the dusty little man entered the room. Chabot leapt to his feet. "Dubois, I did not authorize you to issue Marcel with the naval code. Why did you do it, you incompetent oaf?" Dubois pushed his spectacles up his nose. "Citizen, you indeed did not authorize it. You gave the code-book to him yourself. In the main office. I saw you do it, and so did everyone else there. Now, if you will excuse me, I am busy."

Chabot sat down suddenly. Dubois turned on his heel, nodded to Lessard, and left the room. Lessard sat down on a chair by the window. "So what do you propose to do now, citizen?"

❧

At a third desk, this time in the house at Rolvenden, Henri Poitiers beamed at the two men who sat opposite him. One was his son, the other was Simon Curzon Johnston. Having transferred her passengers back to the lugger near Hastings, *Vixen* had sailed round to Chatham, where she was now in dry-dock for a thorough examination. She would be there for a few days only, so Johnston would not have time to visit his family in Hampshire. Henri Poitiers had, therefore, invited him to join them in Kent. He had accepted the invitation gratefully and, leaving Kirton in charge, had posted to Rolvenden. Now he listened as Poitiers said to his son, "Well, Hugo, if you are determined on this course of action, I have to say that it has my wholehearted approval. What your mother will say is, perhaps, a different matter." He turned to Johnston. "How is this possible, and is he ready?"

"Oh, he is ready, I am sure. It is possible because Sir Charles has pulled strings."

"When is the examination, did you say?"

In three days' time, at Chatham. Mr Midshipman Crocker will be sitting as well, so Hugo will have some company."

Henri Poitiers grunted, then grinned at his son. "At least it means you will wear a decent uniform and pace a quarterdeck as I had imagined for you, rather than skulk around like a vagabond in the company of some very unsavoury characters."

"I wouldn't be too sure of that," countered Johnston. "I don't think 'pacing a quarterdeck' is quite what Sir Charles has in mind for our new Lieutenant, at least not all the time."

Henri, Count of Poitiers, shook his head in mock despair.

# HISTORICAL NOTE

I am but a very amateur historian, and I expect there are a good many historical inaccuracies in this story. What I was trying to achieve in its telling was to give the reader a flavour of the fear and turmoil which pervaded all of Europe as a result of the events in France, a fear which eventually reached into every level of French society and into those of France's neighbours.

HMS *Vixen* is based on a real ship. Brig-sloops of varying sizes, carrying from perhaps ten to eighteen guns, were very popular small vessels, being small and highly manoeuvrable, and a common first command for a Lieutenant. HMS *Badger* was Horatio Nelson's first official command. She was a brig-sloop, mounting twelve four-pounder guns and two swivel-guns. I have enlarged her slightly, increased the number and weight of her armament a little and given her a full poop-deck. *Badger's* poop was not used as a deck – it was simply the roof of the Captain's quarters. The addition of some rails and a couple of ladders was all that was necessary in that area for me to turn her into *Vixen*.

Some readers may have been surprised by my equipping Fletcher's men with air rifles. Surely, they are a modern invention? Not so. The earliest reference to an air weapon I have found dates to the sixteenth century. Bartholomäus Girandoni (1744-1799) was an Austrian gunsmith. His air rifle was a lethal weapon, much feared by the French. There is an apocryphal story that Napoleon decreed that anyone caught with a Girandoni was to be executed on the spot, as a result of an NCO who had been standing next to the Emperor having been killed by an Austrian sniper using one of the weapons. The weapon did not really catch on, being expensive and requiring special training in its use, though the Austrian army did indeed have a regiment equipped with it. A strange weapon carried by Lewis and Clark on their expedition across North America in 1804-1806 may have been a Girandoni.

L. M.
July 2009